MY COUSIN BRIAR, WHO SITS NEXT TO

me, leans in close. "Zephyr, what's going on?"

"I don't know, Bri," I admit. "I'm just as lost as you are." Briar came to live with my family and go to school here a month ago, so she considers me the "expert" on Brooklyn, but the truth is, I'm still pretty clueless.

"I can't even guess. A talking tiger could come out from behind those curtains and I wouldn't be half surprised."

She presses herself against me and whispers in my ear. "Do tigers talk here?"

I shake my head and laugh. "No. Only owls in Alverland," I assure her.

Despite all her questions, I love having my cousin at BAPAHS with me. We're not your average fifteen-year-old girls with our straight, white-blond hair, pale skin, and green eyes. Not to mention that we tower over most people because we're both nearly six feet tall.

Oh, and we're elves. Did I mention that?

SPEAK

Published by the Penguin Group

Penguin Group (USA) Inc., 345 Hudson Street, New York, New York 10014, U.S.A.

Penguin Group (Canada), 90 Eglinton Avenue East, Suite 700, Toronto, Ontario, Canada M4P 2Y3
(a division of Pearson Penguin Canada Inc.)

Penguin Books Ltd, 80 Strand, London WC2R 0RL, England

Penguin Ireland, 25 St Stephen's Green, Dublin 2, Ireland (a division of Penguin Books Ltd)

Penguin Group (Australia), 250 Camberwell Road, Camberwell, Victoria 3124, Australia
(a division of Pearson Australia Group Pty Ltd)

Penguin Books India Pvt Ltd, 11 Community Centre, Panchsheel Park,
New Delhi – 110 017, India

Penguin Group (NZ), 67 Apollo Drive, Rosedale, North Shore 0632, New Zealand
(a division of Pearson New Zealand Ltd.)

Penguin Books (South Africa) (Pty) Ltd, 24 Sturdee Avenue,
Rosebank, Johannesburg 2196, South Africa

Registered Offices: Penguin Books Ltd, 80 Strand, London WC2R 0RL, England

Published by Speak, an imprint of Penguin Group (USA) Inc., 2010

1 3 5 7 9 10 8 6 4 2

LIBRARY OF CONGRESS CATALOGING-IN-PUBLICATION DATA IS AVAILABLE

SPEAK ISBN 978-0-14-241674-7

Printed in the United States of America

selfish elf wish

heather swain

speak
an imprint of penguin group (usa) inc.

For the real Nora, Levi, and Angelica

Special thanks to Stephanie Kip Rostan,
Monika Verma, and the staff of Levine Greenberg;
editor extraordinaire Jen Bonnell and her amazing staff at Puffin,
especially Christian Fuenfhausen for his magical cover art;
my extended clans of family and friends; Dan, Clementine,
and Graham for all their love;
and a special shout to Zephyr's fans.
Hup ba and thanks for reading!

chapter 1

GRIPPING TIMBER'S SLEEVE, I worm my way through the noisy crowd filling the seats of our cavernous school auditorium. It's first period on the Wednesday before Thanksgiving break, and nearly all of the students from the Brooklyn Academy for Performing Arts High School pack the rows of red velvet seats. Excited voices bounce off the high blue and gold ceiling that looks as if the first evening stars are peering down on all of us. Timber follows Mercedes and Ari to an empty row near the front. I wave to my cousin Briar and our friend Kenji, who make their way through the throngs of people to join us.

"What's Padgie got up his sleeve?" Ari asks as we settle into our seats. He shakes brown bangs out of his eyes.

Mercedes cups her hand over her mouth and pretends to narrate a movie trailer, "A twist so BIG," she announces, black curls bouncing around her face, "it will blow your mind."

We all snort and snicker because Mr. Padgett, the director of the winter musical, has been saying this exact thing for two weeks, and we're all sick of it.

1

"All I can say is, it better be good." Ari props his feet up on the seat in front of him.

From the other side of me Timber says, "Whatever it is, it won't live up to everyone's expectations. The guy needs to tone it down."

We all nod in agreement, but despite that, the room crackles with energy as everyone talks about what "the twist" might be. All we've been told is to prepare a song if we want to audition, but we have no idea what we're auditioning for or why the whole school is here.

This is my third month at my new school and my first audition for a musical. That's exciting enough to blow my mind. Where I'm from (a teeny tiny speck called Alverland in the woods of the Upper Peninsula of Michigan) we never have this kind of excitement. Even though the place is magical with streams and bluffs, lakes and wildlife, it's also entirely predictable. Which is why I like Brooklyn. Because here I can try something new every day for a year and not exhaust the possibilities, which both terrifies and thrills me. What if I'm horrible and make a fool out of myself at this audition? Then again, what if I'm great? This is why I begged my parents to let me come to this school—one of the best performing arts schools in the country. So I could find out which I will be—horrible or great.

I look down the row at my friends. Ari and Mercedes huddle together at one end. Mercedes points toward the stage then the crowd with grand, sweeping motions, because everything the girl does is full of drama. If she's not making you laugh, she makes you want to cry. Ari listens intently with one finger pressed against his lip, and I notice that he's not wearing his usual black nail polish today. I wonder if he took it off just for the audition.

Mercedes and Ari were my first friends when I came to BAPAHS in September, and they saved me from being eaten alive by the mean girls. We've had a few rough patches, but now things are all good between us.

When Ari glances up at me, I raise my eyebrows and point to Mercedes as a question. He rolls his eyes and shrugs then goes back to listening to her.

My cousin Briar, who sits next to me, leans in close. "Zephyr, what's going on?"

"I don't know, Bri," I admit. "I'm just as lost as you are." Briar came to live with my family and go to school here a month ago, so she considers me the "expert" on Brooklyn, but the truth is, I'm still pretty clueless.

"But what do you think is going to happen?" she asks.

"Bri, seriously, I have no idea," I tell her again. "I can't even guess. A talking tiger could come out from behind those curtains and I wouldn't be half surprised."

She presses herself against me and whispers in my ear. "Do tigers talk here?"

I shake my head and laugh. "No. Only owls in Alverland," I assure her.

Despite all her questions, I love having my cousin at BAPAHS with me. She's been my best friend since we were born (ten days apart). When we were little, we learned to do everything together—how to track deer, tap maple trees, smash herbs to heal a rash, build a fire in the rain, and cast our first spells. The wilds of Brooklyn seem so much more manageable now that she's with me. Plus, I never realized how important it is to be with someone who looks like me. We're not your average fifteen-year-old girls with our straight, white-blond hair, pale skin, and green eyes. Not to mention that we tower over most people because we're both nearly six feet tall.

Oh, and we're elves. Did I mention that?

Not that it's such a big deal. I mean, other than the fact that we're magic and we live a couple hundred years, we're not all that different from erdlers (that's normal humans). My family might be the only elves in Brooklyn (the rest are up in Alverland, where we've lived for hundreds of years), but we pretty much act like everybody else around here.

"Well," says Briar, clearly frustrated with my lack of info, "maybe Kenji can explain it to me." She uses her thumb to point to Kenji, who's slouched in the seat between Briar and Mercedes, then she raises her left eyebrow and gives me a sly grin. Briar took a shine to Kenji the moment she came to BAPAHS. In fact, Kenji didn't hang out with the rest of us until Briar showed up, but now he's with the group wherever we go. Which was awkward at first, because Ari says he used to have a crush on me, but now it's fine, I guess.

"Kenji." Briar pokes him on the thigh. He flinches then pulls one bright yellow earbud out from under the blue fringe of his hair. Briar leans closer to him. "What's going on?" she asks him.

"Checking out some tunes," he says with a shrug. "What's up with you?"

I laugh and turn away to talk to Timber, who sits on my right. Every time I lay eyes on this boy, with his thick, dark hair and startling gray-blue eyes, my heart beats double time and my palms prickle with sweat. I lean closer to him and breathe in the fresh piney smell that wafts off his skin.

What I wish most in my life right now, is that I knew what was going on between Timber and me. Sometimes I think he's really into me. We hang out a lot, but mostly with our group of friends. Every time I think things between us are shifting, turning us into boyfriend and girlfriend, he pulls away. He says that he wants to take things slowly because he was with Bella, his ex-girlfriend, for over a year before they broke up and he doesn't want to rush into something. I try to respect that and act all nonchalant and unbothered when I'm with him, but I'm half dying inside, because the truth is, I'm madly in love with Timber Lewis Cahill.

It doesn't help that his friend Chelsea (and her crew, Riena and

Darby) seems to be around every time I might have Timber all to myself. Like right now, for instance. Just as I'm about to tap him on the knee to ask what he thinks is going on, Chelsea beats me to it by jabbing him in the ribs with her elbow and pointing to the curtains ruffling on the stage. I've tried to like Chelsea because I know she's Timber's friend, but she used to be best friends with Timber's ex, Bella from Hella. Even though Bella and Chelsea hate each other now (because Chelsea got caught blogging smack about Bella, as Mercedes likes to put it), I'm still leery. I might tolerate Chelsea for Timber's sake, but I wouldn't trust her to beat blueberries off a bush. As far as I'm concerned, once a mean girl, always a mean girl.

The lights dim and Briar grabs my hand as two spotlights swirl across the curtains and an electric guitar swells over the loudspeakers. It's a song I've never heard, but the crowd around Briar and me recognizes it. They clap and whistle or sing the melody. I squeeze Briar's hand just as the curtains sweep open to reveal a backlit staircase. The spotlights focus on Mr. Padgett standing at the top, but instead of his usual jeans and sweater, he's in a gray suit. His brownish-blond hair's slicked back off his face and he struts down the steps with a mic in one hand, the other hand in his pants pocket. He stops at the bottom and booms over the music, "You've watched it on TV. You've followed the winners— Kelly, Carrie, Jordin, David, and Kris. You've dreamed it was you."

People scream. Girls jump up and down, waving their arms. Mercedes is on her feet, her dark curls bouncing as she yells, "Is this for real? Are we auditioning for *Idol?*" Even Timber, usually so calm and cool, has moved to the edge of his seat and grips the chair in front of him, ready to stand up at any moment.

"Now it's your turn, BAPAHS," Mr. Padgett says into the mic.

"Did he get us an exclusive?" Chelsea asks, but Timber shrugs, his eyebrows flexed in confusion.

"Is Simon here?" Ari yells.

Briar buries her head into my shoulder. I know she's scared, but so am I. As usual, I'm lost and have no idea why everyone is freaking out like this.

"This is . . ." Mr. Padgett raises one arm above his head and points to the back of the stage. A bright yellow neon light pops on just as he says, "*Idle America!*"

A loud whoop goes up from the crowd, but then, just as suddenly, the screaming, clapping, and stomping dies, replaced by murmuring and discontented grumbles. "What'd he say?" Mercedes asks Ari.

The lights come up and Mr. Padgett stands center stage, pleased as a cat that just dropped a dead mouse on your toes.

"*Idle?*" Timber asks, reading the sign. "As in not moving?"

"He got the name wrong?" Ari pushes his hands through his mess of dark hair. "What a loser."

All around us people drop into their seats, confused, but not as confused as Briar and I. We're pop culture morons because we grew up under a rock in the woods. Literally. My family got our first television a few weeks ago, and we never had a phone until we moved to New York.

"This year, BAPAHS," Mr. Padgett continues, "instead of staging an existing musical production that's been done hundreds of times, we'll put on an original show." He pauses and struts to the other end of the stage. "One written just for you and one that reflects the times." Mr. Padgett holds the mic loosely in his hand and begins to pace. "As most of you know, I have both a music degree from the prestigious Berklee College of Music in Boston and an MFA in creative writing from Columbia University."

Ari groans and rolls his eyes at Mercedes, who pretends to strangle herself because Mr. Padgett never tires of reminding us about his pedigree.

"So, I have put those degrees to good use and penned the script, songs, and score to the first original BAPAHS production of *Idle America*!"

"What is this man talking about?" Ari asks, but everyone in our row just shrugs and looks bewildered.

"Are we not auditioning for *American Idol*?" Mercedes says. "Because I just about peed myself and now I want to kill him."

"That guy's got some nerve," Timber mutters, slumping back into his seat.

Briar and I look at each other, more confused than anyone else in the room, because whatever they think Mr. Padgett is talking about and whatever he's really talking about are lost on us.

"But that's not all, BAPAHS," Mr. Padgett says.

"This *pendejo* better redeem himself now," Mercedes says loudly, "or I'm gonna whoop his ass into Tuesday."

"Auditions for *Idle America* will be held *American Idol* style." Mr. Padgett pauses for effect and is met only by silence. "Right here. Right now."

"What the . . . " Mercedes says as my heart rolls up into my mouth.

"Did he say 'right now'?" I grab Timber's arm.

He half laughs and pats my leg. "You have to be ready for anything in this business."

Onstage, Mr. Padgett keeps right on talking. "Students will vote for their favorite performers today. The top vote getters will be cast in the lead roles. Second best get supporting roles, and so on. So get ready, BAPAHS, because . . ." He points to the back of the auditorium, cuing the lights, which go down, and the music, which comes up. A spotlight hits him once more, and he says, "This is *Idle America*!" Then everything goes dark.

chapter 2

AFTER MR. PADGETT'S little performance, everyone who's auditioning hustles backstage, clutching our CDs and MP3 players with our background music that we were told to bring. We quickly draw numbers, then boys go to one side of backstage and girls go to the other to start the excruciating process of waiting for our turn to sing in front of the entire school.

From behind the green velvet curtains, I peek onto the stage and nearly hyperventilate when I see Chelsea under the spotlights belting out a song called "Rock Star" by some band called Hole. Her hair is cardinal red today to match her slinky red halter top. The diamond in the side of her nose twinkles then flares under the lights, and her short black skirt inches up her fishnet stockings as she shimmies from one end of the stage to the other, stomping her black boots to the downbeat of the song. I scan upturned faces in the audience. They smile, sing along, hoot, and holler as if they don't want her song to end.

I turn to Mercedes, my eyes as round as moons. "I don't think I can do this," I tell her, because I'm next and my heart's thumping so fast I think it will flop out of my chest like a suicidal fish. "I can't follow *that*."

"Yes, you can," Mercedes says, reaching up to rub my shoulders. "You're better than she is."

"But she's so, so, so . . ." I watch Chelsea, knees bent, arms stretched, hips swaying side to side as she hits a deep resounding note. "Sexy," I whisper.

"You mean slutty," Mercedes says.

"There's no way I can compete." I scan my body sheathed in my Alverland uniform: a long green tunic, golden-brown leggings, and soft leather boots up to my knees. "Compared to her, I look . . . I look . . ."

Mercedes looks me up and down. "Amish," she says. "You know I love your style and everything, but . . ."

"What am I going to do?" I plead, wishing that Briar were backstage with me, but she's in the audience with Kenji because they're not auditioning. "I'll be such a letdown when I walk out there," I whisper. "No one will know my song and I'll bore everyone into a coma." I feel my throat begin to close because the worst part is, Chelsea isn't even my biggest competition today. "And now that Bella's back . . ." I groan.

"This would be fifty times easier if Bella from Hella were still off at rehab," Mercedes adds.

Rumor has it that after she made an ass out of herself at the last BAPAHS audition (thanks to me, but that's another story), her parents shipped her off to detox, her talent agent dropped her, and she lost a speaking part in an upcoming ABC Family TV movie. Somehow, though, she miraculously recovered and came back to school just in time for the winter musical auditions.

"Can you believe how she's been strutting around school?" Mercedes asks. "Like she'd been off at the spa instead of out in the woods getting sober."

I nod in agreement. Just a month ago, Bella was bad-mouthing everyone on her secret blog, until one of her best friends burned her by making the blog public. But, and this is what I can't understand about erdlers, even though most of the school cheered when Bella got sent away, the minute she stepped foot in the building this past Monday, everyone scurried out of her way and watched her with awe, like she was some lone wolf on the prowl. In Alverland, someone that evil would be shunned forever!

Mercedes continues, "I heard she sent out a tweet saying she feels *rested and relaxed.*" She exaggerates the words, making them breathy and ridiculous. "And *better than ever* and she couldn't be *happier* to back at BAPAHS, surrounded by her *closest friends*, preparing for the winter musical." Then she clutches her stomach. "Pardon me while I barf." She pretends to puke all over the floor.

I press one hand over my mouth and wrap the other around my stomach to keep from laughing too loud.

"But you better watch your back, girly," Mercedes says, poking me hard on the shoulder.

"Me?" I ask, swallowing the last of my giggles. "Why?"

"That tweet can only mean thing," Mercedes says seriously. I blink at her because I have no idea what it could mean. "Bella from Hella's back to prove she's still the top dog around BAPAHS. And you know she's already vowed to get even with her number one enemy: you." She pokes me hard again.

I stumble to the side. "But, but, but . . . " I sputter.

"I know, I know," Mercedes says. "But in her mind, what you did is worse than her BFF dissing her. In her mind, you're the reason Timber dumped her, and for that, she hates you the most."

"Oh," I groan. "Will this ever stop?"

Mercedes smacks my arm and points back at Chelsea on the stage. "Just look at that girl shaking her booty. My grandmother would lock me in a convent if I acted that way."

"Yeah, but she's good," I say. "Definitely better than everyone else who's gone so far." We've already seen half the performers, and other than Ari (who had to go first, poor guy, and hit a clam at the end of his Elton John song), Chelsea is the best.

"You're right," says Mercedes. "And everyone would vote for her legs even if she couldn't sing." We stand there for a moment, both miserable, then Mercedes turns to me and grabs my tunic. "Give me your pants," she says as she hikes up my shirt.

"What are you doing?" I squeal, batting her hand away.

"Give me your pants," she demands. "At least you've got long legs. I'm stuck with these *piernas rechonchas*. So if you can't beat 'em . . ." She gets my tunic up to my hips and takes hold of the sides of my leggings. "Join 'em and make them sorry they ever put on a mini." She yanks and my leggings fall.

"Great horned owl, Mercy!" I push my tunic down over my exposed thighs.

"Get your boots off," she hisses. "Hurry. She's almost done."

"I can't do this!" I say, but I am doing it. While I kick my boots off and strip my leggings away, Mercedes unbuckles her wide, brown leather belt.

"Here." She shoves the belt at me. I loop it around my waist and fumble with the metal buckle, trying not to think about what my mother would say if she saw me in a tunic with no leggings. "Loose!" Mercedes says. "Like this." Her fingers work quickly to buckle the belt and push it down around my hips. I tug on my boots again.

Mercedes steps back. "One more thing." She reaches up and undoes two clasps at the top of my tunic then she plunges her hand inside my shirt.

"Hey!" I try to squirm away, but she's got ahold of the amulets around my neck—interlocking Petoskey stones for harmony that my father gave me for my last birthday and the crane's feather for good luck that my mom gave me this morning at breakfast.

"Stoop down and turn around," she commands. I do what she says. "Lift up your hair." She tightens the leather thong of my necklaces until the stones and the feather hang in the hollow where my collarbones meet. "Let me see."

I spin around and face Mercedes as the last notes of Chelsea's song reverberate through the hall. Applause erupts, people shout and whistle.

"Yeah," Mercedes says, grinning, then she chants, "Oh yeah. You're a hottie!"

Ari pops out from behind the backstage curtain. "Just came to say—Hey, whoa!" He takes a step back when he sees me. "Who's this?"

"Good, huh?" Mercy asks.

"Oh honey, superhot," he says, sounding half surprised. "If you're into that kind of thing. And according to Zephyr," he says, pretending to announce to everyone in the wing, "I'm not into that kind of thing." Nobody else pays attention to him, but I toss my arms around his neck and give him a peck on the cheek. Ever since I accidentally outed him as gay, he likes to rub it in. "What song are you going to sing?" Ari asks.

"One of Dad's," I say, but my voice creeps up like it's a question.

"Awesome," says Ari, who was a fan of my dad's gothic folk band since before we met.

"Enough girlfriends!" Mercedes grabs my shoulders and spins me around toward the stage again. Chelsea finishes her last bow, comes up smiling, waves above her head, and struts toward us. As she stomps past, Chelsea shakes her head to cool down, spraying us with sweat.

"Great job," I mumble.

"Thanks!" She smiles, her eyes wild. "That was fun." She pauses for a moment. Her eyes scan my body. "New look?" she asks, and I want to shrink then scurry away to a hidey-hole like a tiny mouse. "It works," she says, then mutters, "Good luck," before she's past us and down the stairs.

Mercedes gives me a push. "Go!" she shouts in my ear.

I stumble into the back curtain then grab it to get my balance. When I look across the stage, I see Timber in the opposite side wing. He stares at me with his mouth and eyes wide open, but I can't tell whether that's a good thing or bad. I look onstage in front of me. Mr. Padgett's in the spotlight, mic in one hand, introducing me, but I can't hear him because my head buzzes and my ears ring like I'm under water. I stare out into the crowd, terrified of what's about to happen, but then my eyes land on Briar. She's on her feet, both arms overhead, cheering. When she blows me a kiss, my ears pop open and my mind clears. People clap, cheer, and chant my name as I get my balance and I walk forward.

As soon as I step into the light, my heart slows, my breathing calms, my body relaxes as if I'm floating on top of a placid lake. Applause ruffles past my ears like I'm in the midst of a flock of mallards rising off the water. My right hand raises, almost with a mind of its own, and I'm waving as I reach for the mic from Mr. Padgett. I take my mark center stage, breathe in, and let the energy from the crowd wash over me. Since I don't know much popular music, I chose one of my dad's songs that charted for a week on the Billboard Top 100 last spring. It's my favorite one about sandhill cranes. They migrate south in the winter, then come back to Michigan in the spring where they find their life mate by doing a song and dance duet. Still, I'm worried that not enough people will know it.

When the intro music to "Flying Dancer" rains down on me, though, all my fear drains away. My dad might not be a hugely famous singer, but his music gets enough play that I see people clapping along in the crowd. I lift the mic to my lips and begin to sing.

* * *

> Flying dancer, cold air flows
> you're leaving again
> when the north wind blows
> But you'll be back
> in early spring
> for the one you love,
> you'll return to sing

Despite my nerves, once the first notes leave my throat, I soar with the music. I keep my feet planted for the biggest notes, then let my body move with the dancing melody. I feel the words and as I sing, I hold Timber in my mind. Really I chose this song for him. Is he watching? I forget about the crowd, the contest, Bella, and Mr. Padgett, and I sing only for Timber.

> A passionate dancing duet
> a song you haven't sung yet
> you'll find the one, don't fret
> to sing your song in spring
> Fly, dancer, fly
> Don't let life pass you by
> Spread your wings and soar
> To find the one you adore

I'm having so much fun that I don't want my song to end. I could sing all day, all night, stopping only now and again for a breath to keep me going. But, like every other song in the world, my song has to end. The fiddle and mandolin fade. I lower the mic and bow my head, pausing for just a moment before I lift up and let the last notes echo through the speakers like the song of a sandhill crane ringing across reedy marshes.

Then the applause hits me like a forceful wave. I take a step back and laugh as I lift my arms above my head and smile. I can hear Briar's voice ringing out above everyone else, and I blow her a kiss. Then, I turn slightly to the left and see Timber clapping with his arms raised. I'd like to run into the wings, tackle him, and disappear into the folds of that curtain. But Mr. Padgett was very clear on the rules. Girls on one side. Boys on the other. I wink at Timber, then nearly skip off the stage back to Mercedes.

She grabs me. "Girl! You rocked that song like nobody's business."

"Was it okay?" I ask, my breath fluttery. "It felt good. Was it as good as it felt?"

"It was better," she tells me, and I hug her. "Here, take your belt." I unbuckle it as quickly as I can and hand it over.

While Mercedes rearranges her long white shirt, I see Bella lurking in the shadow. She looks at me and lifts her hand, even with the floor, then tilts it back and forth as if to say, *So-so.* "You got a little pitchy near the end," she says.

"What's that, Bella?" Mercedes asks. "You're a little bitchy and you have no friends?"

Bella cocks an eyebrow. "Who are you again?"

I feel Mercedes shrink beside me, so I sling my arm over her shoulders. Everyone else might tiptoe around this girl, but I won't. "You know exactly who she is," I say. Bella shrugs as if it doesn't matter. I stand up tall and step closer so that I look down into Bella's fierce green eyes. I was meek like a scared little bunny when I first came to this school, but I won't let her intimidate me anymore. "You better watch out, Bella," I say. "Mercedes and I are on fire."

"Yeah, you might get burned," Mercedes adds.

Bella rolls her eyes and turns away. "Dream your little dreams," she says, and flips her long dark hair. Then she casts one more evil glance our way. "I'm back and everybody already knows this audition is mine."

Two guys sing before it's Mercedes's turn. When Mr. Padgett calls her name, she bounds out from behind the curtains, grabs the mic, and starts clapping while high stepping across the stage to the rhythm of "We Ride" by Mary J. Blige. "Come on, let me hear y'all," she shouts into the mic, then she starts to sing. Mercedes's energy ricochets off the walls and gets inside the crowd, making people hop out of their seats and dance. And she works the crowd, getting close to the edge of the stage, bending down, singing to the front row, then standing up and reaching toward the back of the house. She's told me that that comes from years in her grandmother's church, where people dance in the aisles while the choir stomps and sings. When she's done, the crowd goes nuts and Mercedes looks a little bit shocked. She stands center stage for just a beat as if she can't imagine who they're clapping, hooting, and hollering for. Then she smiles big, bows low, and runs off the stage, bouncing like an unbridled colt running free.

In the wings, she jumps into my arms. "You were smoking!" I tell her.

"They like me," she says, laughing. "They really like me!"

Only Timber and Bella are left to sing. Mr. Padgett claims that was the luck of the draw, but nobody believes him for a nanosecond. Ari and Mercedes think he made up the order according to who he wants to see win because as any dodo knows, the last performer has the momentum of everyone who came before. Mercedes and I wrap our arms around each other and huddle in the wings with all the other girls, including Chelsea and even Bella, as Timber takes the stage. The crowd is stoked, stomping, clapping, and chanting, "At the playground!" because this was Timber's signature song when he was famous.

Timber was the lead singer of a boy band called TLC Boyz from the time he was eight until he was twelve years old. He toured all over the world and sold tons of records. Until his voice changed. And his parents divorced. And his manager stole most of his money. And the band broke up. Same old story, he likes to say when I ask him about it, but it's new to me.

I think the problems his fame caused are the reason he's never tried for a comeback. Like the old pro that he is, he takes the chanting and clapping all in stride, pressing his hands together in front of his heart and bowing a little as if to thank the people who might adore him or might be making fun of him. Before I got to know Timber, I would have thought his actions were fake, but now I know he's sincere. He knows what it's like to have a million fans and then how it feels to watch what you thought you had crumble into little bitty pieces at your feet. So whenever people applaud, he's grateful.

Unlike anyone else who's sung today, Timber owns this stage like he built it and lives on it. While the rest of us jumped around, desperate to pound our songs into people's minds, Timber is smooth. He hangs back and never rushes through a note, a move, a moment. Time slows down when he sings this song about the rain. I've never heard it before, but he told me it's by an old New Orleans R&B singer named Irma Thompson.

I look out at the crowd. No one yells or screams because everyone is mesmerized. I see why he was a star and how easily he could be again if he ever tried. There's something about him. I don't know how to describe it, but it's the thing that makes my stomach flutter and my heart race when I catch a glimpse of him in the hallway or when I hear his voice on the phone. Despite that, watching all these people fall in love with Timber makes me wonder if he and I will ever be more than friends.

I look over my shoulder at Bella. She stands off to the side, alone, one arm crossed over her belly, propping the other one up so her fist covers her mouth. I see real sadness in her eyes, but she's not crying, and this sends a chill down my back. I don't know if she was ever really in love with Timber or just liked having him around, but to me, it looks like she's calculating how she's going to win this audition and then get Timber back. Life is all casting to her, and in her mind, she and Timber should always get the lead.

She catches me staring, but I don't look away. It's like my father taught me when we hunt. If you're in the middle of the forest, facing down a mountain lion who wants the same buck you've got in your arrow sights, look them in the eye and let them know you're in charge.

Timber's voice, climbing up and up now, ends our staring contest. He's center stage, head back, eyes closed, arm up, microphone cocked to his mouth. The golden light bathes him as if the sun has broken through the night sky to illuminate only one thing on this earth. "I wish the rain would hurry up and stop," he sings, letting the very last note quake before he snaps up, smiles big, and drops down for a bow.

There's a half-second pause, and then the crowd goes berserk. Kids are on their feet stomping and clapping. Anybody else would either fall down from the power of this reception or let themselves swell up until they floated, but Timber only shakes his head and presses his hands over his heart, mouthing *Thank you* over and over again as he makes his way offstage.

But Mr. Padgett pulls him back to the center of the stage. "Give it up for Timber," Mr. Padgett says into the mic. Timber bows again, then motions to Mr. Padgett, as if he should get all the credit. Mr. Padgett laughs and slaps Timber on his back. Then he slings an arm around Timber's shoulders and Timber does the same to him.

"Vomit," someone says behind me. "Why don't they just make out."

I wrench around to see who's talking, but everyone is whispering together so I have no idea who said it.

"If you liked that, BAPAHS, wait till you see what's next." Keeping one arm around Timber, Mr. Padgett points toward our side of the stage. "Let me hear you make some noise for Bella D'Artagnan!" Mr. Padgett shouts.

Bella straightens up, tosses her hair over her shoulder, and rearranges her face from cold and calculating to the picture of warmth and beauty.

"How's she change her face like that?" I ask Mercedes as we watch Bella glide onto the stage.

Mercy just shakes her head. "Dang, she is a hell of an actress."

Mr. Padgett keeps Timber in his grip, so that he has to reach across his body to hand Bella the mic. For the smallest moment, Timber and Bella are side by side onstage and I see Mr. Padgett grin over his shoulder.

"This is bull," Chelsea says from beside us. And for once I have to agree with her. "If Mr. Padgett wanted to cast the show, he should have just cast it and not make us go through this."

We all turn back to the stage as the first few notes of Bella's song come over the PA system.

"No she didn't," Mercedes says, shaking her head.

"Of course she did," Chelsea says with a snort.

"What is it?" I ask Mercedes.

"'Girlfriend' by Avril Lavigne," says Mercy. "Get a load of the lyrics."

Bella's alone now, standing in the spotlight, reaching toward the crowd. The thing I realize as I watch her is that Bella isn't the best singer today. Chelsea and Mercedes could sing her into a ditch, but Bella is the best performer. It's as if she means every word as she struts around singing, "I don't like your girlfriend." I'm sure she's singing it to Timber, which makes me boil. But what's weird is even though I can't stand her right now, she still has some quality that makes me want to watch her. Like how you can't look away when a fox catches a squirrel.

When her song ends, applause rings through the auditorium and Mr. Padgett comes back onstage. He holds Bella around the waist. "Brilliant," he says as if he's speaking only to her, but since he says it through the mic, everyone hears. "Now, BAPAHS," he says, quieting the crowd. "It's time to vote. The computer lab is open until the end of the day. Log on and cast your vote. Only one vote per student. If you want to know the results, be back here at 3:05 sharp for the announcement of who will be . . ." The lights lower, a spot circles the stage, and a guitar wails. Then the light hits Mr. Padgett and Bella. "The first BAPAHS idol!"

chapter 3

FOR THE REST of the day everyone who auditioned walks the halls like a zombie, staring slack-jaw at each person passing by, wondering, *Did he vote for me? Did she? Was I good enough? Or was I so bad that I should never show my face at BAPAHS again?* At least I changed into jeans and a long-sleeve T-shirt after the audition so no one can point at me and say, "Hey, there's the girl with no pants who sings like a Canada goose."

Timber finds me in the hallway on the way to lunch. He puts his arm around my shoulders and smiles, which makes my hair and skin prickle with excitement. "You were amazing!" he says, giving me a quick hug, then just as quickly letting go to give some guy a high five.

"So were you!" I say, but he's distracted by the forty-five other people telling him the same thing as we make our way down the steps.

When we get to the lunchroom, we find Ari, Mercedes, Briar, and Kenji already in our new corner of the cafeteria. We had been sitting at a table in the center of the room, because that was Timber's table before he broke up with Bella and she was shipped off to detox. But on Monday, Bella's minions, Tara and Zoe, staked out that table and held it for Bella

21

before anyone else could get to it. Mercedes wanted to put up a fight to get the table back, but Timber said it wasn't worth it.

I like the new table better, anyway, because from here I can look out and see the packs in the cafeteria. On the right, skoners (that's what Ari calls the skateboarding stoners), and jazzers on the left. Drama kids in the front, symphony dorks in the back. Ballerinas to one side, nibbling on lettuce, opera singers hunkered down on the other, chowing on pasta. And now, front and center once again, Queen Bee Bella, still surrounded by her buzzing drones, Zoe and Tara, sipping Diet Cokes and sharing a bag of unsalted pretzels.

Erdlers have stronger packs than wolves, Briar said to me after her first day at school, and I have to agree. Except for our misfit group: a drama girl, a gay goth boy, an emo punk, two dorky blond elves forever trying to hide our magic, and superpopular Timber. Sometimes I wonder why we all get along so well.

Mercedes bumps me with her elbow. "See that home slice?" she asks, nodding to a tall, lanky guy loping across the cafeteria. He's in black, head to toe, wild black hair gelled into a sloppy, half-curly Mohawk, black T-shirt with a silver hollow-eyed alien's face across the chest, super-skinny black jeans, black studded belt hanging low on his narrow hips, clunky black boots. "That's Bella's new conquest."

I look to my left at Timber, who shovels in his lunch like he's been trapped in a cabin for a week with no supplies. He glances across the room where everyone else stares. We all watch the guy slide onto the bench beside Bella. She turns to him, her eyes fluttering like two emerald green butterflies alighting off a milkweed plant. A smile slowly spreads across her face. The guy leans forward and they kiss, longer than a peck hello. I can almost feel every girl in the room sigh and every guy bristle with envy.

Timber rolls his eyes at me. "That's Gunther," he whispers. "I'm pretty sure Bella was screwing around with him behind my back for most of last year."

"No way," I say.

"Yes way," he says, and laughs. Then he turns back to a burrito the size of his head.

"Who cares about them," Ari says. "Let's talk about how much I hate Mr. Padgett."

"Let's castrate him." Mercedes sits back in her seat, arms folded over her chest. "Turn him into a eunuch."

"You could tell he was so proud of himself. Like this audition was the greatest idea in the world," Ari complains. "I've never known a person who can get his own knickers in a twist more than that guy."

"What are knickers?" Briar asks as she crunches into a bright orange carrot.

"Underwear," Ari tells her, pointing toward his lap.

"Under here?" Briar asks, looking under the table.

"Huh?" says Ari.

"The knickers," Briar says.

"Is she joking?" Mercedes asks me.

"Skivvies," I say to Briar, using our word for underwear.

"*Knickers* means skivvies?" Briar asks.

"Yes," I say, laughing. "But usually they call it underwear." Ari still looks confused.

"But why are his skivvies twisted?" Briar asks.

"You can tell they're related," Mercedes says, pointing from me to Briar, because before Briar came I was always asking these kinds of questions.

"I just mean he gets really wound up about his own ideas," says Ari.

"When he's not mentioning his music degree from Berklee and his MFA from Columbia," Mercedes adds.

"You'd think the guy has been asked to direct the newest Sondheim revival at the Met," Ari says.

Briar looks at me puzzled. I shrug because like her, I have no idea what they're talking about. The difference is that I've learned to keep the questions to myself and figure things out as I go along so I don't seem entirely clueless.

"I don't think Mr. Padgett's that bad," Timber says between bites.

Mercedes snorts. "You wouldn't."

"What's that supposed to mean?" asks Timber.

"It means you already got your fifteen minutes," Mercedes says. "But the rest of us are still waiting in line."

"Fifteen minutes for what?" I ask, because even I have to ask sometimes.

"Fame," Kenji tells us. "It's an old Andy Warhol quote."

"Huh?" Briar says, but I shrug and let it pass.

"It was longer than fifteen minutes," Timber says, which is true. "And it's a lot less glamorous than most people think. Sometimes fame can suck," says Timber.

"Then why does everyone want it?" Briar asks.

Timber shrugs. "At this point, I just want to play music, and if people like it and want to listen, that's fine. Fame is beside the point. And anyway, TLC Boyz probably put me at a disadvantage today."

"How's that?" Mercedes asks, one eyebrow up and a hand on her hip.

"Backlash," says Timber.

"What are you talking about?" Chelsea asks as she puts her tray down beside Timber. For once Darby and Riena aren't tailing her.

"I'm just saying," Timber goes on. "People might not vote for me because I already had my moment in the sun."

"Hell to the no," Mercedes says. "They'll vote for you. And they'll vote for Bella from Hella. And all the other popular people in the school." She gives Chelsea a withering look. "Whether they can sing worth a damn or not. This won't be about singing. It'll be about who everybody wants to see strutting their pretty little asses across that stage. And it ain't. Gonna. Be. Me." She shakes her head, and I worry that she might cry. "It's always the golden ones."

"Who's golden?" Briar whispers to me.

"I'm not a golden boy, Mercedes," Timber says. His spork clatters against his tray. "I work just as hard as anyone else."

"Oh yeah." Mercedes looks down and pokes at a lump of mashed potatoes on her tray. "You and Bella both deserve Oscars for your performances today, and I'm not talking about your singing."

Briar and I look up from the goat cheese sandwiches we brought from home. "Who's Oscar?" we ask at the same time.

Only Kenji laughs. Even our ignorance doesn't amuse our friends right now. "It's an award," Kenji explains. "For great actors."

"You think he was acting?" I ask Mercedes.

Mercedes looks up from the design she's making in her potatoes and stares at Timber, who stares back at her.

Briar's hand inches across the table to find my arm. She clings to me. "Why are they mad at each other?" she whispers.

"Good question," I say. "Why are you mad at each other?" I ask, trying to break the tension between two of my best friends, but they're caught, like snakes facing off.

Finally, Mercedes drops her spork and ends the staring contest. "Chelsea already called it backstage. This is crazy." She stands up and snatches her tray from the table. "Was that all rehearsed? Did he already give you and Bella the script?" she asks Timber.

Timber rears back in his seat and blinks. "What are you talking about?"

Kenji, Briar, and I look at each other bewildered, but Ari avoids our eyes. He slumps down on the table with his head on folded arms.

"Or is Padgie in love with you, like everybody else?" Mercedes asks, motioning all around the cafeteria. "Because you're the Golden Boy." She jabs her finger toward Bella's table. "And she's the Golden Girl. And the rest of us don't get crap!" Then she slams her tray back down on the table and careens as close to Timber as she can get. "So I need to know," she says more quietly, but anger makes her voice quiver. "Was that audition for real? Or am I just another jerk who thought I actually had a shot for ten minutes."

Timber lifts his hands. "Mercedes, I . . ." He shakes his head and his voice trails off.

I look at Mercedes and see that beneath the hard line of her eyebrows, tears brim around her lower lashes. She shakes her head, curls bouncing. "I'm sick of this," she says, and stomps off between the tables.

We all sit in stunned silence for a moment.

"What just happened?" Briar asks.

I shake my head. "If this is what an audition does to all of us," I say, "it isn't worth it."

Ari lifts his head and peeks through his floppy bangs. "You have to understand, she never gets the part."

"But she was really good," Briar says. "Didn't she see all those people dancing while she was onstage? Didn't she hear us clapping for her? I screamed my head off."

"Will it matter in the end?" Ari asks, then he shrugs. "Probably not."

"You guys don't know—" Timber says, but Ari cuts him off.

"Look, man, nothing against you, but you didn't see how Mr. Padgett treated you and Bella up there."

Timber looks to Chelsea. "Really?"

Chelsea hesitates, but then she sighs and says, "It was pretty clear what Mr. Padgett wants to happen. I mean, he put his arms around you guys. He held you onstage longer than anyone else. It was kind of jive."

"But that doesn't mean everybody will vote that way," Timber says. "That's the beauty of something like *American Idol* or *Idle America* or whatever stupid title Mr. P gives it. It's the power of the people."

"Yeah, well, sometimes the people are just dumb sheep," Ari says. "Just ask Adam Lambert."

"Time will tell," says Kenji, pointing to the large round clock above the exit. "In two and half hours we'll know."

Two and half hours feel like twenty years. By the time we drag ourselves into the auditorium for the second time today, I could swear I'm an old woman. It's not as packed as it was this morning, but the room is still crowded with kids jostling for the seats down front. I stop in the center aisle and stand on tiptoe, looking for Mercedes, who I haven't seen since she stormed out of the cafeteria.

"I can't find her," I say to Briar, who's climbed up on a chair to look.

"She's nowhere," Briar says.

"I texted her and called, but she won't pick up." Ari flips his phone closed.

"You don't think she went home, do you?" I ask.

Timber tugs on my arm. "We should get a seat."

As soon as we sit down the lights dim and the same routine starts with the spotlights circling, the guitar wailing, the backlit staircase with Mr. P at the top. A collective groan ripples through the crowd.

"Jeez," Ari leans over and says. "Enough with the *American Idol* parody already."

This is when I really miss Mercedes, because she'd say something funny right now and we'd all sink into our seats snickering while Mr. Padgett struts down the stairs announcing, "This is *Idle America*!"

"I really do hate this man," Ari says.

"Well," says Mr. Padgett, a cheesy grin plastered across his face. "You all voted and we tallied the results. For the first time in BAPAHS history you, the audience, have cast the winter musical. To begin let's bring up all the guys who auditioned today. Come on, guys, come up onstage."

Timber and Ari rise along with eight other guys who make their way down the aisles and up the steps onto the stage. They line up in the center, a mishmash of tall and short, dark and light, smiling and nervously swaying.

Mr. Padgett walks down the line. "Jonah, Ben, Henry, Kwan, Levi, Timber, Ari, Cuyler, Graham, and Omar. These were your competitors and you decided which five guys will have parts." He stops at the other end of the line. "The guy with the most votes will have the lead. Second most votes get the supporting role, and on down until all five parts are cast. So, only half of these guys will make it. Who will they be?" He sticks his hand in his pocket and pulls out an envelope. "In here are your results." He turns back to the guys. "Are you ready?" he asks.

They all nod and Timber says, "Yes."

"Okay then." Mr. Padgett opens the envelope and takes out a card. He reads it for a moment, then nods. "Jonah, Henry, Cuyler, Graham, and Ari please step to the right. And Timber, Levi, Ben, Omar, and Kwan step to the left." The guys make two lines on either side of Padgie.

I watch Timber onstage, a pleasant grin on his face. He's taller than the other guys in his group, and he seems to stand in front of them by an inch or so.

"One of these groups will be your cast. The other will not," says Mr. Padgett. Briar and I grab hands and squeeze together because no matter what, one of our friends is going down. "Who will it be?" Mr. Padgett asks, then stops again.

People in the crowd get restless. Someone whistles and someone else shouts, "Get on with it."

"The group to my right," Mr. Padgett says, motioning to Ari's group, then hesitating. "Are . . ." He pauses again, and I think my head is going to explode. Which way will it go? Timber said there could be backlash. Mr. Padgett takes a breath. "NOT in the show."

I watch Ari's face fall and his shoulders slump while the crowd mutters and murmurs. Mr. Padgett ushers them toward the steps down from the stage. People yell their names and clap as the guys exit. Briar stands up. "Hup ba! Ari rocks!" she screams. Kenji and I clap. We welcome Ari back into our fold, pulling him down into a seat beside me.

"You okay?" I ask him.

He shrugs. "You win some, you lose some," he says, but I hear weariness in his voice.

"That leaves one question," Mr. Padgett says. "Who gets what part?" Despite the fact that I now officially hate Mr. Padgett, too, I turn my attention back to the stage to see what part Timber will get. "Supporting roles go to . . ." He stops again and I wish I had something to throw at him. "Kwan, Ben, and Omar." They step forward, slap each other on the back, and smile. "You guys step over here," he says and moves the threesome to the side. "Will Levi and Timber step forward?" Timber slings his arm across Levi's shoulders. They step forward together and wait. A low rumble starts in the crowd.

"Timber!" someone yells from the back.

"Levi!" someone else yells.

"Who will be your lead?" Mr. Padgett asks.

"I swear I'm going to turn Padgett into a badger," Briar says to me, and I shoot her a warning look just in case she's not kidding.

"This year, the BAPAHS winter musical lead role for *Idle America* goes to . . ." He looks at the guys, turns to the crowd, then back to the guys. "Timber Lewis Cahill!"

Levi nods his head. He turns and gives Timber that kind of guy hug where they bump chests. Timber pats him on the back and says something into his ear. Then Timber is standing beside Mr. Padgett.

"Congratulations," Mr. Padgett says.

"Thanks," says Timber. He waves to the crowd. "And thank you."

"You ready to find out who your leading lady will be?"

Timber nods.

"All right then, let's bring up the ladies."

Briar and Ari pat my back as I sidestep out of the row. "Good luck," Ari says to me. "It's hell up there."

I make my way toward the stage, looking for Mercedes, but I don't see her in the line of girls heading down the aisles. We climb up the steps and line up, just like the guys did. Mr. Padgett starts his pacing and blathering again, but I can't even listen. It's taking all my willpower not to zap the guy for being such an irritating boob.

"We seem to be missing someone," says Mr. Padgett. He runs through his list again, "Chelsea, Zephyr, Nora, Riena, Jaden, Angelica, Ellie, Mimi, Bella, and . . ."

"Ena," the tall girl beside me says. "Like Tina without the stupid T."

Mr. Padgett blinks at her as if he can't believe anyone would dare speak. "Yes, you're on my list, but be that as it may, we're still short one girl." He looks down at the card in his hand. "Mercedes?" He turns to the crowd. "Does anyone know where Mercedes is?" People in the crowd mumble and crane their necks to see if she'll make an appearance, but she doesn't show. My heart sinks. I can't believe she'd miss this moment. Instead of standing next to her, holding hands, I'm beside Ena without the T and Chelsea, who's still in her teeny tiny skirt and boots—at least she's put on a sweater.

As Mr. Padgett goes through all the rigmarole of making us step to the left and to the right, all I can think is that either Mercedes or I need to have a part in this play because who else will keep an eye on Bella now that Ari is out? And since Mercedes didn't even show up, she's probably not getting cast, so that means I have to get a part. I can't keep track of which group I'm in and whether we're the lucky or unlucky ones until I hear a simper from the left of me and see Riena, Angelica, Jaden, Mimi, Ellie, and Ena, leaving the stage. I whip my head around to find Timber, who's grinning straight at me. I'm in! I'm in! I'm in!

I step forward with Chelsea, Nora, and Bella, but before Mr. Padgett can speak again everyone turns toward the back of the auditorium.

"I'm here! I'm here! I'm here!" yells a crazy girl, running down the aisle.

I jump. "Mercedes!" I yell as she bounds up the steps.

"I'm here!" she says one last time as she makes it onstage and bends over to catch her breath while people in the crowd whistle, clap, and laugh.

"She's here," Mr. Padgett says with a tight, forced chuckle. "Thank God," he says drily, "and you are in, Mercedes." I reach out and grab her hand, then pull her to my side.

"Where were you?" I ask, but she just shakes her head.

"So here we go, BAPAHS," Mr. Padgett says. "Let's see how this whole thing is going to pan out." He turns to us. I hold Mercedes's hand and shut my eyes. "Will Nora, Chelsea, and Zephyr please step forward?"

I let go of Mercy's hand, but before I step forward I look back at her. She stands, stunned, a few feet away from Bella, who's as cool as a lake breeze. Chelsea, Nora, and I throw our arms around each other and smile. "You're our supporting cast. You can move over there with the guys."

I skip across the stage and jump into Timber's arms. He hugs me tightly, then lets go and hugs Chelsea, too. We stand on either side of him and turn our attention back to center stage, where Mercedes stands, barely able to contain her energy, next to Bella, who seems to be made of marble, she's so still.

"The supporting actress role in the spring musical goes to . . ." Mr. Padgett stops and I want to kill him but not for long because then he says, "Mercedes Sanchez, which means the lead is your very own Bella D'Artagnan!"

Mercedes offers a quick hug to Bella, who barely pats her back before shoving her aside and wrapping her arm around Mr. Padgett's waist. Bella and Mr. P both turn toward our line and call Timber to center stage. The audience applauds, strong and polite, but not wild like at the auditions.

"Well, BAPAHS," says Mr. Padgett. He stands between Bella and Timber, holding each of their hands. "Here you have it." Then he lifts their arms and steps back, joining their hands together overhead. "Your lead actors for . . ." Everyone groans as the lights go down, the spotlights come up, and that same annoying guitar lick whines through the speakers as the neon sign flashes in the background. *Idle America!* Mr. Padgett yells.

The last thing I see is Bella and Timber illuminated by a spotlight, arms around each other, waving and smiling to the crowd.

chapter 4

AFTER WE LEAVE BAPAHS, Timber, Ari, Mercedes, Briar, Kenji, and I grab a table at Galaxy, the funky little coffee shop with mismatched furniture and funny mugs, across the street from the school. Several small groups of BAPAHS students huddle around the tables blowing on steaming mugs of coffee, latte, and hot chocolate, except for me. I'm all about the double chocolate crinkle cookies here. Chelsea and Darby have settled at the table next to ours to comfort Riena, who cries into her mug with a goofy, grinning picture of Elmo on the front.

"I don't even like *American Idol*," Ari says as he dumps cream into his coffee.

"I like when the people audition then argue with the judges about whether they can sing," Kenji says. "It's totally delusional."

"I only watch it because my little sisters are into it," Mercedes says. "I think it's hokey and the people I like never win."

"At least you know what it is," I say, and pop a piece of cookie in my mouth. Briar nods.

"I like it," Timber says, looking up from his iPhone. He hands me the phone. "Check out these clips from YouTube." Briar and I watch a dark-haired woman with a small nose ring singing on the tiny screen.

"For real, you like it?" Mercedes asks him as if nothing weird went down in the cafeteria today.

Timber shrugs. "Sure, what's not to like?"

"It's all so contrived," Ari says.

Timber reaches over and pushes some buttons on his iPhone screen, then another singer, a guy with black, spiky hair and eyeliner, comes on the screen to belt out a tune. "Sure, it's TV, it's got to be contrived. But that doesn't mean the contestants don't work hard. They're all legit."

"True," Mercedes says, and smiles at Timber. "Just like us." They slap a high five across the table, then they reach for me. I slap hands with them, but I'm confused. Weren't these two furious with each other earlier? Erdlers amaze me in this way. One minute they're mad at each other, the next they're friends again.

"What about these guys?" Mercedes asks, looking to Kenji, Briar, and Ari. "We can't do this show without them."

Ari shrugs. "Mr. Sax already tapped me, Angelica, and Gunther to play in the band."

"Gunther?" I ask. "As in Bella's boyfriend?"

"The very one," Mercedes says. I steal a glance at Timber, but he's busy messing with his iPhone.

"Well, that's great about the band, Ari," I say, then I turn to Kenji and Briar. "I wish you could be in the show with us, too."

"Our man Kenji will be there," Mercedes says. "Don't you know about his secret superpower?"

Briar and I both stare wide-eyed at Kenji. He freezes with his coffee halfway to his mouth, which is funny because the mug says CHEER-LEADERS DO IT WITH SPUNK in the exact bright blue as the tips of his otherwise black hair.

"Actually," I say, stopping to think for a moment. "I know why all of us go to this school except you. Timber's here for music. Mercedes wants to be an actress. Ari sings and plays piano. Briar got in because she dances beautifully. I'm here because I can sing and play the flute. But you . . ."

"He's a tech nerd," Ari says.

"Not just any tech nerd," Mercedes adds. "The best tech nerd in the school."

"Stage production and visual design, thank you very much," says Kenji.

"What's that mean?" Briar asks as she licks whipped cream from the top of some chocolaty coffee concoction in a mug with a picture of a Chihuahua dressed in a red hat and a white beard.

"Kenji's the man for set design and production," Ari explains.

"Hey," Mercedes says to Briar. "You could be a techie, too." She cuts her eyes to Kenji. "If the boss here will hire you."

Briar grabs Kenji's arm and begs, "Please, please, please."

"Do you even know what a techie is?" Kenji asks her.

She smiles. "Nope. But I still want to be one so all our friends are together."

"Dude," Timber says with a laugh. "The girl's begging you."

"Do you know where the wings are?" Kenji asks her.

"On the backs of fairies," Briar says brightly.

"How about the pit?" he asks.

"Of despair?" says Briar with wide eyes.

"What's baffling?" Kenji says.

"All of this," says Briar.

"What's the Best Boy?" Kenji asks.

"You are," Briar says with a sweet smile, and we all crack up.

Kenji shakes his head and laughs. "You might not know anything about the stage, but I like your enthusiasm. You're hired."

We all cheer and Briar squeals. She claps her hands like a little kid. "Hup ba!" she shouts, which makes me laugh harder. "We're going to have so much fun!"

"Aren't we though?" The voice comes from behind us, but no one needs to turn around to know who it is.

Bella stands with a guy and a girl I've never seen before. The guy has thick, straw-colored hair down to his chin, a square jaw, and eyes as blue as a jay's tail feather. The girl could be his twin except she has long hair twisted into a messy bun and she looks younger than he is, but still older than we are. They're both as tall as Briar and I. Tara and Zoe, Bella's minions, stand back a ways as if waiting for a command.

"Talking about the audition?" Bella leans over Timber's shoulder. My body tenses as her soft, cream-colored sweater brushes Timber's neck. "I thought it went extremely well."

"Shocking!" Mercedes says, with mock surprise.

Bella blinks at her and then she says, "Congratulations, Mercedes. You must be very excited. You were definitely due for a bigger role this time around. I'm looking forward to working with you." For once, there's not a trace of sarcasm in Bella's words, which makes Mercedes sputter. I notice that Chelsea has wrenched around in her seat to watch the performance at our table. Bella turns to face Timber. Her lips are so close they're practically grazing his cheek. "And you," she purrs. "I'm really looking forward to singing with you again."

I'm about to zap her, Mother Earth help me! Turn her into a toad. Give her a case of the warts and farts. My fingers are moving, my lips forming the words, but before I get it together, Timber shrugs her off. "Are you going to introduce us?" he asks, eyeing the couple beside her.

Bella stands up straight. "Yes. This is Clay and Dawn Corrigan," she says. "They're my new managers."

The guy steps forward and sticks his hand out to Timber. "Great to meet you," he says, leaning too close with a smile so big it looks as if he could swallow Timber's head. "I'm a big fan of your work, Timber. Today proved that you've still got it."

Timber blushes a bit. "You were at the audition?"

Clay slings an arm around Bella's shoulders and pulls her close to his body. She looks like a tiny owlet beneath his wing. "Oh yes. We're planning a big relaunch of Bella's career. We think it's time for her to go in a new direction and showcase some of these amazing stage talents that have been wasted on two-bit television parts. We're looking ahead to some off-Broadway auditions in the spring, then Broadway next fall. This is just a warm-up."

"Speaking of which . . ." The girl steps forward and hands us a stack of red flyers. "Bella will be performing tonight at our all-ages club in Red Hook." Each of us takes a sheet. "The show is free, so bring all your friends," she adds.

"Hope you can all make it," Bella says with a pert little grin. "It'd be great to have the cast there supporting me."

"Great to meet you all," Clay says, flashing us that weird toothy grin again. "And Timber," he says, leaning down and slipping Timber a small card, "if you're in the market for new management, give us a shout." Then he and Dawn follow Bella to another table, no doubt to promote her show some more.

"Just once," Mercedes mutters as Bella walks away, "I'd like to see that girl get what she deserves."

"Rehab wasn't enough?" Timber asks as he tucks the card in his pocket.

My stomach rolls because (a) he doesn't know Bella's stint in rehab was my fault, and (b) if he starts working with those two big blond goons, they'd probably cast him in more things with Bella. I wad my flyer into a ball and toss it to the center of the table. "Haven't you guys had enough of Bella for one day?"

"Yeah, but . . ." Ari holds up his BlackBerry. "This place looks awesome." He hands his phone around and we all look at Clay and Dawn's Web site for the club.

"And it's free," Mercedes adds, pointing to her flyer.

Chelsea scoots her chair closer to us. The little diamond stud in the side of her nose catches a light and sparkles as she grabs for a flyer. "You guys going to check it out?"

"What else have we got to do?" Timber asks.

I can think of about fifty better things to do with my time than watch Bella sing, like scrub my toilet with a toothbrush or stand in a bucket of leeches. But I don't say anything because if Timber's planning to be where Bella is going to be, then I need to be there, too. "Briar and I are free," I say.

"We are?" she asks.

I step on her foot under the table. "Yes," I tell her.

"Oh yeah," she says, yanking her foot away from mine. "We're totally free."

"Great," Timber says. "Let's all meet there at eight."

chapter 5

WE ALL GO our separate ways when we leave Galaxy. Ari's band has rehearsal. Mercedes has to babysit her twin sisters. And Timber promised to go Christmas tree shopping with his mom. Briar and I ride the train back to our station, but instead of going straight home, we slip into Prospect Park. Even though I love my school, by the end of the day I feel like a trapped raccoon ready to claw my way out a closed window. Despite the slushy gray snow covering the sidewalks, I need to be outside, to breathe some fresh air (well, as fresh as air can get in Brooklyn), and see the sky (even if the sun is already sinking at 4:30). I can tell Briar feels the same by the way she lifts her face and inhales the crisp, cold air.

After we've walked for a few minutes in silence, I say, "I can't believe we have to listen to Bella sing tonight."

"Could you believe her hanging all over Timber, then having the nerve to invite everyone to her gig? You should've zapped her," Briar tells me.

"I wanted to," I admit.

"Why didn't you, then?"

"Because," I say, "the last time I zapped her, it came back to bite me in the butt."

She ducks under a large cedar tree and heads up a hill dusted lightly with fresh white snow. I follow, happy to be off the cement walkways erdlers stick to in the park.

"Besides," I trudge behind Briar, "what good would it do? It's not like Timber's even my boyfriend."

"First off," Briar says, "he'll never be your boyfriend if you don't do something."

"Like what?" I ask miserably.

She turns around to face me. "Like zapping Bella when she's hanging on him!"

I roll my eyes at her.

"Or getting the part you wanted today," she says.

"I had no control over that."

Now she rolls her eyes at me. "You're an elf!" She wiggles her fingers. "You can work magic! You have all the control you want."

"No, Briar." I peer around, making sure no one's near. "At school, we're ordinary kids."

A small, mean smile lurks on Briar's lips. "You think *ordinary* kids wouldn't use every advantage they have to get what they want?"

"We can't use magic here," I tell her. "We could get caught."

She scoffs and continues walking. "You wouldn't have gotten caught."

"You don't know that," I say.

"You've always been afraid of getting in trouble." Briar points to a low-hanging branch over my head. She shakes her finger and makes the branch quiver, dumping snow on my head. "Then you complain about what you don't have."

"Hey!" I yell, dusting myself off and frantically looking around to make sure no one saw what she just did.

"Relax," she says as she walks away. "Nobody's around."

"You've always been a troublemaker and you don't fight fair!" I scoop up a handful of snow off the ground and whiz it at her, but she jumps out of the way. "We have to play by erdler rules now," I say as I think back to how sick I got after I cast my last spell on Bella—the spell that caused her to botch the audition so badly that everyone thought she was on drugs (which she was, but that's not why her audition was so bad). I got sick because I used my magic for ill will, a big elfin no-no.

"Whatev," Briar says.

"We have to use our magic for good," I remind her.

"Come on," Briar says. "A tiny little hex when she's singing tonight."

"That's how it starts," I warn.

"Just the hiccups, that's all. It'd be funny."

"Dark elves cast spells for mischief," I say. "Not us."

"There's no such thing as dark elves. Grandma Fawna made that up to scare us. Besides, I'm not a dark elf. I'm me, and casting spells is part of who I am."

"Not here it's not."

"No wonder your sister hated it here." Briar pulls away from me. We're in the midst of bare sycamores and snowy evergreens with only the squirrels to overhear us now.

I think back to my sister Willow sitting in the window seat on the third floor of our Brooklyn house, looking out over the red and gold autumn trees. She was miserable when my family moved to Brooklyn and she had to leave her boyfriend. "Willow was unhappy because she was away from Ash," I say. "Not because she couldn't use her magic." Now she's back in Alverland, engaged to Ash, and preparing for her wedding, which makes her happy, but the rest of us miss her terribly because elf families always stick together.

From the top of the hill, we stop and look down at the fence separating the park from the sidewalk and street. On this side of the fence is an open meadow where dogs run free in the mornings and people play soccer on the weekends. Beyond that, farther into the park, is the copse of maple trees where Timber kissed me this past fall, back when Willow still lived here and before Briar came. The memory gives me happy shivers. Or maybe it's the cold as the sun sinks behind the pale pink clouds in the sky.

"What do you think Willow and Ash's wedding will be like?" Briar asks, a little dreamy.

I shrug. "Probably like every other wedding in the history of Alverland." My sister is traditional, to say the least.

"Isn't it exciting that she's going to get Mama Ivy's land?"

"Ivy's not dead yet," I remind Briar as we tromp through heavier snow dotted with squirrel prints and a few bird tracks.

"She's 199!"

"Grandmother Aster lived to 206," I say, but then I sigh. "I do love Ivy's house, though." We're quiet as we think of the small stone cottage in a glen, surrounded by giant red pines and goldenrod, that my sister will inherit because she's the firstborn daughter in a long line of first daughters—my mother, my grandmother, my great-grandmother, and all the way back eight generations to Ivy, who's the oldest living matriarch in our family now.

"It's so romantic!" Briar says with a sigh. Then she stops. "But if you marry Timber you wouldn't be allowed to live in Alverland."

"Stop," I say, but a little ripple of excitement goes through my chest at the thought of marrying Timber. "I'm not going to marry him. I can't even get him alone. And besides, who says I want to live in Alverland?"

"I know," Briar says. "But it could be a problem. Falling in love with an erdler."

We turn at a big Norway maple and head down a steep hill with old sled tracks packed into the snow. This trail will take us to the road that goes by our house.

"You know what I miss most about Alverland?" Briar asks.

I shake my head because I can think of twenty things I miss right now.

"Dancing," she says.

"You dance every day at school."

"No, not that kind. With you and our sisters." She reaches out and spins herself around the trunk of a small tree. "The fresh snow makes me want to dance an elf circle."

I smile. "I miss that, too."

We follow the track down through the trees, talking about our favorite dance spots in Alverland, but before we get to the road, we both jump when two people come out from the midst of the pines. Both of us fling our hands up, ready to cast mischief if we need to, but a guy and the girl in puffy white coats and white knit hats step back.

"Sorry," says the girl.

"We didn't see you there," the guy adds.

It takes a second for all of us to register that we know each other.

"Hey," Briar says. "Didn't we just meet?"

"At the coffee shop," the girls says, nodding and smiling.

"You were with Bella," I say.

"And you were with Timber," says the guy, then he laughs. "Guess we all had the same idea about a snowy hike off the beaten path." He sticks out his hand and reintroduces himself. "I'm Clay Corrigan. This is Dawn."

Dawn smiles as we all shake hands. Her teeth are as white and straight as the guy's. "Not many people like to come up this far in the woods." She looks up into the graying sky above the trees. "Especially when the sun is starting to sink."

"We're on our way home," Briar says.

"You live near here?" Clay asks.

"Yeah," Briar says, and starts to point toward our house.

I grab her arm. "We should be going, before it gets dark."

"You look familiar," the girl says to me. "I'm sure I've seen you before. I mean before we met at the coffee shop today."

What's funny is, they look familiar to me, too, but I'm sure we've never met. "Probably seen each other around the park."

She shakes her head and steps closer to me. We're almost exactly the same height. "Nope. I know I've seen you somewhere. Are you an actress or something? I feel like you've been on TV."

"I'm not an actress," I say, walking away. "We should be going."

As we crunch past them in the snow, Dawn yells, "Aha! I've got it. You're the daughter of that singer, Drake Addler, aren't you? I saw some documentary about your family on VH1 a few months ago."

I cringe. We were on VH1, trying to show what a normal, happy family we are when my dad was trying to prove that he isn't the leader of a weird pagan cult (a chat-room rumor I think Bella started). "I didn't think anybody saw it."

"Oh, yeah. I've seen everything about your dad," she says.

"We're big fans," Clay adds with his signature toothy grin. I wonder if he's going to hand me a card to give to my dad.

I try to smile graciously, but my stomach knots up. "I'll tell him." I start down the path again.

"Hey, what are your names?" the girl calls after us.

"I'm Briar!" Briar shouts over her shoulder. I elbow her hard in the side, but it doesn't do any good. "And she's Zephyr."

"Will we see you tonight at Bella's gig?" Dawn asks.

"Yes!" Briar says, waving to them. "We're all coming."

"Bring your brother Grove," Dawn says. My stomach flutters. The fact that she knows so much about my family might mean she's one of those nut-job fans. They have Web sites and chat rooms to speculate on my family's life. A few months ago, one of them tried to find Alverland.

"See you at the club," Clay says.

I yank hard on Briar's arm and pull her down the path away from them.

"What is your problem?" she asks, wriggling away.

"Could you be friendlier to those weirdos?" I whisper as I maneuver through the trees.

"Just because they rep Bella—" Briar starts to say.

"That's not it." I look over my shoulder to make sure they aren't following us. "They're creepy. Walking around up here in the woods."

"We're up here in the woods," Briar points out.

"Exactly," I say as we come down from the hill onto the road that circles the park. "And we aren't your normal, average erdlers, are we?"

"You're paranoid," Briar says.

"And you're naïve," I say.

"But they like your dad."

"This isn't Alverland, Bri. Not everyone is nice." I stop and look over my shoulder one last time. The woods are quiet and we seem to be alone. "Besides," I whisper, "they could have overheard us."

"They wouldn't know what we were talking about."

"That's just it," I say. "We can't let anyone know. Ever. Don't you get it? We're different from everybody else and we have to protect that."

"Whatevs," Briar says, and snatches her arm out of my grip. We walk side by side out of the park, to the main road. "But," she says as we wait to cross the street to our house, "it was kind of cool that they recognized you, don't you think?"

"They only recognized me because of Dad," I say, pausing for the traffic to clear.

"What difference does it make?" she asks.

"If I'm going to be recognized," I say, "I wish it'd be for something I do, not because Drake Addler is my father."

I can smell the fire crackling in our living room as soon as I open the front door. As much as I miss our house in Alverland, I've grown to like this place with its cozy rooms, creaky steps, and wheezing radiators.

"Zephyr and Briar are home!" Bramble shouts as he catapults from the middle of the stairs. His brown tunic flies up behind him like a cape, and his little green cap tumbles off his head. "Did you see that?" he asks, looking up from a crouch near our toes. "Seventh stair because I'm seven years old. I bet I could jump from the third highest rock at Barnaby Bluff. There's no way Lake could do that."

"I don't know," says Briar, unwinding her long, red scarf that her mom (my aunt Flora) knit for her. "My brother's a good jumper. I think he was already jumping off the third rock when I left."

Bramble bounces up and climbs the steps again. "I'm going to keep practicing so when we go back I can jump farther than he can."

"Where is everybody?" I ask as I shrug off my coat.

Bramble climbs to the eighth step. "Kitchen or out back, maybe. Doing Harvest stuff. I'm a bobcat!"

"It's called Thanksgiving here," I remind him.

He growls then leaps again. Briar and I hop out of the way of his crash landing. "Be careful, would you?" I tell him. "And don't call it Harvest Festival when everyone is here tomorrow, okay?" But he's already back up the stairs, ignoring me.

Ever since my mom had the bright idea to invite all my friends and their families over for "Thanksgiving" at our house, I've been half dreading tomorrow. First off, elves don't celebrate Thanksgiving. We have a Harvest Festival, which from what I can tell is similar, but not the same.

And for that reason I'm absolutely sure that my family will do something embarrassing in front of everyone.

In the kitchen, we find my mom, my older brother Grove, and my little sisters, Poppy and Persimmon. Grove sits on a stool in the corner, noodling on his guitar while the girls plunge their arms deep into a mixing bowl full of thick dough. Mom chops something at the side counter. Cinnamon and nutmeg permeate the warm, moist air. Usually, I love when my mom bakes, especially for special occasions like the Harvest Festival, but now I'm worried. "What are you making?" I poke my finger in the bowl.

Mom turns around and smiles, radiating her familiar blond-haired, green-eyed charm. "Hello, my little fawns." She opens her arms to us and we both accept a hug. She's wearing her blue tunic, so soft and worn that it feels like a blanket against my cheek. Her amulets click together as she embraces us. "How was your day?"

"We went to the co-op to buy apples," Poppy tells us, proudly, before Briar or I can speak.

"For bumblings," Persimmon adds.

Mom laughs and wipes flour off Percy's nose. "Dumplings."

Persimmon nods. "Daddy likes bumplings."

"But Mom," I whine. "Erdlers don't eat apple dumplings for Thanksgiving!" I march over to the refrigerator and pull down the list of traditional erdler foods that I printed off of Wikipedia. I turn to page two. "Right here it says they eat pumpkin pie or pecan pie."

"But I don't know how to make those," Mom says.

I shake the papers at her. "I printed recipes for you."

"Not everyone has to follow your directions," Grove says.

"Where's Dad?" I ask, hoping at least he'll understand what I'm saying.

"He's at a meeting with his agent," Mom says, then she cocks her head to the left and looks at me for a moment. "Zephyr, honey, tomorrow will be fine. Your friends will bring the traditional erdler food, and we'll share our food with them. That's what Thanksgiving is about."

"And we'll look like big freaks," I mutter as I toss the papers aside.

Briar swipes a bright green apple off the counter, then tosses one to me. "Are these apples any good?"

"Surprisingly, yes," says Mom.

"There was cow's milk in a purple carton with a picture of a cow on it," Poppy tells us. "And I tried a banana. Have you ever had Pirate's Booty?"

My sisters are still amazed that you can buy food at a store. I'm still amazed that my mom joined the Park Slope Food Coop. When we first moved here, she hated going out among the erdlers. Although, after going to the co-op with her, I realize that we probably aren't the weirdest family in Brooklyn. All kinds of strange people shop there.

"Where's Grandma?" I ask, crunching into the apple that is surprisingly good—something I never thought I'd say about erdler food other than pizza.

Mom bites her lip then turns back to her cutting board. "Outside."

"You want some help?" Briar asks her.

"You girls can roll out the dough and start cutting circles," Mom says.

"In a minute," I say, heading for the back door. "I want to say hi to Grandma first."

Sometimes I swear my grandma Fawna is the only person in this house who really understands me. For example, she's the only one who studied the sheets I printed with the Thanksgiving traditions.

I find her in the garden, bent over the round wooden picnic table where she's made a small pile of dried twigs and leaves. She's mumbling as she adds more from a leather satchel tied around her waist. If we were still in Alverland, Briar and I would start our spell-casting apprentice-ships soon. That's when we study with one of our grandparents. I'm not sure how my other cousins in Alverland are coping with my grandma gone, but Fawna says there's plenty of magic to go around, so she's not worried.

Even though everyone in our family still dresses in Alverland clothes every day (except Briar and me when we go to school), Grandma Fawna kicks it seriously old school. Her pine-green tunic nearly sweeps the ground it's so long, and she wears dozens of amulets around her neck, plus bands up her left arm. When I was little, I loved sitting on her lap, counting the amulets then the bands, taking in every detail of the feath-ers, claws, tufts of fur, and smooth rocks. She'd catalog their uses: speed, grace, cunning, stealth. Then we'd look at her tiny bags of moss, herbs, leaves, and dried berries, and she'd tell us each one's healing properties. Elf children aren't expected to memorize all of those things until we're sixteen, but growing up with it makes it easier when the time comes.

I wrap my arms around myself to keep warm in the chilly air, but Fawna doesn't seem to notice the cold. She takes a short, smooth stick from a pocket of her tunic. I recognize the intricate designs my grand-father carved around the base. She closes her eyes, lifts her head, and mutters something as she points the stick at the table. The pile of twigs and leaves ignites, sending a puff of orange fire then a plume of purple smoke curling toward the sky.

"Grandma!" I rush toward her, waving the smoke away. "You can't do that here," I whisper harshly. "What if someone sees you?" I look all around at our neighbors' windows surrounding us on every side, making sure there are no curious faces peering out.

Fawna continues watching the smoke as it rises for a moment, then she turns to me and blinks. "No one cares what a crazy old woman does in her garden." She turns her attention to the ashes on the table. With her stick, she traces the design. "Look here," she says to me. "What do you see?"

I can definitely see a symmetrical pattern with interlocking loops and maybe some kind of square in the center, but I don't know what any of it means. I shake my head.

"Hmmm." She looks troubled for a moment with her eyebrows flexed and her mouth in a tight, straight line.

"What's it mean?" I ask.

She blows the ash away, scattering it across an empty azalea bush. There are no marks from the fire on the table. "Who knows?" she says with a shrug.

"You do."

"Perhaps." She smiles and puts her stick back in her pocket.

"You're supposed to teach me these things."

"Ah." She puts her hands on my shoulders and brings her face close to mine to look deeply in my eyes. My heart slows and my stomach calms like the surface of a pond after the wind dies down. "You're getting old enough now," she says quietly. "Your apprenticeship should start soon. But we must start with something simpler than that."

I look over my shoulder at the ash sprinkled across the snow-covered ground. "What were you trying to figure out?"

Fawna pauses and looks down at me. Then she lifts her head again. "I'm not sure yet," she says. I follow her gaze. Night has nearly enveloped the sky, turning it charcoal gray with a few streaks of fading pink. "Something feels off to me."

"Grandma," I say, "can I ask you a question?"

"Of course, my dear."

"Are dark elves real or did you make them up to scare us?"

Grandma sighs. "Aha, that's the question of someone ready for her apprenticeship."

"Well?" I ask, waiting for a real answer.

"What do you think?" she asks.

"Grandma!" I whine, because it's always the same with her. Ask a question, get a question in return.

"I had a cousin," she tells me. "Her name was Hyacinth. She is the daughter of my aunt Iris, my mother's youngest sister."

And if it's not a question, you get a long story. "Is there never a straightforward answer?" I ask. "A yes or a no?"

She ignores me and continues. "Hyacinth left Alverland, you know. Married a man from a different clan. We were all heartbroken."

"Where'd she go?" I ask.

Grandma shrugged. "No one knows for sure, but some people believe she turned dark."

I lean closer to her. "What's it mean, when someone turns dark?"

"What do you think it means?" she asks.

"Again with the questions!" I say, but this time I laugh.

"Consider this an apprenticeship question," Grandma says, putting her arm around my shoulders. "Get back to me when you think you know. Now," she leads me toward the back door, "let's go help your mother."

"She's in there making apple dumplings for tomorrow, not pumpkin pie," I complain.

Grandma leads me up the steps to the back door. "Ah, well, what can you do?"

"But Grandma . . ."

She holds up her hand. "My dear, you can't control everything."

"But . . ."

She pats my arm. "But what?"

I look in the kitchen window. My mom and the kids have formed an apple dumpling assembly line. "Couldn't you cast a spell or something to turn our food into erdler food?"

Grandma shakes her head. "Good granite, my dear. That would be a waste of my magic when your mother's food is so good."

"So that would be dark magic," I say, half kidding.

Grandma laughs. "It'd be a start. Now then," she says as she opens the door, "tell me about your day. What was the twist so big it was going to blow your pipes?"

"Our minds, Grandma. It was going to blow our minds." I laugh as we enter the warm cinnamony kitchen. "You're not going to believe what happened at the auditions."

"Or where we're going tonight," Briar adds, handing Grove a red flyer.

chapter 6

MUSIC PUMPS THROUGH the speakers overhead and crashes to the red, yellow, and blue puddles of light on the dance floor. The crowd jumps in time to the rhythm of the drums and bass. I'm so sweaty I feel like I'm grooving under a waterfall. It may be 30 degrees and snowing outside, but inside this club, I'm wearing my tunic with no leggings and my boots (which was Briar's idea), and everything's sticking to my skin like it's the middle of summer.

Timber reaches out to me. He's down to his jeans and a white tank. Sweat slicks his hair off his forehead, and his gray-blue eyes sparkle under the roving lights. Watching him dance makes me feel something inside, like a flower blooming behind my belly button, and I want to move! I grab his hands and we jump, twirl, shake, and sing with the other hundred people who've showed up at Clay and Dawn's Red Hook club.

Timber yells something to me, but the *boom-chick* rhythm of the music drowns out his words. I try to maneuver closer to him between the flailing arms, whipping hair, and gyrating hips of all the other people. Ari and Mercedes dance on one side of us. Briar and Kenji on the other. Kenji's movements are sharp and jerky, but Briar flows like a wild river. I have to smile because dancing is her thing. It's what makes her most happy in the world and she's great at it. My brother Grove is somewhere in the crowd, too. I saw Chelsea and her gals earlier, but I lost track of them once the lights dimmed. I even caught a glimpse of Bella and Gunther when we first came in, but I'm hoping the wall of people around us will keep them at a distance, especially because, at this very moment, Timber is so close to me that I can see the beads of sweat on his upper lip.

When the song ends, the lights come up slowly and the DJ shouts, "How y'all doing tonight in Red Hook?" Everyone claps and yells. "I said, how y'all doing?" he repeats, and we yell and clap and stomp louder. "That's more like it. Now, don't go anywhere, stay right where you are and turn your attention to the stage because right here, right now, we've got a special performance by the belle of Brooklyn, Ms. Bella D'Artagnan!"

Music swells over the polite applause from the crowd as Bella struts onto the stage under a white spotlight. She's wearing a short, black, see-through dress and a body-hugging lacy thing underneath that looks more like a bathing suit than clothes. She hits her opening mark center stage with legs wide, arms up, light and wind hitting her from behind so there appears to be a halo around her long, whipping hair. Warm air wafts out into the crowd and I smell camellias and roses and the faintest trace of sandalwood, which reminds me of something else. Home? My mother? Walking in the woods? I don't know, but the smell is soothing and I almost relax into it as I gaze up at her from the dance floor. Her legs seem impossibly long covered in black fishnets as she changes from one pose to the next while the music builds. Then she begins to stomp to the rhythm in her spiky black heels.

I look at the crowd. Everyone stands still as if mesmerized, watching her dance to and sing some song about shaking your booty tonight that I've never heard. I would expect this kind of ogling from the guys, but most of the girls seem entranced by her every move, too. And even though I'd like her to fall off the stage, I can barely take my eyes off her, either. I swear, if I didn't know better, I'd think she's the one who's magic.

Worst of all, Timber stares at her like he couldn't look away if he wanted to. The more she sings and moves onstage, the more beguiled the crowd seems to become, and pretty soon people are dancing along with her, mouthing lyrics to songs I don't know. I turn to see if Briar understands why everyone is so captivated, but then I realize that she's not next to me anymore.

My stomach knots and suddenly I'm panicked. I can't find Briar in the crowd, but since Bella's show is going so well, I assume that Briar's keeping her promise. I warned her before we left the house not to use magic to ruin Bella's performance. *We can't interfere,* I told her. She rolled her eyes at me. *Whatev, cuz,* she said. I squeezed her arm tightly. *Promise,* I demanded. *I promise,* she said. *Elf swear,* I said, and formed my first two fingers on each hand into a V. Then I crossed the Vs together in front of her mouth. She bit her lip and narrowed her eyes at me. *Do it,* I said, *or I'll tell Mom you're planning on casting a spell tonight and she'll keep you home.* Briar shifted from one foot to the other but she relented. *I swear I won't use magic to mess with Bella's performance,* she said, and I caught the words in my hands.

I, for one, have had enough Bella for one day. Between songs, I tap Timber on the shoulder. At first he doesn't react, so I poke him harder. He shakes himself, as if waking up from a daydream, and looks at me. "I'm thirsty," I yell. He leans in close to hear me over the music. "I'm going to get a drink," I shout into his ear. He pushes my hair behind my ear and leans down. "I'll go with you," he yells, making my ear ring.

"Great!" I scream back.

I follow him as we weave through the jumble of bodies to the front of the club where the music is slightly less deafening and the cool air smells like beer and sweat and slushy snow, which is strangely refreshing after the warm woodsy smell on the dance floor.

I plop down on a red vinyl couch and almost slide to the shaggy orange rug because I'm so slippery with sweat. Timber brings over two big plastic tumblers of ice water from the bar.

"You made it!" We turn around to find weirdo Dawn leaning between us from behind the couch. She slings her arms around our shoulders and hugs us both tight to her neck. "Did you bring your friends? Is your cousin here? What about your brother?"

I try to wriggle away from her a little, but she's got a tight grip on me. "Grove drove us all here," I tell her. "And I've seen tons of people from our school, too."

"Hurray!" she squeals, and hugs me tight again. "Clay and I worked so hard to get the word out about Bella's show. E-mail, Facebook, Twitter, flyers, smoke signals!" She laughs and finally lets go of us, but then she climbs over the back of the couch and ends up sitting between us, smoothing down her body-hugging white dress. I scoot away. I don't care what anybody else says, this girl is one odd duck. "What are you drinking? Water?" She grabs my cup and peers inside. "I can get you something better." She waves to a skinny waitress with scraggly bleach-blonde hair and three eyebrow piercings.

I hold up my wristband, red for underage. Timber has the same. We don't have fake IDs and I have no interest in drinking anyway.

"No, no." Dawn pats my leg. "What do you think we are?" She laughs. "How about a Red Bull or a Fuze?"

"I'll take a Bull," Timber says, but I shake my head.

"Water's great for me," I say.

"Come on. It's on the house," says Dawn. "For bringing all these kids out. A lemonade at least?"

"Okay." I peel my legs off the couch, where I'm sticking as the sweat dries. "Lemonade would taste good right now."

"And bring me a cranberry juice," Dawn tells the waitress. "Isn't this so much fun?" She turns back to us. "You guys have to come a lot. We want to have more live music and dancing. You can perform anytime you want."

I look at Timber, wondering if he'll take her up on the offer, but instead he says, "Our friend Ari has a band. They're really good."

"Tell him to get Clay a demo and we'll book him," she says. The waitress returns with our drinks. From the crowd on the dance floor we hear cheers erupt. The applause goes on for several seconds, then the DJ shifts the music back to some dance tune.

"She must be done," Dawn says. She grabs my leg. "I think it went well, don't you? I think people liked her."

"Uh, yeah," I say then take a big gulp of lemonade so I don't have to talk.

"She's star material," Dawn says as people flood toward the bar.

In the midst of all the people, Briar comes bopping off the dance floor with Kenji trailing behind her. She spins, loops her arms overhead, and runs toward us all in time to the music. "What's up, Zeph!" she screams then falls on top of me, splashing lemonade everywhere.

"Bri!" I yell, pushing her off. She tumbles to the floor, her feathery green top poufing up so her pale belly shows. She's nearly in hysterics, she's laughing so hard as she tries to pull herself upright.

Dawn rushes to Briar's side and offers her an arm. "Oh my God! You're so cute. I just love this girl. And did you see her dancing? Oh my God. We should get you on *So You Think You Can Dance*, girl!" Suddenly Briar is on her feet, hugging Dawn as if they've known each other for years. I look at Timber. He laughs while pounding his Red Bull.

"And who is this?" Dawn asks, one arm around Briar's waist, the other reaching for Kenji, who sidesteps her, never taking his hands out of his jeans pockets.

"Kenji Kenji Kenji Kenji!" Briar sings, then she snorts, then she laughs again.

I lean close to Timber. "What's wrong with her?"

He raises his eyebrows. "She sounds a little tipsy."

"You mean drunk?" I ask, too loudly.

"Oh poo on you, Zephyr-poo," Briar says, wagging finger at me. "Party pooper all the time. I'm not drunk. I don't even drink." She's not very convincing since her words are slurry and she's swaying. "Just having a good time." She lifts one arm and yells, "Hup freakin' ba!" which sends Dawn into a fit of giggles, and they hug again. Make that two odd ducks.

"What's with the *hup ba*?" Timber asks me.

I shake my head. "It's just something people say where we're from." I look to Kenji. He shrugs, face blank. I can't imagine he'd give her booze.

"Your boyfriend is so funny," Briar says to Dawn.

"Boyfriend?" Dawn asks, confused. "I don't have a boyfriend."

"Clay," Briar says.

"He's my brother," Dawn says, slapping Briar on the arm.

"Aha!" Briar shouts. "That makes more sense. He showed me all around your . . ." Briar leans too far forward and nearly stumbles. "Establishment," she adds, righting herself again. "Grove's with him checking out the back room, which is gorgie, by the way."

"*Gorgie?*" I ask no one.

"It's a smaller stage. More intimate. It'll be perfect for singer-songwriters or poetry readings," Dawn tells us. "My God, we'd about die if your dad would come do a set."

I ignore her.

"And they have a fox!" Briar says. "A fox in a box!" She hops with excitement, which sends her stumbling backward, pulling Dawn with her to the couch, where they tangle together laughing.

"A fox?" Dawn asks, breathless with laughter. "You must've seen our cat." At this they both dissolve into hysterics again. I can hardly take these two.

Out of the corner of my eye, I see someone else leaning over the couch on the other side of Timber. Hoping it's Mercedes, who might know why Briar's acting so weird, or at least what *gorgie* means, I spin around and lean across Timber's lap to come face-to-face with Bella.

"What the . . . ?" I rear back.

"Oh, it's you," she says, as if she's surprised.

"Why wouldn't it be me?" I ask. I probably look like a sweat-soaked troll right now with a rat's nest for hair. That would only be fitting because although Bella just sang and danced under a spotlight for thirty minutes, she's still as fresh and dainty as an orchid in a hothouse. The girl is not even perspiring. Her hair is silky, her eyeliner's in place, and the black dress hardly looks mussed.

"Timber's got lots of friends," she says.

I tighten my grip around the sweating cup in my hand. I want nothing more than to throw my lemonade in her face or zap her, which I won't do.

"So," she says to Timber. "What'd you think?"

He reaches out and pats her shoulder. "You were great, Bell," he says, and now I want to zap him, or at least throw my lemonade at him.

"That's just a little bit of the show Clay is helping me work up," she says. "We wanted to test-drive it tonight. But of course, now I'll have to put it on hold to work on *Idle*." She stops and rolls her eyes. "Can you believe what a waste of time that whole audition was today? Anybody could have told Padgie what would happen."

Where is Mercedes when I need her?

"If he'd just gone ahead and cast the thing a week ago, we could already be learning lines and blocking scenes. I'm afraid the whole thing is going to blow."

"There's plenty of time," says Timber.

"Have you even seen the whole script?" she asks. Timber shakes his head. "Me either, but I do have the first act. We should get together and start running lines before he gets the whole cast together."

Now my blood is boiling. Rehearsing alone! She's got to be kidding. Briar crawls across the couch to sit beside me. "I hate that girl," she fake whispers to me, but if Bella hears, she doesn't react. "Why's she all up in your boy's grille?"

"First off," I whisper to her, "he's not my boy, and second, are you sure you're not drunk?"

She rolls her eyes and sticks out her tongue. "Yes I'm sure, and why aren't you more worried about that?" She flicks her fingers toward Bella, who's massaging Timber's shoulders now.

"Moose crap," I say.

"Let's get her," Briar growls in my ear.

"No," I whisper. "We can't." But I want to! I want to more than anything.

"Just a little one," Briar pleads in my ear. "Harmless. No one will know," she whispers.

Bella's leaning so close to Timber now that her cleavage is practically in his face. I know that I made Briar promise not to use magic. But this time I've had it. It's time to fight fire with magic. I look at Briar. She grins, one eyebrow up, the corner of her mouth twitching. "Skunk breath," she whispers.

"And belches," I add.

Briar and I mutter incantations behind our fingers then zap our spells at Bella. It only takes a second before her hand shoots up to her lips. Her cheeks puff out, her eyes bulge, but she can't hold it in. Briar and I fall over each other, stifling our laughter as the first burp rips from Bella's pretty mouth, spewing everyone nearby with the putrid scent we've cursed her with.

Timber jumps back in his seat, nearly landing on top of me. "You okay?" he asks her.

Bella stands upright and presses her hand to her belly. "Jesus," she moans. "I think I'm going to be sick." Her hand shoots up to her mouth again and another belch comes up. She groans.

"Honey!" Dawn rushes to her side. "What's wrong?"

"I don't know," Bella says, flustered and embarrassed. "Maybe it's the heat or something I ate before the show or . . ."

Another belch. Dawn steps back, her face squinched from the odor.

"Maybe I'm getting the stomach flu," Bella moans, clutching her sides.

I bury my face in Briar's lap and shake from trying not to laugh, but when I look up, Grove is standing across from us, looking furious with his eyebrows down and his mouth tight.

"Uh-oh." I jab Briar in the side.

"Scat, crap, dung," she says when she catches Grove staring hard at us.

He shakes his head and then as quick as a sneeze, he flutters his fingers, casting a counter spell to take our hexes away. By now Bella is on the couch beside Timber. He rubs her back.

"We need to get you home," Timber tells her. "Is Gunther here? Did you take the train or drive?"

Bella looks up at him, her green eyes swimming. "We took a cab, but I don't know where Gun is," she whines. "Will you take me home?"

"Faker," Briar whispers to me.

"Actress," I say.

Grove steps forward. "We drove," he says. "We can get you home."

My mouth drops open. He has got to be kidding. But he shoots me another harsh look and I keep my thoughts to myself.

"Go tell Ari and Mercedes that we're leaving if they want a ride," Grove says to me. I push myself up off the couch.

"I'm not going." Briar flops back and crosses her arms. "I'm still having fun."

"Your fun is over," Grove tells her.

"Kenji can get me home," Briar argues. "Can't you?" She smiles up at Kenji, who remains off to the side with hands shoved in his pockets. He looks to Grove, who shakes his head.

"Guess not," Kenji mumbles.

Briar huffs. "Pansy," she says not so quietly.

Grove looks at me. His face is stony, and I know I'm in trouble. I shuffle off to find Ari and Mercedes on the crowded dance floor.

By the time I drag Ari and Mercedes back to the red vinyl couch, Bella is sipping a club soda and smiling. "Really, I'm so much better now," she says with her hand on Timber's knee. Gunther stands behind her, punching buttons on his little sideways phone thing like he couldn't care less.

"Is she okay?" Ari asks. "What happened?"

"She thought she was going to barf," Kenji tells him.

I glance at Briar, who pouts on the other end of the couch, and I ball my fingers into fists to keep myself from zapping someone out of sheer frustration.

Grove squats down in front of Bella. "You sure?"

"I'm sure." She blinks like a baby deer. "And I don't want to ruin your night." She lays her hand on his shoulder. Could she touch more people?

"You're not ruining anything," he says.

Dawn reappears, leading Clay by the arm. He moves through the crowd like a snow leopard in white jeans and a rippling linen top unbuttoned so his smooth pale chest peeks out. He steps in front of Bella and squats down beside my brother. "Everything okay?" He reaches out and holds Bella's face in his hands. "Let me look at your eyes."

Now I want to barf.

Mercedes digs her fingernails into my arm. "What the frig?"

I shake my head, unable to explain how our hex backfired and wound up making Bella the center of all male attention in the universe.

"Truly," Bella says, staring at Clay while he "examines" her. "It was just a passing thing. I felt so sick there for a minute. Thought I was going to faint but then it went away."

"Perhaps it was too soon for you to perform," Clay says.

"Oh no," Bella assures him. "Must have been something I ate, but I'm really okay now. Thank you."

Grove stands and holds out his hand. "Let us get you home safely," he offers.

Clay stands, too. "We'll call a limo."

Bella turns around. "Gun?"

Gunther glances up from his phone, his Mohawk up like a shark's fin on top of his head. "Yeah, whatever."

Bella turns back to my brother. "I don't want to trouble you," she says. "You've already got your hands full." She smirks at Mercedes and me, then she turns back to Clay. "If you could call me a car, that would be great."

"Anything for our star," he says, and strides off.

Grove turns to us. "Get your things."

"Who put you in charge?" Briar asks.

Grove steps closer to the couch. He towers over Briar, who cowers in the fold of the red vinyl behind her. Grove doesn't have the most powerful magic in our family because he's spent most of his energy on playing music with my dad, but still, he's stronger than Briar and I are. I hear his voice in my head. *If you ever want to see the inside of this club again, you'll get your things and be out front in three minutes.*

Briar pops up from the couch. "Fine," she mutters.

After we drop Ari, Mercedes, and Timber at their houses, Grove drives Dad's van through the empty streets of Brooklyn. He's been silent the entire way, except to say a terse good-bye to our friends. As we near the park, he clears his throat.

"Do you know what could happen if someone caught you casting spells?" he asks.

"Ugh!" Briar groans from the second row of seats. "We only made her belch. What's the big deal?"

"It was my fault," I say to Grove. "I made Briar promise not to cast spells tonight, but then I got mad and . . ."

"What'd you mean you made her promise?" Grove asks. "Have you been casting other spells, Briar?"

"No," she says.

"She wants to," I tell him, like a little kid tattling, then suddenly I'm mad at her for talking me into doing it tonight. I spin around to face her. "And what was wrong with you? Were you drunk?"

Briar crosses her arms and huffs. "I already told you I wasn't drinking. Clay gave me a Red Bull. It made me feel zippy."

"You were acting really stupid," I say.

She rolls her eyes. "That's called having fun, Zephyr. Ever hear of it?"

Grove sighs and stops for a red light. He turns in his seat to look at both of us. "You're both idiots. This isn't Alverland. It's not okay to use your magic. Ever. Especially for something as stupid as that. You jeopardized all of us tonight. And you, of all people," he says to me. "You should know better. You already did this once. If I told Mom and Dad—"

"Don't!" Briar says, sitting up straight now. "We got carried away. That's all. It wasn't a big deal and it won't happen again."

Grove stares at me. I shake my head. "It won't," I say. "You're totally right. I should know better. I do know better."

The light changes and Grove drives on, around the traffic circle to our street. "That place was weird," he mumbles.

"You thought so, too?" I ask. "I think Clay and Dawn are kind of creepy."

"They're a little strange," he says.

"You guys are so lame," says Briar. "You wouldn't know fun if it bit you in the ass."

"If that's what you call fun," I say, "I wouldn't want it to bite me."

"Lame," Briar says. "So lame."

But I don't care. Tonight ended up sucking, and now I'm even more worried about Timber and Bella being in the musical together. He couldn't take his eyes off her when she was onstage, and then he was doting over her like she was a hurt bunny. It makes me wonder if I'm delusional to think he'd ever toss aside a girl like that for me. What's worse is I can't use magic, the one thing that could make Timber choose me over Bella. I'm stuck, like every ordinary erdler girl, and it makes my elfin heart ache. We park the van and I climb out. All I want is to get in my bed and forget about tonight, but then I remember what's coming tomorrow. I'll have another chance, because Timber will be at my house for Thanksgiving.

chapter 7

I BARELY SLEPT last night. All I could think about was Timber coming to my house today. There will be no Chelsea getting in my way when I want to have a conversation with him. No Bella rubbing up against him like a cat on a tree. Sure there will be eighteen other people here, but this will be the first time in a long time that I'll have Timber mostly to myself.

And it's freaking me out!

"Zephyr!" Mom calls from the bottom of the stairs. "I need you to come down here and set the table. We have no idea where everyone should sit."

"I'm coming," I holler. "As soon as I'm dressed."

"You've been saying that for half an hour," Mom says. "Hurry it up."

I sigh, exasperated with myself. I've been standing in front of my closet, staring at my clothes for at least forty-five minutes.

Briar comes into our room with one yellow towel wrapped around her body and another twisted on top of her head. "Still here?"

"Help me," I plead. "He'll be here in less than an hour."

"Chill," she says.

"Easy for you to say." I look at a skirt, a pair of pants, and a dress. Nothing is right. "You're not trying to impress anybody."

"And you're trying too hard." She flips the towel off her head so her long blond hair hangs in wet strands down her bare back. "Anyway, who says I'm not trying to impress someone?"

I take out a sweater then shove it back in. "Kenji's not coming."

"He's not?" she asks with a grin as she pulls a lacy pink bra and matching panties out of her top dresser drawer.

"Is he?" I ask. My stomach tightens and my scalp prickles. Before Briar moved to Brooklyn, Kenji made a manga for me. The manga is one of the sweetest presents I've ever gotten. I wrapped it in a linen cloth and hid it under my summer tunics in my bottom dresser drawer.

"His parents are Japanese," Briar says. "They don't do Thanksgiving." She stands beside me in her underwear and a light pink, lace-trimmed cami. "So your mom said I could invite him."

"What's going on with you and Kenji, anyway?" I ask, and wait. I used to think he had a crush on me, but then when Timber acted all interested, Kenji backed off. And now Timber acts like he's not interested in me, but Briar likes Kenji. Sometimes it's enough to make my head pop.

Briar slumps against the closet door. "I don't know. We're friends, I guess."

"Do you want it to be more than that?" My palms get moist and my stomach flutters, which is stupid because what do I care?

Briar sighs. "One minute I think we're more than friends, then poof!" She tosses her hands up. "The next minute, nothing."

"Yeah," I say. "Tell me about it."

"What's wrong with boys?" she asks as she reaches in the closet and pulls out a flouncy pink skirt.

"Hey!" I grab for the skirt. "I was going to—"

"No way," she says, tugging. "You've had plenty of time."

"But it's my skirt," I say, yanking.

Her left hand starts to twirl and I immediately counter, holding my forearm up to block whatever mischief she's going to cast. "Don't!"

"Give me the skirt, then."

I hold tight. "What am I going to wear then?"

"That's not my problem," Briar says.

"I'll help you," my little sister Poppy chimes in from the doorway. I let go of the skirt so Poppy doesn't see Briar and me acting like silly erdler girls fighting over clothes. "Thanks, Pop," I say. "But I can figure it out."

Briar slips into the skirt then pulls on a soft gray bolero sweater.

"You look so cute!" Poppy squeals.

She's right. Briar does look cute. "Why didn't I think of that outfit?" I moan.

Poppy reaches inside the closet. "Why don't you wear this?" She pulls out my dark red tunic with intricate black embroidery around the edges.

"Because," I tell her as I scoot more hangers across the bar in my closet, "I want to look normal."

Poppy frowns down at her beige tunic and brown leggings. "I wish Mom and Dad would let me wear normal clothes."

"You look great," I tell her. "I love all the pink pansies Grandma embroidered around the collar. And when you go to erdler school, Mom and Dad will let you buy other clothes."

"She's right, you know," Briar says from the bed, where she puts on gray tights.

"See?" I say to Poppy.

"No," says Briar. "Poppy's right. You should wear that tunic."

"So you'll be the only one dressed in erdler clothes when everyone gets here?" I ask. "Real nice."

Briar looks to the ceiling and waggles her head. "No, because Timber likes you in tunics, duh."

"Without leggings," I say, and Poppy giggles. "Mom would flip."

"You're so unimaginative." Briar digs through our drawers. "Wear tights." She holds up a pair of lacy black hose. "And black boots."

My eyes light up. "You'd let me wear your black boots?"

"If . . ." She pauses. "You let me wear your pink rhinestone ballerina flats."

I hold out my hand for the tights. "Deal," I say.

By the time the doorbell rings, I'm dressed and ready to go. I even had time to put name cards around the table so that Timber will be beside me for dinner. The food is cooked and my family appears to be reasonably well adjusted despite the fact that everyone but Briar wears a different colored tunic. There's only so much one girl can do in a day. Changing my entire family will have to wait for another year.

The first person through the door is Mercedes. She marches in, rolling her eyes and shaking her head. She hands me a bouquet of pine boughs and holly leaves. "My family is whacked!" she growls at me. I look over her shoulder at her mom, dad, and younger twin sisters who seem perfectly harmless.

Briar takes a covered dish from Mercedes's mother. "That's yams with marshmallows," Mrs. Sanchez says. "An old family recipe."

Mercedes raises one eyebrow at her mother. "Straight off the Jiffy Marshmallow bag."

"Hush now," her mother says.

The doorbell rings again as I introduce Mr. and Mrs. Sanchez to my grandmother, who's doing her best to look less kooky by taking off most of her amulets and armbands today. My stomach flips as I look over my shoulder to see if it's Timber at the door, but it's not. Ari stands between his parents with his arms crossed and a scowl on his face. "Maneschewitz is such crap wine!"

"You won't be drinking it, so why do you care?" his mother snaps as they enter.

Ari pushes past her and shoves a bottle of wine into my hands. "Could they be any more annoying?"

The doorbell rings again, and this time a shiver goes down my back as I glance around to see Timber and his mother on our threshold.

"Timber!" Dad hollers. He pulls Timber into a deep hug, which makes me cringe. I'm sure my dad is the only father in the universe who hugs his daughter's friends every time he sees them. When he lets go of Timber and opens his arms to Timber's mom, I think I'd like to crack open the bottle of wine and guzzle it, then fall down and pass out. But Timber's mom graciously accepts my dad's embrace with a happy laugh.

"Happy Thanksgiving!" she says from somewhere in the folds of Dad's brown tunic.

"Mom." Timber leads his mother by the wrist across the entryway. "This is Zephyr. Zephyr, this is my mom, Laura."

My pulse zings and my cheeks flush. I set the wine aside and walk forward with my hand extended, but instead of shaking my hand, Laura holds open both arms. "Finally I get to meet you!" she says as she hugs me. She's petite, coming up only to my shoulder. Her hair is sandy brown and curly, pulled off her face in a large tortoiseshell clip. "I've heard so much about you and your family."

Which means he's been talking about me at home! *Is that good or bad?* I wonder.

Laura steps back and smiles up at me.

"I see where Timber got his dimple," I say, pointing to the little comma at the edge of her mouth, which is identical to his.

"That and his grace and charm," Laura says with a laugh.

Then Timber leans toward me. I don't know what to do with my body. Are we going to hug? Kiss? Shake hands? Do the cha-cha? He puts one hand on my shoulder. I melt like maple sugar over a fire. He passes his lips by my cheek and whispers, "Is it just me, or is my mom insane?"

Everyone mingles in the living room where we've laid out little bowls of spiced pecans, platters of goat cheese and home-baked crackers, and plates of smoked fish surrounded by dried fruits. I watch carefully as my friends and family chat and sample the food. No one seems to think anything is too odd, and for the first time I take a deep breath because this whole thing might work out okay. Until I look at my grandmother.

Fawna has stationed herself in her favorite armchair in the corner, and as usual, she's watching everything like a hawk. You have to know what's going on around you to cast good spells, Fawna always says, which is why she's making me nervous. Usually, Grandma is as placid as a lake on a still spring day, but now she looks stormy. Her eyebrows push into a V, causing wrinkles on her forehead like cracks in dry dirt. I follow her eyes across the room to see what's troubling her. My gaze lands on Timber.

Timber's been to my house a few times, and it was no surprise to me that he had trouble keeping everyone's name straight and knowing how to fit a word in edgewise as my sibs pestered him. But now he seems perfectly at ease. He squats down with Poppy, Bramble, Persimmon, and Mercedes's twin sisters surrounding him so he can show them some app on his iPhone. He doesn't even flinch when a green and yellow parakeet swoops by his head then perches on a curtain rod above him. So I can't imagine why my grandmother is staring at him like this.

"How'd you do that?" Bramble asks Timber when the phone starts to sing.

"Magic," Timber says.

Poppy's mouth falls open. "You, too?" she asks. I rush forward and clamp my hand over her lips.

I laugh. "There's no such thing as magic, remember?" I keep my hand over Poppy's mouth even when she tries to wrestle away.

Persimmon's eyes are wide. "Grandma Fawna is magic."

Briar rushes over. "Persimmon's so cute!" She ruffles Percy's hair. "Always making stuff up."

"Your grandmother is magic?" asks Timber, indulging my littlest sister. "Really?"

Timber looks to my grandmother and smiles, but Fawna narrows her eyes at him. I've only seen her look this fierce a few times, once when a sick wolf came prowling near the glen where my cousins and I were playing. The wolf was probably rabid, and my grandpa Buck disposed of it quickly with one arrow.

Then the doorbell rings again. Briar scurries out of the room before anyone else can move. "I'll get it!" she yells, then swings open the front door to reveal Kenji standing on our stoop. Tonight the tips of his black hair are orange and he wears a bright green ski parka, skinny jeans, and heavy winter boots. He tugs his earbuds and lets them dangle around his neck before coming in the house, only to be mobbed by the same gang of crazy elf children who attack anyone who enters our home. Briar grabs their arms and legs and pulls them off Kenji, who stands stiff, as if he's being licked by a bear.

"Everyone's here!" Poppy shouts with glee.

"Just in time," my mother calls from the kitchen doorway, where she emerges into the dining room carrying a giant platter with a beautiful, crisp brown turkey. We all ooh and aah at the bird, its scent drawing us to the table.

After the serving dishes have been passed around, my dad taps his fork against his glass and stands.

"Please, for the love of the north wind, don't let him embarrass us," I whisper to Briar as I scrunch into my seat.

"I'd like to thank you all for joining us today," Dad says while lifting his glass of cold elderberry tea. "Brooklyn was a lonely place for my family when we first moved here."

Briar and I look at each other. My cheeks begin to burn. "Does he have to admit that we're such freaks?" I whisper.

"But the longer we live here, the more we realize that there isn't much difference between life where we come from and life here."

Briar screws up her face and shakes her head. "Has he lost his mind?" she whispers back to me.

"In the end," my father says, "what's important to us is the same that's important to anyone else. A good meal, good conversation, and good people to share it with. And so, today I'd like to propose a special toast to my daughter Zephyr."

At the mention of my name I sit up straight. Briar and I stare at each other. I have no idea why he's toasting me.

My dad looks at me with his glass in the air. "Zephyr was the first one to go out in Brooklyn and make friends, then bring the world back to us. So, sweetie, thank you for bringing these fine people to our table today."

I smile at my dad, both relieved and proud. Then I look around the table at Ari and Kenji, Mercedes and Timber. I'm not exactly sure what Thanksgiving is all about for the erdlers, but I do know that I'm grateful for my friends and for my family (even if they are hanging on to normalcy by the tips of their elfin fingers).

"Now," says Dad, "I hope you all enjoy this wonderful meal and maybe even some good conversation, too. Cheers!"

"Cheers!" everyone shouts, glasses clinking.

I lift my glass and mouth the words *Thank you* to my dad. He winks and then we all dig in.

Just as I'm cutting into a big juicy slab of turkey breast on my plate, Timber turns to me and says, "I've never seen you eat meat. I thought you were a vegetarian."

I stop, fork halfway to my mouth, which gives Poppy, who's sitting across the table from us, enough time to butt in.

"Usually we only eat the meat from animals that we kill ourselves," she explains with her mouth full of sweet potatoes.

I glance at Timber's mom, who's on Poppy's left. She leans forward and cocks her eyebrow. "Really?" Laura asks. I glare at Poppy. I should have never seated her so close to me. In fact, I should have made her sit in the pantry.

"When you think about it," Bramble says from the other side of Poppy, "if you hunt your own wild turkey, you know it's probably had a pretty good life out there in the woods, doing happy turkey things like eating acorns and roosting in the trees, so then you don't feel so bad eating it."

"I never thought of that," Laura says.

"They all know how to hunt," Timber tells his mom. "With bows and arrows."

Laura raises both eyebrows. "In Michigan?"

"It's very rural," I say quietly, as if that can explain why my seven-year-old brother knows how to take down a wild turkey.

"She texted me from a tree the last time she went back," says Timber.

Even though this is true, I slap him on the thigh under the table to let him know he's embarrassing me. He flashes me a playful smile and keeps right on going. "They don't even drive where they're from."

If he were my brother or cousin, I'd slap him with a short mute hex to shut him up. Instead, I shake my head and say, "We drive sometimes. We just walk more."

"Like New Yorkers," says Laura, and Poppy bursts out laughing.

"Alverlanders are nothing like New Yorkers," she says. I kick her foot and she squirms in her chair, but it shuts her up.

"What other Thanksgiving traditions does your family have, Zephyr?" Laura asks.

I hesitate. So far Laura has heard that we kill wild turkeys with bows and arrows, and we don't drive but we do sit in trees to text. We sound like Neanderthals with BlackBerries. What will she think if I tell her that we don't actually celebrate Thanksgiving? That we don't celebrate any of the same holidays as most other Americans? Not Christmas, or Hanukkah, or Kwanzaa. No Easter or Passover or Fourth of July. We don't shop for presents or buy singing cards or send e-mails on someone's birthday. And, no matter what my dad said in his toast, that barely scratches the surface of how my family is different from Timber's family. I can't say all that, but I also can't lie.

"We eat a lot at this time of year," I say, which makes Laura laugh.

"That's what Thanksgiving is all about," she says.

I nod, but technically I'm not talking about Thanksgiving because our pilgrims came from Scandinavia by way of Greenland then Canada, and they showed up long before the Plymouth Rock crowd.

"And we have a festival," Poppy tells her.

Bramble catches wind of this and leans over again. "That's when we reenact the first feast. The boys act out the Big Hunt, when Grandfather Tjern and the other men shot a twelve-point buck."

"And the girls act out Aster, our first mother, and her sisters harvesting the original crop of corn, beans, pumpkins, and squash," Poppy says. "And the little kids pretend to be the first children, who found berries, nuts, and wild onions in the forest."

"Then we all feast to celebrate the good fortune of our ancestors finding Alverland and—"

Before they can say any more, I clear my throat and quickly flick my fingers toward Poppy and Bramble, saying, "Ribbit" under my breath. Then I lift up the platter of turkey and ask, "Would anyone like some more?"

Timber hands me his plate. "I'll take more," he says. "This is delicious."

"Sure, I'll have some, too," says Laura.

Poppy and Bramble's mouths move but only raspy noises come out as they try to clear their throats.

"You okay?" Laura asks them.

"Frog in my throat," Poppy croaks while glaring at me.

"Here, have some water." Laura picks up a crystal pitcher and refills their glasses.

"What's Thanksgiving like at your house?" I ask Timber.

He shrugs. "Since it's just Mom and me, we usually go somewhere else."

I feel it then. Like a quick electric shock through my brain that sizzles down into my mouth. I look across the table, horrified. Poppy and Bramble smirk at me. I don't know which one hexed me or if it was a group effort, but no matter how hard I try to control myself, I can't stop the words beginning to spill out of me. "Like to your grandparents? A lot of people do that around here, don't they? That's what we'd do in Alverland. Everybody gets together at the grandparents. So many people. I have, like, a hundred cousins. And everybody has to be together for every little holiday. And believe me, we celebrate a lot of hmfrdls," I shove a roll in my mouth to stop the words.

"Um, no," Timber says, eyebrows flexed. Across the table Poppy and Bramble huddle together, their shoulders quaking as they try holding in their laughter. "My grandparents aren't around."

I swallow the bread and press my lips together as hard as I can, but the words, "Maybe you go to a restaurant then?" pop out. "I always wanted to go to a restaurant for a holiday. Just once, you know? It'd be so fun." I scramble for the bread basket, knocking over the salt shaker as the words keep blobbing out. "Ordering food off a menu instead of cooking it all and having someone else do all the dishes would be great. And you wouldn't have to eat turkey if you didn't want to and . . ." Quickly, I butter another roll. "Of course, there are no restaurants where we're from so we'd have to mmmfrld." I shove the bread in my mouth.

Now Timber is looking at me like I'm crazy. "We just go to a friend's house."

"What kind of friends?" I ask and I start to sweat. "Family friends or school friends?" More bread. I'm starting to feel sick from all the rolls in my stomach.

"School friends." He looks at me, puzzled. I'm sure he wants me to stop grilling him, but I can't. Even when I stuff my mouth full of mashed potatoes, I can't stop myself from talking. "Which friends? Anyone I know?" I ask, potatoes spilling from my lips. Bramble falls out of his chair because he's laughing so hard.

Timber looks at me. "The last couple of years we spent it with Bella's family, okay?"

Now I'm really sweating and my stomach hurts. I try biting my tongue, but that doesn't work either. "It's always good to have someplace to go," I chirp. "Does Bella's mother make turkey? Do they have a cook? Are they rich? I bet it's really nice there. They probably have candles and music and stuff while they eat." My brain races through all the ways her house is probably better than my house and I can't stop talking. "And pumpkin pie. They probably always have that. But we don't because my mom didn't know how to make it even though I printed out a recipe. And Bella doesn't have any brothers and sisters, right, so there probably aren't like a million little kids running around and . . ."

I feel a tap on my shoulder. Behind me Mercedes and Ari stand on either side of my chair, staring daggers at me while I keep right on yammering about Bella's family. "Could you show us where the bathroom is?" Mercy says. They both yank my chair away from the table. "Right now." They lift me up by the armpits and usher me through the dining room, my lips flapping all the way.

Ari shoves me in the little bathroom behind the kitchen. They squish in with me and lock the door behind us.

"Okay, intervention," Ari says to me.

"What the hell are you doing?" Mercedes asks.

"I know! It's terrible. I can't stop talking. It's just blurting out and blurting out and blurting out . . ." I bury my face in my hands.

"You've got to pull it together, girl," Mercedes says. "Or I'm going to slap you."

I grab her sweater. "Please do," I beg, wondering if that would reverse the hex. "I can't stop myself. What am I going to do? I sound like such an idiot." But as soon as I say this, I feel the hex start to fade. These things don't last long. Especially when someone as little as Poppy or Bramble casts them.

"For God's sake," Mercedes says. "Get ahold of yourself."

I take a few deep breaths. The tingling feeling on my tongue has almost disappeared. "Okay. All right. I'm better."

"At the very least," Ari says. "If you're going to talk a thousand miles an hour, stop talking about his old girlfriend."

I groan and flop down on the toilet. "Oh stars! What am I going to do? Now he thinks I'm a complete freak."

"You can recover," Ari assures me. "Make the boy laugh. Ask him questions. Sing a song. Tap dance. You know, work your magic!"

"What?" I ask, staring up at him in a panic. "Why would you say that? What makes you think—"

"Not literally," Ari says. "We know you're not really going to sing and dance, but stop acting like such a frickin' spaz."

Mercedes turns to the small mirror over the sink and fluffs out her curls. Then she turns back to me. "This is your chance," she says. "Don't screw it up."

By the time we get back to the table, the buzzing feeling in my tongue is gone, but so are Poppy and Bramble, who've finished dinner and disappeared upstairs with the twins. Good thing, too, because I'm as mad as a hornet. But I don't have time to think about getting them back, because my grandmother has moved into the seat next to Timber's mom and appears to be grilling her.

"And where are your ancestors from?" Fawna asks.

"Poland and Germany," Laura says. "And one grandmother was Italian. I'm a regular American mutt."

"Hmmm," says Fawna, biting her lip. "And his father?" She nods toward Timber.

"They're French," says Laura.

Fawna's eyes become little slits. "From the coast or the mountains?" I can tell by the look on her face she's not just making polite conversation. Fawna is fishing for some piece of information, but I don't know what it is.

"The Alsace-Lorraine area," Timber says. "We still have cousins there. I used to go back with my grandfather."

"A dangerous area," Grandma mutters.

"Actually, it's really nice there." Timber looks at me, confused.

I have no idea what's going on, so I do what I always do when I'm uncertain; I change the subject. "Did you get a Christmas tree yesterday?" I ask.

"We did," Laura says. "You should come decorate it with us this weekend."

"Oh, wow, um . . ." I say, looking to Timber.

His face betrays nothing. Does he want me to come to his house or not? Instead of answering, he looks at his mom. "By the way," he says, "Dad asked me to go skiing with him for Christmas."

"Okay," she says, but I think she looks disappointed. "What will your family do, Zephyr?"

"Um, uh," I stutter, wondering if Christmas coincides with the winter solstice this year. "The usual, I guess."

"See the tree at Rockefeller? Visit Santa at Macy's? Check out the lights in Dyker Heights?" she says.

"Er . . ." I look at her dumbly. Crikey, I wish I had the talking hex back. Now I sound like a monosyllabic moron.

"This is their first Christmas in New York," Timber says.

"Then you should definitely take her to Macy's," Laura tells him. She turns to me. "You have to see Santa there at least once."

Timber studies me for a second, then he says, "You've never sat on Santa's lap, have you?"

"Well, I, uh . . ." I try to remember what I know about that Santa guy.

"Of course you haven't!" Timber says. "There are no malls where you're from." He turns back to his mom.

Laura shakes her head. "Oh dear," she says, as if that's the saddest thing she's ever heard.

"My grandfather played Santa once at the Yale Club," Timber says.

"His friend Bunny Woolen was supposed to be his elf. Only Bunny was this short, fat little guy. About this tall." He holds his hand four feet from the ground.

Laura starts to laugh. "I remember that. It was hilarious. He was this angry, sour little man who chomped on a cigar the whole time."

Timber laughs along with his mother. "He was nothing like an elf."

The table suddenly goes quiet. A fork clatters against a plate. My parents stop their conversation with the Sanchezes. Grove looks up from his conversation with Ari's family. Briar turns slowly from Kenji toward us. Everyone's eyes are wide, and no one seems to breathe.

"And what, pray tell, are elves like?" Fawna asks. My mouth drops open.

"You know," Laura says, her laughter fading as she realizes my entire family is staring at her. "Goofy, funny little things with pointy shoes and . . ." She trails off.

I brace myself, ready for the worst spells to fly, people to turn into frogs, my grandmother to morph into a screeching hawk. My mother hops up from her seat. I close my eyes and Briar grabs my hand. We hunker down.

"Who's ready for dessert?" Mom nearly shouts.

Suddenly the table comes back to life. Dishes clack and brattle as my mom, dad, Grove, and my grandmother quickly gather up the dirty plates, glasses, and silverware and disappear into the kitchen in a flash.

"Oh my," Laura says, blinking. "That was, um, quick."

Briar and I stop clutching each other. "Whew," she whispers as I slump back in my seat, feeling as if my limbs are full of jelly.

"So you'll be in town for Christmas?" Laura asks me. I have to stop myself from making some sarcastic remark about how we'll be helping Santa.

"We're going back to Michigan," Briar says, saving my butt.

"That's so nice." Laura gently folds her napkin and places it on the table. "So nice to be with family for the holidays."

"Depends on the family," I mutter half to myself.

Timber slaps my back and laughs loudly. "Exactly."

Once dessert is done and the candles have burned down low, my friends and I slip into the living room while the adults stay at the table talking.

"Let me be the first to apologize for how annoying my parents are," Ari announces when we settle on the couches and chairs. I grab a spot on the love seat next to Timber.

"Your parents?" Mercedes slaps her own forehead. "That's nothing compared to my parents. All they could talk about was sausage. Sausage! Who talks about sausage?"

"I think my mom has a crush on Zephyr," Timber says, and everybody stops to stare at him. He laughs uncomfortably. "She's totally in love with you," he says to me, and I blush a deeper red than the fabric of my tunic. "I think she wanted to invite you over for Christmas while I'm off skiing with my dad."

Great, I think, *his mom is more into me than he is.*

"Well," says Timber, grabbing my knee, "at least she has good taste."

Now I have no idea what to think! Does he like that his mom likes me or is that annoying? While I'm trying to puzzle through what it all means and whether or not Timber will ever like me as more than just a friend, the conversation around me takes a hundred twists and turns. By the time I clue back in to what everyone is saying, something has been decided.

"So tomorrow then?" Kenji asks.

"Works for me," says Timber.

"Sorry, I can't go with you," Mercy says.

"I'm out," says Ari.

"Briar? Zeph?" Timber asks.

I blink at my cousin, but she nods. "Yeah, we'll meet you at ten o'clock."

chapter 8

AT TEN O'CLOCK the next morning, Briar and I are on the train with Kenji and Timber.

"So what's the surprise?" Briar asks Kenji when we get settled on the F to Manhattan. The train's not very crowded since it's Friday after Thanksgiving, so the four of us can sit in a row with Kenji and Timber on the outside and Briar and me together in the middle. Last night while I was spacing out, our friends agreed that Briar and I need to get Christmasized, only we don't know what that means.

Kenji leans forward to look at Timber. "Should we tell them?"

Timber grins. "Sure, why not? We've made them wait long enough."

"Okay," says Kenji. "First, you have to take a quiz." He shakes his hair out of his face. Today the streaks are red and green, and he has a red-and-white-striped scarf tied at the top of his black jacket. "Who lives at the North Pole?"

Briar and I look at each other, confused. "You mean in the Arctic?" I ask. Kenji nods. "Well." I lean back against the hard orange seat and think as the train rocks. "Other than the animals, there are probably some scientists and some native people. Are you talking about the Inuits?"

"*Bzzzz*," Kenji says. "Wrong!"

Timber snickers. "Okay, here's another one. If someone wanted to pull a sleigh around the world, what animal would he use?"

Briar thinks about this. "What do you mean 'a sleigh'? Like a sleigh that goes through snow?"

"Is there another kind of sleigh?" Timber asks.

"Are we still in the Arctic?" I ask.

He nods but he can barely contain the silly smirk on his face.

"Then it'd have to be dogs," Briar says. "I mean sled dogs, of course."

"*Bzzzz!* Wrong again!" Kenji says, then he laughs like a little kid with his head thrown back and his mouth open. A few riders look up from their newspapers to stare at us for a moment.

"All right, all right. Try this one," Timber says. "If you had a workshop and wanted to make toys for all the children in the world, who would you hire to help you?"

"Now you're being plain weird," I say, annoyed.

"No come on," Kenji says. "It's a legitimate question."

"How is that a legitimate question?" I ask. "First off, who's going to make toys for all the children in the world? And second, what's that have to do with the dog sleds and the Arctic?" They both blink at me. I think for a moment, then I stop and chuckle. "Oh, I get it. Very funny."

"What?" Briar asks. "I don't get it at all."

"They're talking about Santa Claus," I say, thinking back to the reading I did online about how erdlers celebrate Christmas.

Briar thinks about this. "Ohhhh," she says. "Right, lives at the North Pole, drives a sleigh, makes toys."

"Now you can answer the question," says Kenji. "You got the first one right: Santa lives at the North Pole."

"And what kind of animals pull his sleigh?" Timber asks.

Briar and I look at each other. I think about the pictures I saw of

Santa's sleigh. "Um, elk?" I say, which makes Timber and Kenji snicker.

"No, no. Moose!" Briar says. The guys nearly fall out of their seats laughing at us.

Kenji catches his breath and says, "Reindeer. Santa and his reindeer."

"Right, reindeer," we say, nodding.

"And who helps Santa make all the toys?" Timber asks.

Briar and I shrug. I run through my limited knowledge about this erdler holiday. I know Santa wears a red suit because I keep seeing him on billboards and in shop windows everywhere I go. And I guess he likes to drink cola.

"Penguins?" Briar guesses.

"Dude," Kenji says, shaking his head.

"You should know this," Timber says to me, but I'm drawing a blank. "Elves," he finally says.

Slowly, Briar and I turn away from Timber and Kenji. She takes my hand and we stare at each other. If my face is as white as hers and if her eyes are as big as mine, then we must look like two snow owls right now. I wish my magic was strong enough to get inside her mind, but I can't, so we stare at each other, wondering why they're bringing up elves. Do they know? Did our family give it away last night? Is that why they're being so strange today? And the biggest question of all: where are they taking us? I squeeze Briar's hand. She squeezes back.

"Hey, guys." Timber taps me on the shoulder. "What's wrong over there? Don't you remember the story about my grandfather's friend Bunny Woolen?"

The color comes back into Briar's cheeks and my hearts slows down. "Oh right," I say. "That was a showstopper last night."

"Yeah, what was up with that?" Timber asks. "Your whole family went dead silent."

"Guess we were just curious," I say.

"Yeah," says Briar. "So tell us everything you know about *elves*?" Now it's our turn to swallow our laughter.

"I don't know," says Timber. "Guess they're good at making things."

"Do they hunt?" Briar asks.

Kenji raises an eyebrow. "No. What would they hunt?"

"Reindeer," Briar says. "To eat."

Timber and Kenji both look horrified. I have to press my hand over my mouth to keep from snorting.

"Santa's elves don't shoot his reindeer!" Timber says with a shiver. "Now you're getting creepy."

"And the idea of a fat guy in a red suit who comes into your house while everyone is asleep isn't creepy?" I ask.

"When you put it that way . . . " Kenji says, looking horrified.

"But wait," I say. "What's this have to do with the surprise?"

"Remember last night when you said you'd never sat on Santa's lap?" Timber asks.

"I didn't say that, you did," I point out.

"Yeah, but I was right, wasn't I?" Timber asks.

"I guess so," I say with a shrug.

"We're taking you to see the man himself," Timber says.

"What man?" Briar asks.

"The fat guy in the red suit," says Kenji.

"I thought you said he lives in the North Pole," Briar says.

"And he's made up," I point out.

"Dang," says Timber, hanging his head and laughing. "Sometimes hanging out with you is like . . ."

"Like what?" I ask, my fist on my hip.

"Easy there." He pats my leg. "I was going to say like hanging out with foreign exchange students."

"From Mars," Kenji adds.

"Hey!" Briar punches him on the arm.

"Seriously," Kenji says, rubbing his shoulder. "Even a foreign exchange student would know that Santa's elves don't kill and eat the reindeer."

Timber pops up from his seat as the train pulls into a station. "This is our stop," he says.

"Herald Square?" Briar reads from the sign on the platform as we step out of the train. "This ain't the North Pole, honey."

"You don't have a bow and arrow hiding in your coat somewhere, do you?" Timber asks, patting me down.

"Maybe," I tease. "Deer meat is awfully tasty."

He shakes his head as we climb the stairs. "Don't take down Rudolph, whatever you do. Santa needs him."

Briar and I follow Timber and Kenji out to the crowded midtown sidewalk. Even though I've been in New York for a few months now, I can't get used to seeing erdlers swarm like ants. They come from every direction, moving in droves, looking ahead but not seeing what's right in front of them. The swarm parts to go around a man standing on the sidewalk in a long black coat, ringing a red bell. They come together again on the other side, swallowing him like a rock in a stream. The people are all shapes, colors, and sizes in puffy coats, scarves, hats, and gloves. Most carry bags. Many have on earphones or talk on cell phones, but few talk to one another. I grip Timber's sleeve and look over my shoulder to make sure Briar is with us. She clings to Kenji's arm, like a caterpillar on a leaf during a thunderstorm.

At the street corner, four police officers in blue caps stand in the intersection blowing whistles and waving cars through as people spill off the curbs, eager for their turn to cross.

"What are all these people doing here?" I ask Timber.

He slips his arm around my shoulder and keeps me close against his body. "This is the busiest shopping day of the year," he says.

"What could they possibly need to buy?"

He looks down at me and cocks his head to one side. "Presents," he says simply.

The cops' whistles shriek and we surge forward with the crowd into the street, over a steaming manhole cover, and onto the equally packed sidewalk on the other side.

"Here it is," Timber says, pointing up.

I raise my head to see a huge brown and beige brick building with hundreds of windows all lined with twinkling lights. On one corner of the building hangs an enormous red banner with a large white star and the word MACY'S on one side and WORLD'S LARGEST DEPARTMENT STORE on the other.

"Oh right!" I say, remembering what his mom said last night. "This is where you can visit Santa Claus."

He nods. "Every year."

Kenji and Briar have made it across the street now. Briar gawks at the building, the lights, the people just like I do. "Ready to go in?" Kenji asks. We both nod, although to tell the truth, I'd rather duck back down into the subway to escape everyone pushing by us.

We go in through revolving doors, which I have to admit are pretty fun. I could stay spinning in those doors for at least an hour, but of course, I follow my friends inside. Then I'm glad I did.

The first thing that hits me is the smell. It's powerfully sweet and a little bit musky, like girls who sweep by me at school. I smell roses, pine trees, vanilla, nutmeg, coffee, and rain.

"Wow!" Briar says, looking up, spinning around, taking in all the sparkling lights and shiny decorations wound around cases and cases of jewelry, handbags, scarves, makeup, stockings, and probably everything else anyone would ever want to buy. "It's gorgie!"

"Look, pine trees!" I squeal, and point to a long row of Douglas firs lined up across the middle of the floor. "How do they get them to grow inside?" Each is more elaborate than the next, with tiny lights and silver bows and red shiny balls hanging from their branches. Then I realize what a doofus I must sound like. "Oh right," I mumble. "They're Christmas trees."

"Come on." Timber laughs at us and tugs on my hand. "Let's go upstairs. The line is probably ten miles long."

"That's your idea of an elf?" I ask Timber as we join the long twisty line to Santa's workshop. Briar and I look at each other and lose it laughing. The "elves" all wear oversize green smocks, red puffy pants, black boots, and long red and green velvet hats that jingle when they walk. What's even funnier is they're all different. Some of them are tall, some short, some chubby, some thin. There are white elves with brown hair and brown elves with black hair. There's even a black elf with blond hair twisted into braids. There are men, there are women. Some are old. Some are young. But none of them look like *actual* elves.

"I thought you said they were small," Briar says to Kenji.

"These guys are just out-of-work actors," Kenji says. "Real elves are small."

"*Real* elves?" I say.

"You don't believe in elves?" Timber asks.

"I didn't say that." I wink at Briar.

A little girl about Bramble's age turns around to say, "They are real, you know." Her brown hair is pulled in two pigtails, and she's missing a front tooth. Her mother glances over her shoulder and gives me a worried look. I smile.

"Of course they're real," I tell the girl.

"But they won't make you any presents if you're bad," the girl says.

"That elf has a present for you," Briar tells the girl, pointing to a big brown-haired guy in a smock strolling our way. Briar grins, one eyebrow cocked, the corner of her mouth twitching. My stomach tightens. "Ask him to look inside his hat," she says to the girl. When everyone turns toward the "elf" walking our way I see Briar's lips moving as she flicks her fingers at the "elf's" head.

"Stop," I hiss at her, but she ignores me.

The little girl reaches out and tugs on the "elf's" smock. "Hey, do you have a present for me in your hat?"

The "elf" smiles, bewildered. "I don't think so," he says, but being a good sport he takes off his hat to look inside. A butterfly flutters out and everyone oohs and aahs. The "elf" jumps back. "What the hey?" he says, tossing his cap to the floor.

My grandmother says Briar has a gift for magic if she'd ever choose to use it correctly. It would take me years to learn to conjure up a live animal like that, so I'm not strong enough to counter Briar now. With her coat slung over her arm and everyone's eyes on the butterfly, Briar surreptitiously points to it, catching it in her spell, and flies it to the girl, where it perches for a moment on her nose. The girl squeals happily but stays still. Then Briar blows and the butterfly takes off, flapping up and away toward red poinsettias on the roof of Santaland.

"Hey!" the girl says. "Where'd it go?"

"I guess it flew away," says Briar.

"That's not a real present then," the girl says, and stamps her foot. Her mother glares at the brown-haired "elf" who's turning his hat inside out.

"Tough crowd," Briar mutters.

"How'd you know he had it in there?" Kenji asks Bri.

She shrugs. "I saw him put it there a few minutes ago. I thought it'd be fun to mess with him."

"Cool," Kenji says, smiling.

He might think my cousin's cool, but I'm furious with her. After the other night in Red Hook I can't believe she'd pull this. The line moves forward and I step close, grabbing her arm. "Don't do that again," I whisper in her ear. "Or I'll tell Grove and you'll be in deep trouble."

"You're a good one to talk, Miss Frog-in-the-throat."

"That wasn't in public," I hiss.

"It was in front of them," she motions to Kenji and Timber, then she shrugs me off. "Hey look," she says, pointing to a display. "Ice-skating polar bears and a singing tree."

It takes an hour to get through Santaland and have our picture taken with the man himself. Timber and Kenji try to make us laugh, but I'm fuming the entire way. When we exit and get our photo, Timber holds it out and says, "You look pissed, Zeph."

Briar grabs it. "Like she's going to shoot one of Santa's reindeer."

I snatch the photo from her. "Shut up."

"Touchy!" Briar backs away from me.

The little girl who'd been in front of us earlier comes out with her mom. "But I want my butterfly!" she cries.

"It was a trick," her mom says. "A joke or something. You can't really have it."

Tears stream down the girl's face. "Santa's elves are mean."

I look at Briar. "Happy?"

"Want me to fix it?" She wiggles her pointer finger.

I step closer. "Don't you dare."

"Fine," she says, and walks away.

"Hey," says Kenji, obviously trying to keep the peace. "You guys want to go get some Korean barbecue?"

Briar stops. "I'm up for anything."

I look over at Timber, but he's on the phone, so I just shrug.

"I know a great place really close to here," Kenji tells us. "We can get bibimbap and kimchee, some scallion pancakes."

"I've never had any of that," Briar says, draping herself over Kenji, who's a full head shorter than she is. He stands stiff, hands in pockets, blushing slightly. I can't figure out if he's like that because he likes Briar as more than a friend or if he's mortified by her hanging on him.

Timber slips his phone in his pocket and joins us. "Sorry about that."

"Was it Ari?" I ask. "He said he might meet us later."

Timber shakes his head. "We going to get some lunch? Go for some Korean Q?" He rubs his hands together.

"Follow me," Kenji says, and we do.

At Kum Gang San, we fill our plates with three kinds of spicy pickled cabbage, tiny smoked fish with chilis, and marinated mushrooms sprinkled with tiny sesame seeds. My mouth's on fire but I can't stop eating, especially when the waitress sets a sizzling iron pot with rice, veggies, and a raw egg in front of me.

"That's the bibimbap," Kenji tells me as he uses chopsticks to flip over beef searing on the grill in the center of our table. "Mix it with that sauce and some chili paste."

I do what he says and listen to the rice crackle at the bottom of the hot pot. Timber's food goes untouched because he's on his second call since we sat down to eat. This time he looks agitated, pacing by the coat racks.

Kenji focuses on the meat until Timber comes back to the table, then he asks, "You guys want to see a movie after this?"

Timber grimaces. "I don't think I can."

"I thought we were all hanging out tonight," I say, disappointed.

"Sorry. I have to go back to Brooklyn," he says.

I scoop up a bunch of rice on my chopsticks. "Is everything okay?" I ask, then I take a big bite of the smoky, sweet, spicy food.

"No, nothing's wrong. It's just that . . ." He trails off and plucks some meat from the grill. "Bella thinks we should run lines this weekend before rehearsals on Monday. Today is the only time I can do it because I have plans with my mom tomorrow."

I swallow hard. The rice sticks in my throat and I choke. Briar hits my back and hands me a glass of water. "Here," she says. "Are you okay?"

"Mr. Padgett gave Bella a key so we can meet at school," Timber says.

Now I choke on my water and almost spit it on the table.

"Are you going to be mad if I don't go to the movie with you guys?" Timber asks.

"Why would we be mad?" I ask after gulping more water. "You're free to do whatever you want." Briar gives me a pitying look, and even though I'm still really annoyed with her, I'm glad she's here with me.

"I'd rather be at the movies with you guys," Timber says. "But Bella's right. Mr. Padgett took way too long to go through this whole stupid audition thing and now we've barely got time to get the first act together and I don't want to make a fool of myself."

I stab a piece of meat and dip it in the hot sauce. "So go, then. We're not in charge of you."

"Okay," he says, picking at his rice. "I will."

I pop the meat in my mouth. "Fine," I say, my eyes watering from the chilis.

chapter 9

FRESH SNOW HAS fallen like a clean white sheet over Prospect Park while we were on the train back to Brooklyn. New York feels almost cozy when it snows. People come out, bundled up and smiling, dragging kids on sleds. The sound of laughing and happy shouts replace rumbling cars and belching buses. By the time Kenji, Briar, and I get off the train, people have filled the park. They cross-country ski across the hidden ball diamonds and soccer fields, sled down the hills, throw snowballs, and build snowmen. Briar grabs my hand. "Come on!" she says, tugging me toward the snowy meadow.

I hang back on the slushy sidewalk. "I'm not really in the mood."

Instead of letting me go, Briar holds my hand and wraps her other arm around my shoulders. "Poor you," she says, giving me a hug. This is when it's great to have Briar with me. No matter how mad I can get at her, she always makes it up to me. When I said I didn't feel like going to the movie after Timber left the restaurant, she said she didn't either. When I said I wanted to go home, she said she did, too. "I wouldn't be able to stand it," Briar says. "I'd have to turn her into a toad."

Kenji leans against a black lamppost and laughs. "Just like a fairy tale. Only usually the prince gets turned into a frog."

"You better watch out," Briar tells him. "You might be next."

"Me?" Kenji asks, blinking. "What did I do?"

Briar puts one fist on her hip but keeps the other arm around me. "Nothing," she says. "That's the problem."

"What'd you expect me to do?" Kenji asks. "I couldn't stop Timber."

"You guys," I say. "He's not my boyfriend. He can do whatever he wants to do."

"That's not what I'm talking about," Briar says. "I'm talking about Kenji."

Kenji looks at me, helpless, but I don't know what Briar's getting at either. "Are you really mad at him?" I ask.

Briar looks up into the graying sky. "I don't know what we're doing."

"Well," I say. "We can go home or hang out in the park or call Ari . . ."

"No," says Briar. "I mean, I don't know what this is. What we're doing." She motions between herself and Kenji. "Why do you hang out with me all the time?"

Kenji pushes himself away from the lamppost. "I was under the impression that you liked hanging out with me."

"I do. That's my point," says Briar.

He shoves his hands into his coat pockets. "Then why are you pissed?"

"Because I realized today that you're just like Timber," she says. "You can't make up your mind! But I'm not like Zephyr. I'm not waiting around forever."

Kenji's eyebrows lift. "Waiting around for what? I have no idea what you're talking about, Bri. I thought we were friends."

"That's it? Friends?" she asks.

A slow flush crawls up Kenji's neck and over his ears. "You know . . ." He squirms, kicking a pile of grayish snow. "I don't really want to talk about this right now." He looks at me. "Especially in front of your cousin."

"Fine," says Briar, hands on her hips. "Why don't you give me a call when you do want to talk about it."

Kenji shakes his head. "Timber and I tried to plan this fun day . . ."

"Right," Briar says with a huff. "And then he blows off my cousin."

"Don't get pissy at me because Timber acted like a jerk," Kenji says.

"Hey, you guys . . ." I say, but they're not listening to me.

"I'm not mad at you about Timber. I'm mad at you about you!" Briar almost yells.

"I don't need this," Kenji says, and starts to walk away.

"Fine!" Briar yells.

Kenji looks over his shoulder. "I just thought . . ."

"What?" Briar demands.

"Never mind." He turns and walks away.

"Ugh!" Briar stamps her foot. "Come on." She pulls my arm, and I follow her into the park. "I need to move before I explode or turn someone into a rat!"

We trudge through the snow. Our thick, fur-lined, deerskin boots are perfect for this weather. Instead of heading up into the tree line at the top of the hill, Briar walks toward a pristine expanse of white in the middle of the snow-covered meadow.

I jog to keep up with her. "What just happened?" I ask. "I don't understand."

"I don't know," she says, shaking her head. "Seeing Timber treat you like that today made me realize that I can't do what you do. I can't let Kenji string me along."

I stop in my tracks. "You think Timber's stringing me along?"

She turns around but keeps walking backward. "I don't know what he's doing, Zeph. But that's the point. I won't let that happen to me. Either he's in or he's out."

"You really like Kenji, don't you?"

She nods. "But I don't know how he feels. He's so closed off. It's like hanging out with a tree."

"I know what you mean." I point to an elm and a sycamore at the edge of the meadow. "There's Timber. And there's Kenji."

"No," she says. "Kenji would be a Japanese maple." I snort. Then she lifts her head and yells into the sky. "I need to blow off some steam. I need to dance!"

"I'll dance with you," I say, almost smiling for the first time in hours. "Let's go."

Holding hands, we run through the snow, past groups of kids stockpiling snowballs for an epic battle and toddlers making snow angels on the ground. A couple whizzes past us on skis. I look over at the hill, trying to see if our family might be sledding, but it's too far away to see anything clearly. When we get to the center of the meadow, we are alone. We both stop, facing each other, our breath pluming into the early evening sky. The gray-bottomed clouds, tinted pink on top, hide the sunset, but a pale sliver of moon perches above the clouds calling in the night. The betwixt time, Grandma Fawna calls it, and it is the perfect time to dance.

Briar drags her foot, marking out a large circle in the snow. In the summer we tramp down grass or use rocks and flowers to make the ring. We throw down our bags then take off our coats and scarves before we step inside the circle, Briar on one side, me on the other. We close our eyes, breathe deeply, and silently call the wind, the water, the moon, and the sun. We lift our arms above our heads and clap. Then, we open our eyes and start the dance.

I haven't felt this good in a long time. Skipping after Briar in the circle, hopping with my knees high, a one-footed turn, then sweeping the ground before we jump to the middle to join hands and back out again, not unlike the frenzied dance of the sandhill crane. We sing the ancient songs that we learned as little kids. The words are nonsense to us, but we feel their meaning deep in our chests.

"*Sha we no, hallenschor, um triden fayre la dolly. For maden kling um schaden flang, um triden fayre la dolly.*"

Briar is beautiful when she dances. She has the grace and speed of a young, strong doe who runs for the freedom and fun of moving. When she spreads her arms to spin, she is a majestic crane soaring.

She sings loudly as she dances. "*Sha we no, hallenschor, um triden fayre la dolly. For maden kling um schaden flang, um* KENJI *fayre la dolly!*"

I laugh, hearing her shout his name in our song. It sounds so funny. I try the same thing. "*Sha we no, hallenschor, um triden fayre la dolly. For maden kling um shaden flang, um* TIMBER *fayre la dolly!*"

We howl as we go around and around, singing their names as we dance away all our frustrations about them. I have no idea how long we dance. Ten minutes, two hours? All time gets lost when we're in the circle, but at some point, we're both exhausted. We slow the dance, whisper the chant, let our arms float to our sides. We close our eyes and breathe in deeply until finally we're still. I stand, letting the blood pump through my body, warming me, reminding me that I am alive and no one, not Bella or Timber or anyone else in the world, can take happiness from me unless I allow them. A smile fills me and I sigh, then open my eyes.

I nearly jump when I look up. A huge group has formed around our circle. The snowball fighters, the skiers, families with sleds in tow. People with dogs and backpacks, a guy pushing a bike. They surround us, nearly silent in the gently falling snow. The sun is gone, the sky is gray with only the faint light of the first few stars and thin moon above the trees. Briar turns around, taking it all in. Then she grins, grabs my hand, and pulls us both into a deep bow. The crowd applauds.

As we step out of the circle, people flock to us.

"That was amazing."

"What do you call that?"

"What language were your speaking?"

"Do you do birthday parties?"

Briar and I laugh, gathering our things, slipping on our coats, saying thanks and I don't know and no, we don't do parties. How funny these erdlers can be! Then there's a commotion. People jostle and push until the crowd parts and Kenji stands in front of us. He's breathing deeply, his face is flushed, and his hair is wild as if he's tried to pull it out.

"Briar!" he says, more loudly than I've ever heard him speak.

"What?" she asks, startled

Kenji rushes toward her. "Oh Briar!" he says. "I love you." He flings his arms around her neck and knocks her flat on her back. They lie in the snow, surrounded by strangers as Kenji, for the first time, kisses my cousin.

Briar couldn't be happier as we walk home with Kenji hanging on her arm, but I'm not so sure. He can't take his eyes off her and he's nearly drooling. Everything she says makes him laugh and he wants to stop every five feet to kiss her again.

"What the heck happened to you, Kenji?" I finally ask when we're out of the park and away from the crowd.

"What do you mean, what happened?" he asks as we walk toward our house. "Nothing happened. Everything happened! I came back to talk to you," he says to Briar. "To work this out because I realized that you're right." He holds her hand and rubs her back while we walk. "That this is more than just being friends. And then I saw you. Dancing. Dancing.

Dancing. Shouting my name. I've never felt anything like it. Like some force of nature was pulling me. Like tug-of-war between the moon and sun and I was in the middle. But there you were!" He presses his hands into her cheeks. Strokes her hair. "I realized then that you are the most beautiful person in the world. That you are everything I've ever wanted in my whole entire life." He stops and kisses her again at the corner. Long and slow for the length of the red light. When he comes up for air he says, "That I love you, Briar."

Briar's face blossoms. Her eyes sparkle. She takes his hand in hers and gently pulls him near.

My eyes sting as we cross the street to our house. Kenji's madly in love with Briar. Timber is off with Bella. And I'm alone. How wrong is that?

chapter 10

KENJI STAYS FOR dinner and manages to stop mauling Briar long enough to let her eat, but he stares at her nearly the whole time and laughs at everything she says. Mom and Dad exchange perplexed but amused looks over the turkey dinner leftovers. Grandma Fawna looks slightly worried, but no one says anything until after Kenji is finally out the door.

"Kenji seemed, um . . ." Dad starts to say while we clear dishes from the table.

"Different," Mom adds.

Briar floats around the table, picking up one piece of silverware at a time, lost in her own private la-la land. "I know," she says with a sigh. "He finally realized how he feels about me."

Mom and Dad look at each other. "Do all erdlers act like that when they take a liking to someone?" Dad asks.

"How would I know?" I huff, because obviously Timber has never acted this way around me.

"Oh, Zeph," says Briar dreamily. "Don't be jealous."

"I'm not jealous," I say, wadding cloth napkins into a ball. "I think it's weird. Don't you, Grandma?"

Grandma stops stacking cups. "What?"

"Don't you think it's weird that all of a sudden Kenji's fawning over Briar like he's a bear and she's covered in honey?"

"Is he?" she asks. "I hadn't noticed." She goes back to stacking cups and my mouth drops open. I figured as soon as it was clear that Kenji's into my cousin, my grandmother would go cold on him like she is to Timber.

"But you looked worried," I say to Fawna.

"Did I?" she asks. "I must've been thinking about something else."

"Just remember, Briar," Mom says, "Kenji is different from you. And there are things about our lives that he can't know."

Briar nods. "You don't have to worry about that. I would never put our family in jeopardy."

I glance at Grove. He rolls his eyes at me, then carries a large stack of plates into the kitchen.

"As long as you can keep up with your schoolwork and follow the rules of our family, then Kenji is welcome here anytime," Dad tells Briar.

"Yes, Uncle Drake," says Briar, and I want to gag. She hasn't been so sweet and polite since she was six years old.

Mom and Dad seem to think it's a little bit strange, too, but they just shake their heads and laugh.

When the dishes are clean and tucked away in the cupboards again, my parents gather us all in their bedroom.

"We have a letter from Willow." Mom's face blossoms into a smile as she presses the letter to her heart.

Poppy, Persimmon, and Bramble scramble onto the bed to sit on my parents' laps. Grove, Briar, and I sit side by side on the window seat, and Grandma lowers herself into a rocking chair.

My dad hands me the letter. "Will you read it aloud?"

I nod and feel a twinge of sadness that Willow isn't here with us. I can just imagine her at Aunt Flora's heavy wooden table in front of the open-hearth fireplace, writing this letter that smells slightly of wood smoke. "'Dearest Ones,'" I begin. "'We're all hunkered down like rabbits snug in our warrens beneath the blanket of snow. As you know, winter came early this year and is making quite a spectacle of itself. The drifts have reached the back porch roof now.'"

"The roof!" Bramble throws himself backward onto a pile of pillows. "That's not fair. The snow here is almost melted."

"We'll get more," Mom tells him.

I read on. "'I can imagine how much fun Poppy, Bramble, and Persimmon will have sliding down into the deep snowbanks with all the cousins.'"

"I bet Tulip's been sledding without me," Poppy pouts.

Persimmon crosses her arms, mimicking Bramble and Poppy. "Not fair," she says.

"Oh now," Dad tells the kids. "There'll be plenty of snow when we get there."

I continue. "'Ash made me a new pair of skis this week and we've spent lots of time up at the bluffs. The snowshoes Dad made last winter are still hanging strong. We didn't even have to restring them.'" I look up. "I can't wait to snowshoe," I say.

"I can't wait to do the solstice dance," Briar says with a sigh.

"Keep reading," Mom says, eager for more.

"'Now a bit of sad news,'" I read. Fawna stops rocking and the kids all settle down. "'Mama Ivy has begun to fade.'"

"Oh dear," says Grandma, rubbing one of the amulets. "That must have been what I've sensed."

"Which one is Mama Ivy?" Poppy asks.

"Six greats," says Mom. "Ivy, Hortense, Apricot, Laurel, Jonquil, and Lily."

"Lily is my mother," Fawna says. "Your great-grandmother."

"Is Mama Ivy the one who makes strawberry candy?" Poppy asks.

"That's right," Dad tells her.

"And lives in that house with all the wildflowers around it?" Bramble asks.

"Yes," says Fawna.

"What else does it say?" asks Mom.

"'Grandmother Jonquil sent word through cousin Umber. He says Ivy's comfortable and peaceful, but her magic is dwindling fast.'"

"Hmm." Grandma looks at my mom. "Won't be long."

"Until what?" asks Bramble.

Mom cups Bramble's cheek in her hand. "Until she passes."

"Passes what?" Poppy asks.

"Dies," Dad says.

Tears immediately quiver at the edge of Poppy's eyes. "I don't want her to die."

"A minute ago you didn't remember who she was," I say. Mom frowns at me, then she opens her arms for Poppy.

"Mama Ivy's lived a very long time," Dad says.

"But I want her to live forever," says Poppy.

Mom gives her a hug. "That's not the way life works, my dear."

"Yeah, erdlers don't even live to be a hundred," Briar says.

Poppy wipes her eyes. "I'm glad I'm not an erdler, then."

"What else does Willow say?" Grandma asks me.

I look back at Willow's neat handwriting. "'Jonquil says Ash and I should come look at the house soon, but I can't face that without Mom and Dad and Grandma Fawna.'"

"What's she mean?" Bramble asks.

"Willow will inherit Mama Ivy's land because she's the next first-first in line," Mom explains.

"First-first?" Poppy says.

"Because Willow is my first daughter," Mom says.

"And your mother is my first daughter," Grandma adds. "And I was the first daughter of Lily, and Lily was the first daughter of Jonquil, all the way back to Aster, the very first mother. So we're a line of first-firsts."

"Then what am I?" asks Poppy.

Mom kisses the top of her head. "A middle."

"You all are, except for Briar," Fawna says.

Briar looks surprised. "What am I then?" she asks.

"A youngest daughter of a youngest daughter," Grandma says. "But it stops there because I'm Flora's mother and I'm a first."

I shake my head. "This is all too confusing for me."

"Yes, it's a bit much, isn't it?" Grandma says. "None of it really matters except for true first-firsts and true youngest-youngests, so don't worry about it."

I turn back to the letter. "There's more here for you, Grandma."

"Go on," says Mom.

"'Jonquil also says to tell Grandma Fawna that your aunt Iris shifted and has been gone for a week.'" I look up. When we first moved to Brooklyn, Grandma Fawna shape-shifted into her totem animal, a red-tailed hawk, so she could fly here and check on us. Only the most powerful elves can do such a thing. I won't even know what my totem is until after my apprenticeship.

"What's Iris's totem?" Mom asks.

Grandma thinks for a moment. "A mink, I think. Or maybe a fox."

Briar sits up straight. "That reminds me, do you remember seeing that fox at the Red Hook club the other night?"

"They're keeping a fox at a club?" Grandma asks.

"I wish I had a fox," Bramble tells Poppy.

"No, you don't. It would eat your bunny," Poppy says.

"I'd make him be a nice fox," Bramble tells her.

"You're crazy," I say to Briar. "Dawn told me it was a cat."

"I know the difference," Briar says.

"I saw it, too," says Grove. "It was definitely a fox."

"So very strange," Grandma says with a finger pressed to her lips.

"Clay and Dawn are W-E-I-R-D," I say.

Grandma shrugs. "Aren't all erdlers strange, though?" I think about defending some of the erdlers I know, but then Fawna points to the letter. "What else does it say?"

I continue reading. "'Uncle Logan is worried because before Iris left, she divined something wrong with your cousin Hyacinth.'" I look up at Grandma. "The one who left?" I ask.

Grandma nods. "Read on."

"'I don't remember ever meeting Hyacinth and I can't find her name in the log. Did she marry out?'" I look up again to catch my mom and Grandma exchanging worried glances.

"She's a youngest-youngest," Fawna says quietly, then she and my mother glance at Briar.

"Hyacinth is a pretty name," Poppy tells Persimmon.

"Why do they write names on a log?" Bramble asks.

"It's a book," Mom says. "Not a tree."

Briar shakes her head. "I can't keep all these aunts and cousins and grandmothers straight." She turns to me. "Is that all the letter says? Is there anything from my mom?"

I skim the rest. "Just a bit more about Willow's wedding plans."

Fawna smiles at Mom. "Ah, young love," she says with a sigh, and this irritates me. After the way she glared at Timber, I know she would never say that about me if he and I were dating. I keep skimming the letter for news about Briar's family. "She says your mother misses you, but nothing else too exciting except she can't wait to see us in a few weeks.'"

Bramble jumps up. "A few weeks! Really? Is that all until we go back?"

"The solstice is soon," Mom says.

Briar kicks up her legs. "It's going to be so fun!"

As I hand the letter back to Mom, the phone rings. Briar hops out of the window seat. "I'll get it!" she yells, running out of the room, probably thinking it's Kenji.

My dad scoops up my younger sibs and says, "Time for you little cubs to hibernate for the night." Poppy, Bramble, and Persimmon willingly go with my dad, talking the entire time about what they'll do back in Alverland.

I hang back with Mom, Fawna, and Grove.

Mom goes to Fawna in the rocker. She lays a hand on Grandma's back. "Shall I gather the things for conjuring?"

"What for?" I ask.

"Iris," Mom says. "We must try to help find her."

Grandma looks out the window and sighs. "Later," she says.

"Can I help?" I ask.

Grandma shakes her head. "No, my dear. This isn't something for you to worry yourself over quite yet."

"But you said yourself that I'm ready for my apprenticeship," I tell Grandma.

"So I did," Grandma says. "But it's too early now. We'll wait until after the children are asleep and the moon is up."

All the dancing must have exhausted me because I fall asleep on the couch watching some Christmas special about a kid named Charlie

Brown and his spindly little Christmas tree. When I wake up a few hours later, the house is dark and someone has put a blanket over me. I hop off the couch and hurry toward the garden, hoping Mom and Grandma haven't started the conjuring without me, but the garden is empty. I look out the back door and see a pile of ash on the table where my mother and grandmother must have worked their magic. I'm miffed that they didn't wake me.

I creep up the stairs, trying to avoid the squeaky steps so I don't wake anybody up. I hope Briar's still awake so I can tell her how annoyed I am with Grandma and Mom, not to mention how irritated I am that Timber never called me tonight. But I shouldn't be surprised about that. Why would he call me? He was with Bella. I moan out loud. Just when I thought things might be heading in the right direction with Timber, Bella comes back to ruin my life. Of course, all Briar will want to talk about is how much Kenji loves her, which, if you ask me, is plain weird.

When I get to our room, I go to Briar's bed and whisper her name. "Bri, you up?" I reach down to touch her shoulder, but all I find are pillows. I search around her bed, feeling for an arm or a leg, but everything is soft and mushy. I flip on the lights and find her bed empty. I didn't see her downstairs. And the bathroom door is open, so she's not in there. This is really weird but not totally unexplainable. If she's anywhere, she's with Kenji. I get the phone and dial him, even though it's close to midnight.

He picks up immediately. "Hey, Zeph."

"Is Briar with you?"

"Yep." He giggles like a girl. "She's right here beside me." I hear a smoochy sound and want to puke.

"Where are you guys?" I whisper. "It's midnight. She's supposed to be at home."

"Don't worry," Kenji says. "We can see your house from here."

"Give me the phone," I hear Briar say. Then her voice is strong and clear through the line. "Go back to bed, but don't lock the door."

"Tell me where you are."

She sighs. "Look out the front window." Then she hangs up.

I run to the front of the house and pull back the living room curtains. Sure enough, across the street on a park bench, I see Kenji and Briar kissing under the glow of a streetlight. Idiots.

I pull on my coat and boots and march out the front door, then run across the street. "What are you doing?" I ask the tangled mass of KenjiBri. "You're not supposed to be out here."

Briar looks up, her face warm and flushed. "Says who?"

"You have a curfew!"

"Don't be such a baby," Briar tells me as she winds her fingers in Kenji's red-tipped hair. "I can see our house from here. It's fine."

"What about you?" I ask Kenji. "Don't you have a curfew?"

Kenji hasn't stopped staring at Briar since I walked up. "I don't care," he says dreamily.

"This is ridiculous." I stamp my foot in the crusty snow. "You have to come in the house."

"You go back in the house," Briar tells me.

"You're going to ruin it for both of us," I plead. "You'll get caught and Mom and Dad will make some stupid rule that will apply to me, too. And then we'll never be allowed to go out again."

"I won't get caught if you keep your mouth shut and go back inside," Briar says.

I toss my hands up and groan. "You're impossible!"

"Shhhh!" Briar hisses. "That's how we'll get caught, because you're such a baby."

"I'm not a baby," I say. "You're an idiot."

Briar levels her gaze at me. "Just because you're jealous—"

"I'm not jealous!"

"You should be. If Timber felt about you the way Kenji feels about me . . ."

"Enough," I say, my heart stinging. "You're on your own. If you get in trouble, don't ask for my help because you won't get it." I turn to cross the street but have to wait for a car to pass by.

"I'm not the one who needs your help," Briar says. "You're the one who needs my help."

"What's that supposed to mean?" I ask, looking over my shoulder.

"You wouldn't have even gotten a part in the musical if it wasn't for my help," Briar says.

"What did you do?" I walk slowly toward her again.

She glances at Kenji then blows on his face and says, "Freeze!" to paralyze him. He's stuck, lips pursed, straining toward her.

I gasp and whip around, making sure that there's no one out here who could see what she's done. "You can't do that!" I whisper harshly.

"You asked the question," she says disentangling herself from Kenji's frozen embrace. She stands and walks toward me, leaving statue boy on the bench alone.

I put my hands on my hips. Briar might know more spells than I do, but my magic is quick and I'm strong. If she tries to pull anything on me, I'll be ready.

"Wasn't it funny how calm you felt when you got up onstage at the audition?" she asks me. "You were so nervous and then . . ." She blows me a kiss and wiggles her fingers. "Poof! You weren't anymore."

"You promised not to use magic on the audition," I tell her.

She shakes her head. "No, you told me not to cast any spells on Bella. I didn't." She points at me and I lift my hand, ready to counter. "I put a spell on you." She lowers her hand and grins.

"What was it?"

"I gave you the breeze," she says. "And you rode it. You were great," she tells me. "You really can sing, but you get too nervous. You would have made an ass out of yourself if you had gone out there like a scared little mouse."

"That's not what I wanted," I tell her, and fight back the gathering tears of frustration.

"Maybe, maybe not. But in the end, you got what you really wanted. A part in the musical so you could keep an eye on Bella." She rolls her eyes and glances over her shoulder at Kenji, who hasn't budged from his frozen half kiss. "Fat lot of good it's doing you tonight, though? Did he ever call?"

"What'd you do to him?" I ask, pointing at Kenji.

"Duh, I froze him. You saw me."

"No, I mean how'd you make him fall in love with you?"

Briar knits her eyebrows together. "That's not a spell, Zeph. I know you thought he always had a crush on you, but he really feels this way about me."

I shake my head. "I don't think so. You did something. Erdlers don't switch on and off like that. No one does."

Briar's face clouds over. "It's not a spell," she insists. "He really loves me." She struts back to the bench and rearranges herself between his rigid arms then turns her head so his lips are touching hers. "Unfreeze," she says and kisses him.

chapter 11

HERE'S HOW MY life has been going for the past week.

Sunday: sucked because I had to watch Kenji slobber all over Briar all day and Timber never called.

Monday through Wednesday: super sucked because other than sitting with Timber at lunch, I barely saw him since he's been spending all his free time after school with Bella and Mr. Padgett in private rehearsals while I'm stuck with Ms. Ramachadran and the supporting cast, learning the songs and dance numbers for the first act of *Idle America*.

Which brings me to today, Thursday, after school when Mercedes stands in front of me, feet planted and hand raised like she's going to slap me upside the head. "If you step on my foot one more time, *mija*," she says, shaking her fist at me.

"Sorry, sorry," I tell her. "I can't get that move right. Is it the left foot first?" Chelsea, Nora, and Ms. Ram look at me like I'm hopeless. On the other end of the stage, Kwan, Ben, Levi, and Omar rehearse the same dance number with Mr. Padgett's assistant teacher, Malca, while Ari, Gunther, Angelica, and the rest of the band work on songs with Mr. Saxon in the pit.

"I feel like you're not totally concentrating, Zephyr," Ms. Ram says as she twists her black hair into a bun, securing it with an elastic taken from her wrist.

"Something on your mind?" Chelsea asks, one eyebrow arching up, which is just plain mean because of course there's something on my mind.

All I can think about is what Bella and Timber are doing upstairs in their "private" rehearsal. I bet Bella has Padgie hog-tied in a closet while she seduces Timber in thigh-high combat boots. But of course, if I get myself kicked out of the musical, then I'll never know what they're doing. "Let's do it one more time," I say. "I'll definitely get it right."

We back up to our marks. "Cue music," Ms. Ram says. We wait. Nothing happens. "Music," she says. Still nothing. She throws up her hands in exasperation. "Oh for God's sake. Who's running the sound board around here?"

I know the answer to this one: Kenji and Briar. Which explains why nothing happened, because they're probably lip-locked in the sound booth at the back of the auditorium.

"Music!" Ms. Ram yells.

"Oops, sorry," comes Kenji's voice over the PA system, then we hear giggles from Briar, and instead of music they keep talking. "You have the cutest laugh," says Kenji. "Laugh again." Giggle giggle. "I love that laugh. Wuv that waff. Wuv wuv wuv that waff."

Everyone groans. Mercedes pretends to shoot herself in the head. "KENJI!" Ms. Ram shouts toward the back of the auditorium. "Cut the crap and cue the music before we all toss our lunch."

Kenji and Briar howl with laughter over the PA, then the music starts and, of course, I come in late. But at least this time I don't stomp on Mercedes's foot, or run into Chelsea, or bump Nora, or in any other way spazz out on the dance moves.

"Okay, finally," Ms. Ram says when we all hit the ending pose. "And just in time, too, because it's time for us to put the whole thing together."

A ripple of excitement goes through the pit of my stomach. "You mean, everyone? The whole cast together?" I ask.

"With Mr. P. watching," Ms. Ram shakes her hair loose from the elastic. "So don't make me look bad," she says, pointing at me. As if on cue, the back doors of the auditorium open and in walks Bella, followed by Timber, followed by Mr. Padgett.

"All right, people," Mr. Padgett says from the first row in the auditorium as Bella and Timber climb the steps to the stage. I peek out from behind the other supporting cast members and wave to Timber. He gives me a quick wink and I think I'll burst like a huge, happy firework. "Everyone get settled," Padgie says, "because I have a special announcement." This only makes us all fidget and talk more until he shouts, "Silence!" through a bullhorn, as if he's directing a huge movie set rather than ten kids ten feet away from him. When everyone is quiet, he puts the bullhorn down and says, "We have been graciously invited to give a very special performance next Friday."

Of course this sends more murmurs through the cast as we all wonder what it is.

"Shhh!" Padgie hisses through his horn. He stares at us until everyone is stone still. "As you know, the Rockefeller Christmas tree was lit this week." A collective gasp goes through the cast, except for me. As usual, I'm clueless. Mr. Padgett nods and smiles. "Yep, you guessed it. We've been asked to come and do a few numbers from *Idle America* on the stage by the tree."

Everyone around me whoops, hollers, and slaps five.

"I can't believe this!" Mercedes says. "Rock Center!"

"Quiet!" Padgie yells through the bullhorn. "That means we've got to polish the first three group numbers straight through, starting right now. If you mess up, find your place and keep going. Better yet, don't mess up! Anybody who can't hack it won't be performing with us next Friday. I mean it!" I could swear he's looking straight at me. "Now, find your marks."

I hurry to the back of the stage where Chelsea, Nora, Mercy, and I form the left side of a V with Levi, Ben, Omar, and Kwan making the other side. I'm at the very back since I'm the tallest, which makes Levi my partner. Mercy's at the front, since she's the shortest, which means she's paired up with Ben. It also means she's right behind Bella and Timber, who form the tip of the V, closest to the audience.

"Cue music," Mr. Padgett yells through the bullhorn, and this time, instead of lovey-dovey giggles, the intro music actually comes through the speakers. I lift my arms in a high V over my head and get ready to step forward with my left foot at the top of the second measure of music, but then I see Bella reach out and grab Timber's hand. Not only do I miss the beat, but I stumble over my own feet while trying to see over Chelsea's stupid long arms in front of me. Everyone steps left on the downbeat and I fall on my butt.

"Cut! Cut! Cut!" Mr. Padgett yells. "For God's sake, the first step? Who's back there?" He shades his eyes and everyone onstage turns around to stare as I scramble back to my feet.

"Sorry!" I squeak. "My shoe was untied." I quickly drop down and pretend to retie my already knotted laces. Mr. Padgett sighs through the bullhorn so that his disappointment resonates over the stage and lands on me like a heavy cloak. "I'm ready now," I call out, but really I wish I had clunked my head on the floor and knocked myself out when I fell down. This would be so much better if I were in a coma.

"Take your marks, people," Mr. Padgett yells again.

Chelsea looks over her shoulder at me. "Try double knots," she says sarcastically.

"Very funny," I say, and this time I don't flinch when Bella takes Timber's hand.

We start the number over again and I'm doing fine. Despite the fact that I think Padgie is a putz, I have to admit that I like doing this song. It's when we all introduce ourselves as the contestants in the reality show. My character is Sadie, a sweet farm girl from Indiana who made it on the show singing country songs. Every time it's my turn to sing, I have to step up, put my thumbs in my belt loops and sing, "I'm a little bit country!" Then Levi slides up beside me and sings, "And I'm a little bit rock and roll!" which, for some reason, is supposed to be funny.

Mercedes is Charlie, a spunky girl from a rough neighborhood in Los Angeles. Ben is a guy named Johnny from the 'burbs, and he has to choose between music and pitching for his high-school baseball team in a championship game. Nora plays a nerdy violin prodigy who finally lets her hair down. Omar is the guy version of that, only he's really good at math. Kwan and Timber are supposed to have some big rivalry, and Kwan plays dirty, hiring a thug to whack Timber in the kneecap, only it backfires and Kwan gets kicked off the show. (That's also supposed to be funny because some ice skater from a long time ago named Tonya Harding tried to whack another skater. But again, lost on me. This time it was okay because Mercedes admitted she had no idea what Padgie was talking about with that one either. He told us not to worry about it, that our parents would think it's funny, only obviously he doesn't know my parents!) Chelsea is called Lacy, the rich girl whose daddy buys her voice lessons and pays the judges to let her in. She's supposed to be the favorite to win, except, and here's the big surprise (not) Bella plays the sweet underdog named Maggie who wins everything—including the heart of Timber's character (gag me very much).

We end the first number with the guys down on one leg and the girls sitting on their other knee. We girls kick up our left legs and wrap our right arms around our partner's neck. I have to wrench my head around to see Bella perched on Timber's leg. She's sitting right on his thigh with her cheek pressed against his face.

I hate that girl. I hate her I hate her I hate her! But I don't have time to dwell on how much I despise her because the music changes and we're all scrambling to our marks for the next song, which has Mercedes's big solo in it.

The third song is the final number of act one. This is when things heat up between Timber and Kwan because they're both in love with Bella/Maggie. Chelsea, Mercedes, Levi, Ben, and I circle around Kwan and Timber, who stand on either side of Bella. Mercedes explained that this song is a medley and Ari downloaded all the originals for me. "She's my girl," Kwan sings and grabs Bella's left arm. "She's the one that I want," Timber sings back and puts his hand on her right arm while Bella sings, "Torn between two lovers," with her arms stretched wide between them. The rest of us line up, Chelsea and Ben on Timber's side, Levi and me on Kwan's, with Mercedes behind Bella. We grab and pull, yanking the three of them apart. Just like we practiced Levi, Kwan, and I tumble to the ground in a pile stage left.

This is supposed to be the end of the scene. Or at least this is the way the supporting cast rehearsed it with Ms. Ram, but instead of everyone freezing, soft music comes back in. I peek out from the tangle of arms and legs on top of me to see Bella and Timber walking toward one another center stage. They look into each other's eyes and circle one another. Bella sings, "This love I have inside." She reaches out. Timber lays his hand on Bella's cheek and sings, "And I'll give it all to you." She looks up at him with hungry, wanting eyes. She takes his wrist in her hand and puts her other hand behind his head. He cups the small of her back and pulls her close. "My endless love," they sing together, and then, horror of all horrors, they KISS!

chapter 12

THE ONLY THING that keeps me from tracking Bella down and zapping her into a dust mite after that kiss is Briar. She rushes to the stage as soon as the rehearsal is over. "Come on," she says, reaching for me. "Let's get out of here."

"No, let's find her. Let's zap her."

Briar massages my shoulders. "You're upset," she says. "But you need to walk away."

"Why?" I ask. "You're the one who's always telling me to use what I've got."

"I know," she whispers. "But not now. Not here." She motions to all the other cast members milling around, except for Timber, who's nowhere to be seen. "You're too mad. Your magic will be too strong. Besides, we'll get her later. Maybe I could drop a light on her head or something."

Kenji comes backstage and says, "Easy there, Phantom."

"Phantom?" says Briar. "Who's a ghost?"

"Dropping lights on people is what the Phantom of the Opera does," Kenji explains.

"Well, I've got to do something!" I say. "Or I'm going to explode."

"Let's go to the park to dance," Briar says quickly. "Blow off some steam."

I sigh. "Fine, but so help me, if I see her face . . ."

Kenji, Briar, and I take the train back to Park Slope. Despite the fact that she just bailed me out, Briar is bugging the bejeezus out of me. She sits on Kenji's lap and plays with his hair while he stares at her and they both ignore me. And she's annoying when we get off the train because she and Kenji amble up the stairs tangled together like a four-legged, two-headed, lovelorn yeti. Not to mention how annoying it is going into the park with them because they have to stop every five feet to say really stupid stuff to each other like, "You're my little sushi roll, I'm going to gobble you up" and "You're my sweet butterscotch blondie, I want to nibble you to pieces." Mostly I've learned to ignore them, but sometimes I want to smack them. Like right now when they lean against a tree and Kenji attaches himself to Briar's face as if he's a sucker fish and she's the bottom of a tank. I can't take it anymore, so I scoop up a handful of snow. I take my time forming it into a ball, patting it smooth on all sides. I add a little more snow. Then I aim it and throw, splatting them right where their cheeks meet.

"Hey!" Briar says, wiping snow from her face. "What's your problem?"

"Are you cold?" Kenji asks, pressing his scarf against Briar's cheek. "Do you want me to kiss it? Your cheek is turning red."

"It's the only way I can get your attention," I say, swallowing my smile. Then I turn and point across the field at a crowd of people. "Looks like someone took our spot."

Briar shrugs. "No big deal. We can dance somewhere else."

We're just about to head into a different meadow when someone from the group shouts, "There they are!"

Everyone turns around and waves to us. Briar and I look at each other, confused.

"Do you know them?" Kenji asks.

"I don't think so," I say slowly. "Do you?"

Briar shakes her head, but I can see one of her mischievous grins starting to bloom as she walks toward the waving group. "Let's go see who it is."

As we get closer to the group, I realize it's bigger than I thought. About a dozen people, mostly men, stand around. I recognize a few of them from the past few days when we've come here to dance. A tall guy with short, curly brown hair and glasses. A short round guy in a light blue parka. An old guy walking a beagle. The crowd parts as we near to reveal our circle. All around the edges fresh snow has fallen, but our space is a perfectly matted circle of grass.

"Thanks," Briar says to the guys. "You kept our circle safe."

I stop at the edge of the crowd. I don't mind a few people coming by to see what we're doing, but this feels strange to me. Like we're performing, but that's not why I want to do this. I want to do it for me. To forget what's bugging me and to feel free because when I dance out here with Briar I don't have to worry if I'm better or worse than anyone else or if I'm getting the steps right. There are no wrong steps. I just do whatever my body wants me to do.

"*Sha we no, hallenschor, um triden fayre la dolly,*" says the tall guy, then he bows.

Briar laughs. "Hey, how'd you know that?"

"That's what you say," he tells us, his eyes wide behind the thick lenses of his glasses. "*For maden kling um schaden flang, um triden fayre la dolly.*"

"That's right," Briar says as she lays down her book bag and unzips her jacket. "You've been paying attention." The guy blushes deeply and looks down at the snow, smiling. "Come on, Zeph," Briar says, stepping into the clear circle in the middle of the trampled snow.

Everyone turns to look at me and I shrink back. "I don't really want to."

"Come on," Briar whines. "Don't be a baby. It's so much fun."

"We'd really like to see you dance, miss," the man in the blue parka says politely.

Briar holds her hand out to me. She nods, grinning, her eyebrow twitching. All I can think is that I wish Timber were here. I wish I could dance for him and that he would feel about me the way Kenji feels about Briar. Doing this for anyone else feels creepy.

"*Sha we no, hallenschor, um triden fayre la dolly,*" the curly hair guy whispers. A few other guys join in. "*For maden kling um schaden flang, um triden fayre la dolly.*" They say it again, this time more of them joining in. Their voices are low murmurs, swirling together over the quiet snow as they repeat the words. Briar claps to the rhythm of their chanting and I feel a swelling in my chest. My arms and legs want to move. I can't really explain it, but despite my misgivings, I lay my bag down, unzip my coat, and let their words lead me into the circle.

Briar and I stand facing each other. She smiles at me and nods. We both close our eyes, take a deep breath, then, when we're ready, we open our eyes and start the dance.

I can't totally describe what happens when we dance, because in some ways it's as if time bends and twists. I can see the faces I pass as we twirl around the circle's edge, but I couldn't tell you how many times I pass them. I know the sun slowly sinks and early stars peek out, but I have no idea how long that takes—fifteen minutes or two hours, I couldn't say. At some point, my arms and legs start to feel tired, my body wants to slow down. The crowd around us matches their chanting to the slowing pace of our bodies. And then we're done, standing across from each other again, exactly how we started, only I'm warm instead of cold, happy instead of annoyed, and calm instead of worried. Briar and I bow to each other, then turn to bow to the people surrounding us as they clap.

When we step out of the circle, we're each immediately encircled by smaller, tighter groups. People shove business cards and envelopes at me. Someone hands me a bouquet of pink roses. Another person gives me a small wrapped box. They're all talking at once.

"We could put it on the Web and . . ."

". . . they're all nice guys, it's just a bachelor party . . ."

"I represent lots of models . . ."

". . . off-Broadway for now, but I think it could go big if . . ."

". . . the two of you could be famous . . ."

"Thanks. Thank you. Thanks so much," I say, pushing my way out of the knot of people. I hate this feeling of being mobbed, and I want to run across the open meadow until I hit the tree line so I can disappear. I stand on tiptoe to find Briar. She's still in the midst of her crowd, taking time to speak to every person around her. Offering her hand. Looking into their eyes. Accepting cards and gifts and bouquets of flowers with a huge smile. When I finally break free from the group to swipe my bag and jacket off the ground, I find Clay and Dawn waiting for me.

"Wow," says Dawn. "Wow! Wow! Wow!" She has her hands pushed down in the pockets of her long, white coat.

Clay slinks toward me, a sly grin showing beneath the shadow of his white knit hat. "Briar told us your dance was good, but Dawn's right. Wow!"

I narrow my eyes. "Briar told you to come today?"

"Sure," says Clay. "And she was right. That's some following you girls have there."

I shake my head, furious with Briar. This was why she was in such a hurry to get me out of rehearsal.

122   selfish elf wish

"What do you call that dance?" Dawn asks.

I toss all the stuff in my arms to the ground beside my bag so I can slip into my coat. "It's just a dance," I grouse at them. "Something my grandma taught us. It doesn't have a name."

"Well, those guys love it," Clay says, stepping closer to me. "You've got them pretty riled up." He's nearly in my face, but if I step back I'll bump into the throng behind me, so I'm stuck. "What did they give you?"

Dawn squats down and pokes through the pile of stuff on the ground. "Flowers. Chocolate." She shakes a little box. "This sounds like jewelry." Then she plucks a manila envelope from the pile. "Gisselquist Modeling Agency," she reads.

My mouth drops open.

"You should consider representation for your act," Clay says right when Briar and Kenji walk up.

"That's a great idea!" Briar says at the same time as I say, "I don't think so."

"Oh, don't listen to her. Zeph takes a while to warm up to new ideas." Briar bumps me with her hip, then she turns and kisses Clay on each cheek as if they're the oldest and bestest of friends. Kenji hangs back, but his face goes stony and his arms are rigid at his sides.

Dawn stands and offers Briar a hug. After they embrace, Dawn says, "You could dance at the club."

"It's getting dark," I say to Briar. "I'm leaving." I gather all the stuff on the ground and stuff it into my bag.

"Well," says Clay with a chuckle. "You know where to find us." He rubs Briar's back, and I see Kenji tighten his hands into fists at his sides.

"I'm sure we'll see you this weekend," Briar says, and gives him another peck on the cheek, which makes Kenji wince.

* * *

Kenji and I barely say a word on the way home, but Briar is as chatty as a bluebird. "And that guy in the black motorcycle jacket was from a modeling agency. He said he could get us bookings right away. Magazines love twins and he says we could pass. And that other guy with the goatee and the glasses, I think his name was Brian, did you meet him? He wants to do a documentary."

"I'm not doing any of this. You tricked me into dancing today!" I yell at her.

"God, you're impossible," Briar says. "You needed to get away. You like to dance. And people want to see us. So what's the big deal."

I stop by a trash can, unzip my bag, and dump the contents into the trash.

"What are you doing?" Briar yells, grabbing for the gifts. "Anytime you get what you want, you throw it all away." She pretends to look carefully through the trash. "Look, here's your part in the musical. Oh, and there's Timber. What else is Zephyr throwing out?"

"That's ridiculous," I say. "I never asked for this junk, and I'm not throwing away my part in the musical or Timber. I can't even get Timber to hang out with me. And you're no help at all." I look across the street to the lights in our living room and the smoke billowing from the chimney. I want to be inside the warmth of our house instead of out here sniping at Briar.

"Zephyr's right, you know," Kenji says to Briar. This gets my attention. "You have to be careful about this kind of stuff."

"What kind of *stuff*?" Briar asks.

"You don't know if these guys are legit. They could be running porno rings," Kenji says.

"What's a porno ring?" Briar asks. "Is that like our dance circle?"

Kenji slaps his own forehead. "Oh my God, no! It's when people take pictures of girls, naked, doing stuff."

"What kind of *stuff*?" she asks again.

"You know," Kenji says, his face reddening. "*Stuff* stuff. Like sex stuff."

My stomach turns over and my head feels warm. Briar's eyes widen but then she laughs. "Seriously?"

"Yes," he says. "Seriously. You don't want to get caught up in something like that. It's bad news. Not to mention illegal."

"All the more reason to let Clay be our manager. Then he can see who's legit."

The light changes and I stomp into the street, yelling over my shoulder, "Who says Clay's even legit?"

Briar jogs after me. "At least we could dance at their club. Just for fun."

"No way," I say.

"Why not?"

"Why should we?" I ask when we reach the other side of the road.

"Because they asked us to and they're our friends."

I shake my head and open our gate. "They're not my friends. And you know, Briar, sometimes I wonder if you are, either."

Briar puts her hands on her hips and stares at me. "I'm trying to help you, Zephyr!"

"Oh really? How's that."

"I bet you ten bucks if we danced this around Timber, you'd never have to worry about Bella again." I stop on our walkway and turn back toward Briar. "He'd fall madly in love with you and never look twice at her again."

I shake my head. "That's not the way it works," I say, but I can't help thinking that Briar's right.

"Worked on him," she points to Kenji.

I look at Kenji. He stands beside her, grinning stupidly.

"But you know what?" Briar says, pushing past me with Kenji at her heels as usual. "I'm tired of you, so suit yourself."

I watch them go into the house. It's clear to me that something changed for Kenji after he watched Briar dance, but I don't know what caused it. So maybe the dance would have the same effect on Timber, but the big question is whether this is how I want him to fall in love with me. But if not, what's the alternative? Standing alone on the street corner, always pining away while he's off with Bella?

No matter what I decide, I realize then that it's not fair of me to be so angry with Briar. She can be annoying, but she is trying to help me, and if she doesn't help me, who will? I sigh.

chapter 13

THE WHOLE NEXT week flies by like a goose heading south. All I do is go to school, then rehearsal, go home and do my homework, fall in bed, and start the whole thing over again the next day. Ms. Ram has worked us like dogs every day for six hours. Mr. Padgett has come in and out, cursing half the time at what amateurs we are and how we don't deserve his original script, even though we've never even seen act three and he keeps changing act two so nobody can get their lines straight. Despite all that, act one looks great, so by the time Friday rolls around, I can't wait to perform it at Rockefeller Center.

At three-thirty, Briar and I stare up at the seventy-eight-foot Norway spruce tree standing in the middle of the Rockefeller concourse, but I'm not sure how to react. It seems as if all of midtown Manhattan is packed with people, milling around under the shadows of skyscrapers today, most of them ending up here. On the one hand, it'll be a great crowd and the tree is beautiful; on the other, I hate seeing everyone gawk at this sick joke on nature. "I don't know whether to be impressed or to lie down and weep," I say.

"How could someone cut down such a beautiful tree?" Briar asks, near tears.

I want to reach out and press my hand against the trunk and tell the spirit of this old tree that I'm sorry, but of course I can't get near it because it's surrounded by big metal gates, two guards, and hordes of people trying to take pictures. Not to mention the fact that it's covered with five miles of electric lights.

"Pretty cool, huh?" Timber slides up behind us.

Although a little trill goes through my body at the sight of his blue eyes under a black knit cap, I can't help but shake my head. "Trees belong in the forest," I say.

"This tree didn't come from a forest," says Timber.

"Listen, city boy," I say with a laugh. "Hate to break it to you, but trees grow in forests. Not in concrete in the middle of Manhattan."

"But in forests, they don't grow this big." He points to the top of the tree, where there's a giant star like a goofy hat.

"Obviously, you've never been to our neck of the woods," I tell him.

"Seriously, Zeph. You don't have to be so upset." He lays his hand on my shoulder. I feel like a snowflake in the sun. "Somebody donates a tree from their yard every year. They don't go out in the woods and cut one down."

This makes me feel a little bit better. "Still, I hate to think of this old beauty being chainsawed down for a few weeks of glitz and glamour."

Timber bumps me with his elbow. "Come on. You sound like a Grinch."

"A . . . ?" I start to say.

Timber laughs. "I'll lend you the book. Anyway, just wait until you see the tree lit up when the sun goes down. It's pretty spectacular." Then he turns and points over the railing of a fence behind the tree. "And check out the rink."

"Now that I like," I say when I see the large square of perfect ice surrounded by lights, a waterfall, and a beautiful golden statue of some dude flying with fire in his hand. Above it, around the rim where we stand, are rows of brightly colored flags whipping in the wind. The whole place is beautiful.

"I bet you're a great skater," Timber says. I grin because ice skates are one erdler invention we're very familiar with in Alverland. "And look over there," Timber says, pointing to the other side of the concourse, where a small stage with mics and spotlights wait.

"Is that where we'll perform?" I ask.

He nods. "You have to admit, that's pretty cool, right?"

I imagine us on the stage, singing and dancing, people skating below us and this amazing old tree in the backdrop. "Wow," is all I can say, because in Alverland, nothing like this is possible.

"I've lived in New York City all my life," Timber says, slinging his arm around my shoulder. "And every year Christmas here still amazes me."

Without thinking, I reach up and slip my mittened hand into his.

He gives my hand a little squeeze. "This is going to be awesome."

"Yes," I say, squeezing back. "It is."

Timber lets go of my hand and leans against the railing. He looks at me. "I haven't seen you much this week."

"Guess we've both been busy with rehearsal and stuff." I concentrate on watching the skaters so he won't notice the disappointment in my eyes.

"I've missed hanging out with you," he tells me.

I snap my head around toward him. "What?" I ask. "Really?"

"Sure, really." He laughs. "Why'd you act so surprised?"

I shrug, but I can't contain my smile. "I didn't know it was important to you to hang out with me."

Timber's smile melts into a frown. "Of course it is. You're my . . . my . . ."

I search his face, his dancing blue eyes, the hint of the comma at the corner of his mouth. "Your what?"

He shakes his head and laughs, but his eyes still look troubled. "I don't know," he admits. "But I did miss you."

I can't help it. Now my smile is plastered from cheek to cheek like a chipmunk with a den full of acorns. "Well," I say slowly, "there's something we could do about that."

"Yeah?" he asks, a grin sneaking onto his gorgeous face. "What's that?"

"Why don't we hang out after this?"

As quickly as it came, the grin is gone. "Aw crap, Zeph. I'd really like to, but . . ." He shakes his head and stares down at the rink again.

"But what?"

"It's this stupid musical. Mr. Padgett has Bella and me rehearsing all the time."

"You sure it's Mr. Padgett?" I ask, my jaw clenched. Timber looks at me, confused. "Maybe it's Bella who's demanding all the rehearsal time with you."

He shakes his head. "I don't think so. The whole play is a mess. Padgett keeps changing things and . . ." He leans in close to me. "To tell you the truth, I don't know if he's even finished writing it yet. It'll be a miracle if this thing is ready to go in two weeks."

"So blow him off!" I say, stamping my foot. "He can't make you rehearse on a Friday night."

Timber takes a deep breath, then lets the air out slowly so his face is obscured by the steam. "I wish I could."

"Whatever," I say. "I'm going to find Briar and Mercedes."

Timber reaches out and grabs my sleeve. "Hey," he says. "Please don't be mad at me."

"I just wish . . ." I say, but then I stop, because wishing isn't going to change anything.

What?" he asks.

"Nothing," I say, looking down at the skaters in the rink below. "You do what you have to do."

Mr. Padgett pulls the entire cast aside by the stage at four o'clock to explain what's about to happen. I huddle close to Mercedes to keep warm. "The show starts at four-fifteen sharp," he tells us. Mercy and I wriggle with excitement. "Before we go on, Bella will do a solo performance and then—"

He gets drowned out by everyone saying, "What? How the . . . ? Who said anything about . . . ?"

Mr. Padgett holds up his hand. "Hey, this is showbiz, kids," he says. "Not some grammar-school talent show. Some people get solos. You don't like it, get on the subway back to Brooklyn."

Everyone shuts up, but no one is happy. Except for Bella, who stands slightly behind Padgie with a half smirk on her face. I glance behind her to see Clay and Dawn lurking in the shadows. I elbow Mercedes and point to them. "I bet they're behind this."

"Jerks," she says.

"After that," Mr. Padgett continues, "there will be a ten-minute break to reset the stage and then the *Idle America* cast will go on at four forty-five sharp. Do not be late! We *will* go on without you. Understood?"

Everyone nods and mutters yes.

"Good," says Padgie. "And I hope I don't have to remind you that this is a professional performance. I expect everyone to do his or her best, because if you look bad, I look bad, and I don't like looking bad."

"Jeez," Mercedes says. "Easy there, Herr Padgett."

* * *

When Mr. Padgett has finished with us, Briar slips behind me. "I have an idea," she whispers in my ear. She motions with her head for me to follow her.

Briar leans against the railing overlooking the rink. "Clay just told me that Bella's getting a solo," Briar says.

"I know. What the . . . ?"

"Here's the deal," Briar says. "Clay set this whole thing up. Someone owed him a favor. He couldn't get Bella booked alone, though. He needed the school angle to make it happen, but he made Padgie promise Bella a solo because he brought a bunch of casting agents to check her out."

"I hope she falls on her butt."

"Exactly," Briar says, smiling. "And maybe we could help her along."

"No, Bri. I'm not going to—"

She holds up her hands. "I'm not talking about zapping her. I'm talking about something better than that."

"What would be better than that?" I ask.

"Zapping Timber," she says.

I roll my eyes. "We can't do that! There are hundreds of people here."

"But we can do something else." She points to the skating rink.

"What?" I search the ice for a clue about what's she's thinking.

"Let's do the elf circle. On skates. Down there."

"When?" I ask, still not understanding her plan.

"Four-fifteen sharp."

"That's when Bella goes on."

"Duh," says Briar. "And we always attract a crowd."

"Briar!" I gasp. "You're so brilliant. Evil, but brilliant." But then I stop. "I don't know. I don't think I can."

"Yes, you can." She takes my hand and pulls me toward the revolving doors in the nearest building. "I already checked it out. We just have to rent skates and—"

"But, but, but . . ." I stutter as I let her pull me through the crowd.

Briar stops. "Yes or no?" she says, staring at me. And I think, *This is it*. Briar's getting tired of trying to help me. It could be my one chance to get Timber, and get back at Bella, at the same time.

"Technically we're not casting spells," I say.

"Of course not," Briar says. "We'll just be doing the dance, which we do all the time. Only this time we'll be Elves on Ice."

I bite my lip. Somewhere deep inside I know this isn't exactly the right thing to do. It could all backfire or get us into trouble. But then again, since we're not exactly sure what the elf dance does, I can't really get in trouble for dancing it, can I? Even if I could, do I care? Because for a moment by the tree, I thought Timber was going to blow off Bella to be with me, and that was the best feeling I've had in weeks. And now the best chance I have to make that happen is to get out there on the ice.

"Okay," I say. "Let's do it."

Briar and I lace up our skates and zip out to take three quick laps around the perimeter of the rink, spinning and dancing the whole way. Since winter is so long in Alverland, we start skating as soon as we learn to walk. Even though I haven't been on skates since the end of last winter, I feel great on the ice, and when my path is clear I do a split jump, sending a whoop up from the small crowd beginning to gather near the railing. "No jumping!" one of the workers tells me, and I smile sweetly.

"Sorry," I say. "I won't do it again."

Then I hear someone call my name. I look up to see Mercedes and Ari, waving and yelling from near the railing. "Do some more!" they holler.

Briar comes up next to me, sending a spray of ice shavings arcing into the air. "You ready?" she asks.

I glance up at the stage. The lights are on now and the MC is climbing the steps to introduce Bella. I also search for Timber, but I don't see him. He's not with Mercedes and Ari. Not by the tree. He must be in the audience getting ready to watch Bella. All I can do is hope that Briar and I cause enough of a ruckus that he comes to the railing to watch. "Okay," I say. "Let's do it."

Briar and I skate to the middle of the rink. With one toe of our skates digging into the ice, we circumscribe a large circle in the center, then we step inside it and face each other just the way we do at the park. Before Bella's music kicks in, we start our chant.

Around and around we go, dancing our dance on the narrow steel blades of our skates. The lights, the golden statue, the flags, and the Christmas tree above us blur together as we spin and chant. Within minutes, the other skaters on the ice have formed a ring around us, but I can't make out any faces as I keep going, shouting now, "*Sha we no, hallenschor, um triden fayre la dolly. For maden kling um shaden flang, um* TIMBER *fayre la dolly!*"

Doing the dance on skates feels like flying. Soon I realize that above us, crowds of people have gathered at the railing to watch. I can't slow down enough to see individual faces, but I keep shouting Timber's name, hoping that he feels me spinning into his heart. As usual, I lose track of time and too soon Briar slows the chant, but I don't want to stop. I could keep going until the moon and stars shine down on us.

Briar skates nearer to me and takes my hands. We spin together, a mighty whirl of blond hair flying, until our momentum slows. I close my eyes, whisper the chant, and let my heart beat calm as our skates come to a stop. Briar hugs me close. I cling to her and say, "Thank you" into her ear.

When we look up a roar of applause engulfs us. Briar grabs my hand and pulls me into a bow. We spin around, bowing in each direction, to the other skaters on the ice, to the lines of people by the railing above us, to others who watch from the windows down below. Then I turn and look up at the stage. Even Bella has stopped to stare down at us. She's too far away for me to see clearly, but I can tell that she's pissed. This makes me smile. I press my glove against my lips and toss her a big juicy kiss!

We hurry out of our skates and run up the steps to the concourse. When we burst through the doors near the stage, Mercedes and Ari grab us. "I don't know what that was," Mercedes yells, "but it was off the hook!"

"Oh my God!" Ari's laughing so hard he can hardly stand up straight. "And did you see how many people were watching you? And how many people were NOT watching Bella?"

I grab his arm. "Really?" I ask. "Did they really watch us and not her?"

"Honey!" Ari says, slapping my back. "She had, like, one homeless guy and a Salvation Army Santa on a smoke break watching her. You had like a thousand people mesmerized! What was that?"

Briar and I squeal and jump around, hugging each other. "We did it! We did it!" we yell.

"But come on, Kristi Yamaguchi," Mercedes says, pulling me away from my cousin. "It's time to dance with the stars!"

We head toward the stage where the rest of the cast has gathered. Everyone applauds when I run up, except for Bella, who stands off to the side, shooting fire from her eyes. I swear, if she were magic, I'd be a pile of dog doo by now.

"Where's Timber?" Mr. Padgett yells as he pushes through the cast. "Where the hell is he?"

I crane my neck, looking for those blue eyes flashing in the crowd, but I don't see him anywhere. Then behind me, the crowd parts and

Timber comes running. I step into the center of the group, facing Timber as he skids to a stop. My heart nearly bursts out of my chest. "Did you see?" I ask him.

"Am I late? Did I miss it?" he pants.

"Did you see us?" I ask again, searching his face for some sign of true devotion.

But he blinks at me. "Did we already go on?"

"Who?" I say.

"The cast," he says.

"No," I say, baffled. "Bella did her solo and Briar and I—"

"Whew!" he says and laughs, finally catching his breath. "I ran over to the Sony store to get a new charger for my phone and—"

"It's about time!" Mr. Padgett pushes me aside. "So nice of you to join us." He grabs Timber by the elbow and drags him away. I watch, my heart dissolving into a puddle of slush. He didn't see it. He wasn't there. Mr. Padgett leads him up the steps.

I watch Timber mount the stage with Bella by his side. "How'd your solo go?" he asks her.

"Shut up," Bella says, and pushes him into the spotlight.

I trudge behind the rest of the cast and take my place in the back of the V. The music starts, but I can hardly sing, I'm so disappointed. How could this happen? All through the first song, I do my steps, lackluster, my arms flopping like half-dead fish. How could he miss it? It was my chance. My one chance. The only thing that saves me from crying onstage is watching Mercedes belt out her solo in the second number. She's on fire when she steps forward into the spotlight. Her voice is strong and clear. Her high notes could shatter glass, and her lows make your heart ache. She throws her arms open for her last line. "I have so far to go!" She holds the note until the crowd screams and stomps and claps.

I take my mark for the last song of the first act and I dread what's coming. This is when they kiss. When the song is over, I fall to the stage in the pile of bodies like I'm supposed to, but I want to stay here forever, buried under arms and legs. I know I shouldn't look, but I can't help myself. I lift my head to look at Timber. He's center stage, next to Bella. She pauses, then turns her head and locks eyes with me. She reaches for Timber, wraps both hands around his head, and pulls him toward her. Before their faces meet, she opens her mouth and slides out her tongue, then she plants the biggest, sloppiest, wettest French kiss on him that I've ever seen. Timber leans into her, his eyes closed, like he's lost in a moment of true love, but Bella's eyes are wide open and she's staring straight at me.

chapter 14

WHEN WE COME offstage, we're almost mobbed by people wanting to congratulate us on a great performance, but I want to get away. I need a place to go where I can cry. As I push through the crowd, mumbling, "Thanks," someone taps me on the shoulder. I turn around to see a tall, elegant woman with fiery-red hair wearing pressed black pants and a black and silver wrap. She extends her hand. "Zephyr?" she says. I nod. "My name is Isadora Falcon. I saw you dancing on the ice."

I step back. "How did you know my name?"

The woman points over her shoulder to Dawn, who stands off to the side with her arm around Bella as people surround her. "She told me." She hands me a card. "I'm a booking agent with IMG." I look at her blankly. "We're a modeling agency," she says, and I nod, but I'm not sure what that has to do with me. "I'd like to talk with you and your cousin about putting together a portfolio and booking some work for the two of you. Twins are very hot right now and you girls could pass."

"I don't think so," I say. What is it with the twin thing? Then I see Briar weaving through the crowd to get to me. "But you should definitely meet my cousin." She turns around just as Briar walks up, and I take that as an opportunity to slip away.

As I make my way through all the people, I see Mercedes shaking the hand of a guy in a suit. She's smiling from ear to ear. He takes a card from his wallet and hands it to her. She clutches it with both hands as if she's been given a thousand-dollar bill. Behind that guy is a woman, reaching for Mercy, too. And another on the other side, tapping her on the shoulder. *Good for her*, I think. It's about time someone noticed how talented she is.

I push on until I find a bench by the railing where I slump down, trying not to cry. I bury my face in my hands and stare at my boots, wishing everything was different. Someone else taps my shoulder. Crikey, I hope it's not another casting agent. I look up, ready to politely ask this person to leave me alone, but standing beside the bench is Timber.

"Hey," he says. "You okay? You look sick." He sits next to me.

I cross my arms and shake my head. "I'm fine," I tell him.

"That was some performance," he says with a laugh. "And the crowd was crawling with talent scouts. I think Mercedes has gotten, like, five audition offers."

I try to smile. "Good for her."

"Are you sad because no one tapped you?" he asks. "I'm telling you, it's not all it's cracked up to be. Auditions are grueling and—"

"That's not why I'm upset."

Timber puts his hand on my knee. "Then what?"

That's when the tears leak out of my eyes, even though I really don't want to cry, but then again, I'm tired of pretending that I'm okay when I'm not okay or acting like none of this matters to me when it does. I shake my head. "I can't believe you kissed her like that," I whisper.

"Who?" he asks. "Bella?"

"Who else?"

Timber laughs, but not because this is funny. His laugh is that uncomfortable kind of chuckle when you don't know what else to do. "Zeph, we were acting. You know that."

"But you weren't acting!" I say, all my anger welling up and spewing from my mouth. "I saw you. That kiss was real."

"That *was* acting," Timber insists.

"She wasn't acting."

This makes Timber spit out a hard and bitter *Ha!* "She was acting for the last six months I dated her. And believe me, she's good. Good acting is supposed to make you think it is real. She had me convinced for over a year that she was still into me, even when she was busy kissing other guys, like Gunther. I've kissed Bella a thousand times in my life—"

"Is that supposed to make me feel better?" I almost yell.

"No, I mean, yes. What I'm saying is, if you'd let me finish, only half of those were real. I know how to kiss her and make it look like I have feelings for her because she was my girlfriend for a long time—"

"That's the problem!"

"Was, Zephyr. WAS my girlfriend. Not is." I can tell by his voice that he's getting weary of this discussion, but I can't let it go because every time I stop talking, the two of them locking lips jumps back in my mind.

"You had your eyes closed and then you smiled," I say, remembering how he pulled away from her slowly, a small happy smile dancing around the edges of his wet lips.

"No, Jason smiled. My character is supposed to be happy that they kissed. What'd you want me to do, spit on the floor?"

"Yes!"

Timber's shoulders slump. "Zeph, this isn't going to work if you get crazy like this."

"What's not going to work?" I ask, looking up at him.

"This?" he motions between us.

"What's *this*?" I yell. "I keep trying to figure out what THIS is, but every time I think there might be a THIS, it turns out I'm wrong!"

"I told you I wasn't ready to jump into anything," he says.

"Well, I am. And I'm tired of waiting. And I'm tired of Bella getting in my way."

He shakes his head. "I can't," he says. "Not if you're going to get all crazy like this. Bella was the most jealous person I've ever known. She never trusted me, which is a laugh because she was the one always messing around behind my back. I can't be with someone like that again." He shakes his head. "I thought you were different."

"I am," I say, then I stop. There's part of me that knows he's right. I am acting like a crazy, jealous person. That's not who I am. But that part is buried below this fury, and I can't latch on to it. Because another part of me knows that if he keeps kissing Bella and pretending that he likes her, pretty soon he's going to really like her and really want to be kissing her again and the thing between us will never happen. "What exactly are you saying?" I ask.

He puts his hands in his hair. "I'm saying I thought we had a chance. If we could take it slow and you could let me be who I am, but now—"

"No," I say, my voice shaking. "Don't say that." I move toward him, but it's too late. He's standing up. He's walking away from me. "Timber," I call out. He pauses and looks over his shoulder. Behind him, I see our friends waiting for us. They peer around other people in the crowd, staring while my heart begins to crumble.

Timber shakes his head. "It's not going to work, Zephyr," he says, then he takes off, disappearing into the crowd, and I'm left alone in the midst of strangers. Just then a collective gasp and cheer goes up. I turn around and see the lights of the Christmas tree blink on and I crumple to the bench, sobbing.

Mercedes and Briar are suddenly beside me, helping me up. "Come on, get up, *mjia*," Mercedes says, tugging on one arm while Briar pulls on the other. "It's going to be okay. It'll all get fixed tomorrow."

I search the faces in the crowd for Timber. I see a black knit cap, but it's not him. If I wish hard enough, will I see him coming back to me? I close my eyes, squeezing out the tears, but when I open them, he's still gone.

"I knew she would ruin my life," I wail. "She said she would. She swore she'd get me back."

Briar puts both arms around my neck. "We'll get her back," she says. "I'll help you."

chapter 15

THERE'S ONLY SO much time a person can cry, and I think I've exhausted my quota for a year. Since I got home last night, after we sang at Rockefeller Center, I've pretty much been facedown on my bed, bawling like a motherless kitten. If only I hadn't done that stupid dance, I wouldn't have pissed off Bella and she wouldn't have kissed Timber like that, and I wouldn't have gotten mad, and Timber would still be speaking to me. But I blew it! I wanted so badly to make him like me that I ended up making him run away.

All day long, my mom has been in and out of my room, rubbing my back, bringing me tea, and asking me if I want to talk about it. I don't. My grandma has brought me ointments to sniff and balms to rub into my heart to help ease this heavy ache that's filled up the space between my ribs, but it hasn't worked. My little sisters and brother have sneaked in, one by one, to push my hair out of my face and leave me little presents on my pillow. Dad and Grove even stopped in this morning when they got home for their overnight gig in Boston, but I didn't want to talk. Briar has kept watch over me the whole time, plotting and planning

Bella's downfall through a series of hexes and spells, but I'm afraid that everything I'd try would blow up in my face.

Sometime this evening Briar told me she was going out with Kenji, who, of course, can't be apart from my cousin for more than ten minutes without losing his mind. And so, I think I'll stay in my bed until I have to drag myself to school on Monday. I'll just stare at the ceiling, wishing I could cry some more, except by now I feel like a washcloth that's been wrung out and left to dry.

Then there's a knock on my door. It's not the soft knock of my mother, or the rhythmic knock of my dad, and it can't be Grandma Fawna because she doesn't knock at all. This is more of a quick pounding, followed by, "Enough's enough!" Then Mercedes is in my room, flipping on the lights, yelling.

I pull the covers over my face. "Can't a girl mourn in peace?"

"Get on up, *mija*!" Mercy says.

Ari's close at her heels, tapping away on his CrackBerry. "I got a tweet from Kenji," he announces. "We're going to Red Hook."

I pull my pillow over my head and groan. "You guys . . ." I whine, then turn over and twist myself down inside my covers.

But Mercedes is having none of it. "It's time to celebrate and you're coming with us."

"What's there to celebrate?" I ask, my face still buried.

"Miss Mercedes Isabella Rios Sanchez has landed herself a professional audition," Ari announces.

I pop up in my bed. "Mercy, that's wonderful!" I open my arms to hug her. "Was it one of the talent scouts from the performance yesterday?"

"Hell, yeah," she says with a big grin. "Mama gonna audition for a mayonnaise commercial. First, I run this way with a big group of people, like we're all having the best time." She runs across my room. "Then we all run that way, like we're still having the best time ever." She runs the other way. "Then we all collapse in a big heap on a picnic blanket, laughing our asses off." She falls on my bed beside me. "And then, obviously, we all start spreading mayonnaise on our sandwiches because nothing says good times like mayo."

Without even knowing it, I'm laughing. "I'm so happy for you, Mercy," I say, and hug her.

"Good, now get up."

I fall back to my bed again. "No."

She yanks the covers off of me. "Lordy, you're still in your clothes from yesterday. I'm turning on the shower. Ari, you pick her out something clean and presentable to wear."

I keep my face buried against the mattress, but I can hear Mercedes's quick stomps down the hall, then the squeak of the faucets and the rain of the shower. I also hear Ari opening and closing drawers and pulling hangers across the metal bar in my closet. "Kenji and your cousin are already at the club. He says everybody's there."

"Everybody who?" I ask, my voice muffled by the wrinkly sheets.

He ignores my question and says, "You can't be the only one who doesn't show up, because then the terrorists win."

"What terrorists?" I ask from my cocoon.

"The Love Terrorists," Mercedes barks as she stomps back into my room. "We're not going to let you lie there like some sad sack, brokenhearted damsel on a Saturday night. You'd look like the biggest loser, and I'm not talking about the TV show. Plus, nobody ever got her prince back like that, sister." She pokes my leg. "Get up."

"No," I say. "Nothing I can do will fix this."

She pokes me harder. "Get up, get up, get up."

"Go away," I tell them.

It's silent for a moment, then I hear whispering, then a paper bag crinkles. I smell the chocolate before they speak. I almost lift my head, but I resist. "I've got cookies," Ari sings. "Your favorite kind. Double chocolate crinkle cookies from Galaxy."

He waves it beside my head. As the aroma of the gooey, chewy chocolate and powdered sugar as light as fresh snow hits my nose I realize that I'm starving. I lift my face from the mattress to look at my friends, who squat beside me, waving a giant cookie.

I reach out, but Mercedes smacks Ari's hand back. "Shower first."

"Come on," I whine, reaching.

"Get up," she says, and Ari dangles the cookie above me.

I sigh, heavy, as if my lungs were made of iron when I put my feet onto the floor. My head is spinning and my body is weak. I push my hair out of my face.

"Jeez, you look like hell," Mercedes says.

"I feel worse." I nearly slump back down to my pillow, but Ari breaks off a piece of cookie and hands it to me.

"We can fix that," he says.

I can't resist. I try to take just a nibble, but as soon as I taste the first crumb, I have to shove the whole piece in my mouth. I chew and swallow and realize that I'm parched. The water plinking in the shower sounds heavenly. I want to step in and open my mouth to drink. Let the water wash away all this sadness from my body and refresh my soul.

"That's a girl," Ari tells me. He takes two steps back and breaks off another piece of cookie. "Come on."

Like an obedient dog, I get up and follow, letting him feed me one bit of cookie every few steps until I'm at the bathroom door.

"There's more where that came from," he says, and pats the bag in his hand.

Mercedes gives me a push from behind. "Make it snappy," she says. "We want to get there soon."

The shower does wonders for me, and for a few moments as I scrub away yesterday, I can almost forget how sad I am. By the time I step back into my room, wrapped in a towel, I almost feel normal.

"This?" Mercedes says, holding up my favorite green miniskirt and gold metallic tank top.

"Or this?" Ari asks, pointing to skinny jeans and a tee with embroidered peacocks.

"You guys are the best," I say, but then I start to lose it again. My face crumples. "Remember how much of a superdork I was until you guys helped me out?"

"How could we forget? Your buttons all the way up to your neck and a belt around your waist." Mercy says.

"But now . . ." Tears creep back into my eyes. "What's the point of looking cool?" I sniffle. "When Timber won't even care?"

"No crying," Mercedes warns me.

"That won't get him back," Ari says.

"But this just might." Mercy turns back to my closet and takes out my green tunic and my boots, the ones I wore for the school audition. She shoves the clothes in my hands.

"You can't let them see you broken down," Ari says.

"You're gonna walk into that club looking like the *chica* that owns the joint," Mercy says.

"You want people falling at your feet," says Ari.

I hang my head. "I can't," I tell them, rubbing the soft linen of Timber's favorite tunic. "I'm too sad."

"Then fake it until you feel it, honey," Mercedes says.

"But we're not letting you mope around here for another twenty-four hours," Ari adds.

Mercy pulls Ari toward the door. "You've got ten minutes. And if you're not downstairs looking glam, then I'm coming up here and slapping you into Tuesday."

A tiny laugh bubbles up from my belly when Mercedes says this. I sort of smile. On the way out, Ari hands me another cookie. "For strength," he says.

I'm pretty sure my friends are crazy, but I also know they're trying to help. And I know they're right about one thing at least—sitting around here crying will not change the situation. So I pull on the tunic, find a big belt, grab a few amulets hanging off my bedroom mirror, and pull on my favorite boots. Then I twist my wet hair into a bun so I won't freeze out in the cold. I stand back and look at myself in the mirror. I look like I did at the audition. I remember Timber's hungry eyes. Part of me wants to slump back down on the bed and sleep for the next day and a half until I have to drag myself to school on Monday, because he'll probably never look at me that way again.

But I hear Mercedes calling my name, and I know that if I don't go downstairs, Ari and Mercedes will come up and get me. I might as well give this a try instead of crying. I grab my bag and join my friends downstairs.

Standing here under the pulsing lights while everyone around me shakes and shimmies to the throbbing music reminds me how much I don't want to be at Clay and Dawn's club right now. It's hard enough to act like I enjoy this place when I feel good, but trying to fake it when I really want to drop to the floor and sob because Timber isn't even here is next to impossible.

Beside me, Briar's shaking her groove thing so hard that sweat flies off the ends of her hair like a sprinkler watering grass. Kenji's nearly in a trance, bopping on the other side of Briar, his eyes fixed on her every gyration, a beatific smile playing on his lips. When I watch him watch her, I want to grab Kenji by the collar and shake him, demanding to know what did it and why it didn't work when I tried it. It's not fair that she gets this kind of devotion when I got nothing. How did that stupid dance change him from the cagey guy who was never clear about his feelings for my cousin to this hopeless duckling following her around as if she's his long-lost mommy? And would it have really worked on Timber if he had been watching?

Ari was right about one thing: the club is full of kids from our school, including the entire supporting cast of *Idle America*, who are either dancing or playing Guitar Hero in the other room. I've scanned the club a dozen times looking for Timber, and I don't know whether to be relieved he's not here, which might mean he's at home feeling as miserable as I am, or if I should be freaked out because Bella's not here either, so they could be together.

When the song is over, I tap Mercedes on the shoulder, "I'm taking a break," I yell in her ear.

Mercy shrugs. "Suit yourself," she yells, and starts grooving to the next tune.

I plop down on the red vinyl couch near the bar. If I had a way home right now, I'd leave, but I can't, so I close my eyes and try to block out the music so my brain doesn't explode. "Hey, Zeph," I hear Briar say. She falls onto the couch beside me. "You feeling better?"

I shake my head.

"You look better," she says. "And anyway, sometimes acting like you feel good makes you feel good."

Kenji sits down and wraps his arms around my cousin's waist. "You're so smart," he says. "And pretty. Model," he says, and they both laugh.

"Mom and Dad didn't say yes," I remind Briar, who's been on cloud nine since Isadora Falcon asked her to be a model.

"Yet," Briar says. "They'll come around."

Kenji pulls her down for a long kiss. When they come up for air, I'd like to knock their heads together.

"I have to go to the bathroom," Briar announces. "You want to come with me?" she asks me.

"No," I say. "I'm fine."

She stands, but Kenji keeps ahold of her hand. "Don't go."

"I have to pee," she says, laughing.

"Hurry," he begs, and I seriously think I'm going to barf Vitamin Water all over the red vinyl.

He finally lets go of her hand, but continues to watch her skipping off toward the toilets. I smack him on the shoulder. "Hey," I say. Kenji turns toward me. The green tips of his hair glisten with sweat. "What happened with you?"

He pushes his hair back and blinks at me. "What do you mean?"

"I mean all this lovey-dovey stuff with my cousin. You used to barely pay attention to her and then it was like a switch flipped in you. I don't get it." I know we've been through this before, but I need to hear it again.

He shrugs. "I don't know. Guess I fell in love."

"When?" I ask.

"It just sort of happened," he says.

I shake my head. "No, it didn't." I realize that I sound mad. "One minute you were standing under the streetlight at the park with Briar screaming at you, and then an hour later you were running across the field madly in love. What the heck happened in between? Was it the dance?"

Kenji thinks about this for a moment. He eyes scan back and forth as if he's reliving that day in the park when everything changed. Then he lights up. "Yeah, it was. When I saw her dancing it was like she reached inside of me. It was the way she moved," Kenji says. "Like she was calling to my soul." He blushes. "Sounds goofy, I know, but that's the truth."

I sigh. *Maybe it's not some sort of magic*, I think as he and I sit quietly. Maybe Kenji was ready to fall in love with her and seeing Briar do the thing that she loves to do most made everything click into place. But then Kenji looks at me again.

"And that chant," he says. "There was something about that chant. It got inside my head, you know? Which is weird, because I don't know what it means, but I've never been able to shake it. Even when I go to sleep, I hear it."

My heart revs up. Maybe it is magic, some incantation Briar and I stumbled on, and maybe it could work again if I tried. But when?

My cousin comes bopping across the floor again. "Come with us, Zeph," she says, reaching toward me. "Let's dance some more."

Kenji snaps his phone closed. "I just got a text from Timber. He's heading over here."

"Oh my God!" I say, feeling like I might barf. "What am I going to do?" I look at them with panic in my eyes.

Kenji smiles at me. "You should dance," he says. Then he winks. "Worked on me."

Even though dancing is the last thing I feel like doing right now, I follow Briar and Kenji to the floor. I position myself toward the door and force my feet to keep time with the beat of the music while my head spins through all the possibilities of how to work this out with Timber. I'm so caught up in working out scenarios for what I'll say that I don't see when he comes through the door. It's not until Briar grabs my arm and spins me around to face him that I realize he's already here.

I understand now what it means to melt. My heart thaws, my eyes water, and I feel a gush from the pit of my stomach to my toes. He's not even looking at me. He's too busy talking to everyone who's holding out their hands for high fives and pulling him in for chest bumps. I turn my head and look for Bella. I find her standing in the doorway between the back room and the bar. I see how she cocks her head and studies the situation, like a cat plotting her attack on an unsuspecting bird. At that moment, my chest swells with something fierce. I won't let her have him. I won't let her do this to me. I'm going to get him back.

I turn to Briar. "I want to dance," I tell her.

"Good!" she says, spinning.

I grab her arm and pull her close. "I mean, I want to do the elf circle again," I yell into her ear. She steps back and studies me. I look over my shoulder at Timber then I turn back to her. "For him," I say. "Here."

A slow smile spreads over Briar's face. "Don't move." She scurries off the dance floor.

I keep time to the music, dancing just behind Kenji so that Timber won't see me if he turns this way. I don't know what Briar and I conjure when we dance, why people fall all over themselves for us, or why it worked on Kenji, but right now I don't care. This is my chance and I'm not going to throw it away.

The music fades until it's just a drum and bass rhythm under Dawn's voice over the speakers. "Hey, Red Hook! Holla!" she yells, and everybody yells back. "Y'all having a good time?" The crowd whistles and screams. "Check it out, Brooklyn. We've got something special for you tonight. Two gorgeous girls are here to dance for you."

Briar is at my side, tugging on my arm. "Come on," she shouts in my ear, and drags me toward the stage.

"You've got to see this dance," Dawn shouts. "It's sick."

Briar and I climb up two steps to the side of the little stage.

"Give it up," Dawn shouts, "for Briar and Zephyr!"

I don't know if the crowd goes nuts or stays quiet because the drum and bass swells to fill the room. Before I can change my mind or think about what I'm doing, Briar and I stand across from each other, bouncing on our toes to the beat. She nods at me and then we start the chant over the rhythm of the music. Once again, I insert Timber's name. "*Sha we no, hallenschor, um triden fayre la dolly. For maden kling um shaden flang, um* TIMBER *fayre la dolly!"*

I dance in a way that I've never danced before. I'm lost in the music, in the rhythm, in my movements, in the sound of my voice mingling with Briar's under the heavy drums and bass, but mostly I'm consumed by thoughts of Timber. He fills my mind, and every time I spin around the stage to face the front, I find him, standing in the center of floor. I feel as if he's in a spotlight, that he's all alone, that the entire room has cleared out except for Timber in the middle of the floor and me on the stage dancing for him. I feel a connection to him, like Kenji described, as if I'm reaching into his soul and pulling him toward me. My heart is full, as if my chest will burst and a hundred birds will fly free. I harness that feeling and put it into my body, dancing, spinning, jumping, chanting. Over and over again I chant his name until his name becomes my name.

"Sha we no, hallenschor, um triden fayre la dolly. For maden kling um shaden flang, um TIMBER *fayre la dolly!"* I pull him into me, and slowly he steps closer and closer to the stage. I lock my eyes with his. I lose the room, the sound, the smell of the club until I'm in a meadow with Timber under a blue sky, dancing for him for all eternity. I feel a white-hot rush burst through me until I know what I have to do. I rush to the edge of the stage. Timber stands at the foot, looking up, eyes connecting to me and on the last chant, *"For maden kling um shaden flang, um* TIMBER *fayre la dolly!"* I rush forward. I spread my arms and I leap.

chapter 16

TIMBER'S MOM'S APARTMENT in Brooklyn Heights is closer and quieter than my house, so we catch a cab from outside the club. I cannot keep myself away from him. I want to devour him. I kiss his lips, his cheeks, his neck, and behind his ear. I drink in his slightly musky, fresh piney scent. "You smell so good," I moan into his ear.

"I can't believe I've been so stupid," he says. "How come I never realized how I feel about you?" He covers my neck with kisses.

"I thought this would never happen," I say, burying my face in his shoulder.

He unwinds my scarf. Unzips my coat. Presses his lips against the flesh on my neck. "I can't believe you wore this outfit. I love this outfit." I have goose bumps all over my body, half from the cold and half from the excitement of Timber's touch.

"Hey, lovebirds," the cabbie says, and knocks on the Plexiglas partition between the front- and backseats. "Which side of the street you want me to let you out on?"

Without glancing up, Timber says, "Left side, please," then he attacks my earlobe, sending me into a fit of giggles and squirms.

"Sheesh," the cabbie says. "Take it inside, would you?"

Timber shoves a twenty-dollar bill at him. "Keep the change," he says, and pushes the door open.

Timber wraps his arms around my waist and lifts me up. The streets in his neighborhood are quiet, with only a few people walking dogs or hurrying up stoops with their keys ready to take them out of the cold. "I'm so glad I came tonight. I'm so glad you were there. I can't believe how sucky yesterday was." He holds me tight against his body and I press myself against him.

"I know, it was horrible and I'm sorry that I ever acted like—"

"Shhhhh," he says, pressing his hands against my lips. "I should have never walked away from you yesterday. It was so stupid. It wasn't until I saw you up there tonight that I realized it."

We kiss as he unlocks the front door to his building. We kiss in the foyer. We kiss in the elevator going up to his mom's apartment. We kiss so much that my lips begin to ache, but I don't want to stop kissing him or feeling his hands under my coat, exploring my back, squeezing my waist. He fumbles to put his key in the lock and we continue kissing. "Don't worry, Mom's not here."

"Is it okay if we're here then?" I ask as we step into the dark apartment.

"Sure, why not? I live here, too."

I'm not sure if I'm supposed to be at his apartment without his mom, but what am I going to do? Go back out in the cold and hail another cab? There's no way I can do that, especially not now that we're here, alone. "Seeing you dance up there," he says. "I felt like you were only dancing for me."

I hold his face in my hands and look straight in his eyes, those gray-blue wolf eyes that make me shudder with fright and excitement. "I was," I tell him.

"Wow," Timber says, settling down now. "Wow, wow, wow." He steps back and takes off his coat. "I'm so glad you're here. Do you want something to drink? Some tea or something? You like tea, don't you? Your family drinks a lot of tea."

"We do drink a lot," I say and laugh because he's never noticed little things like that before. I hand him my coat, which he drops on a chair by the door. "But I'm fine for now."

"Let's go sit on the couch and talk. I want to talk. I have so many things to ask you. There's so much I don't know about you and . . ." As I follow him into the living room, his phone beeps. "Who could be texting me?"

My stomach tightens. It's probably Bella. After I jumped off the stage into Timber's arms, almost everyone in the club burst into applause. Timber swung me around, hugging me, and we kissed. One of the last things I saw as we gathered up our coats and headed out the door was Bella staring after us. The very last thing I saw, though, was Briar, standing between Clay and Dawn, her arms wrapped around their shoulders and all of them smiling, giving me big thumbs-up. I think I've misjudged Clay and Dawn. If it weren't for their letting us dance, I wouldn't be back together with Timber.

"That's weird," Timber says. "There are three messages from Kenji, but I don't understand what he's talking about." He holds the phone out to me. I scroll through the three messages:

> Tell Z 2 come bck B went w/ c & d cant find
> smthng wrong B missing come bck to club
> Need HELP!!!!

I roll my eyes. "Kenji is way too into my cousin," I say. "She can't even go to the bathroom without him freaking out."

"Yeah, but this is weird," Timber says as he dials Kenji. "He's not usually panicky like this. It's going to voice mail. Probably can't hear it ringing. I'll text him."

As soon as Timber punches in the message, the phone beeps again. "It's from Ari," he says.

Where r u? K freaking out!

"Something's wrong," I say.

The phone beeps again. "Mercedes," Timber says.

We need Z.

As soon as we've read that one, another one pops up from Kenji.

COME BACK NOW! B in trouble. Need help.

"Oh my God!" I say, jumping up from the couch. "We have to go."

Timber's ahead of me. We grab our coats and bolt out the door.

It's so late and the neighborhood is so quiet that we can't find a cab. Nobody at the club will answer their phones, so Timber texts everybody that we're heading back.

"Can we take the train?" I ask.

Timber shakes his head. "There's no subway to Red Hook. I'll call a car service."

"It'll take forever!" I'm starting to panic. "We should have never left."

"It'll be okay," says Timber as he dials.

"I should call my parents."

"Not yet," he tells me.

"Look!" I see a black town car bumping down the street. I jump off the sidewalk and wave my arms.

The car pulls over and the driver rolls down his window. "Where you going?"

"Red Hook," we both say in unison.

He shakes his head. "Nah, I'm off duty in fifteen minutes, I don't want to go that far."

"No!" I bark, and grab the door handle. "You have to take us. It's an emergency. My cousin's in trouble." I try to open the door but it's locked.

"Sorry." He rolls up the window.

I zap the window and jam it, then I stick my head inside the car as the guy messes with the controls, confused by why his window won't go up. I whisper, "Don't mind, change mind, mind the mind to change." I draw back and say, "Open the door now, please."

The man shakes his head, bewildered, but he says, "Yeah, okay. I can do that."

I grab Timber's hand and pull him into the car behind me. "Hurry," I tell the driver.

As we cruise over the bumpy side roads leading down to Red Hook, I take Timber's phone and call Grove's cell. "I'll feel better if he comes," I tell Timber.

"I'm sure everything is fine," he tells me, and pats me on the knee.

"I don't know." I shake my head. I can't understand what went wrong and if something is really wrong why I haven't already sensed it, which could mean that nothing's wrong and Kenji is freaking out because Briar went off somewhere without him. Then again, Kenji isn't the type to freak out and he's even freaking out Ari and Mercedes, which has me worried. Grove's phone goes straight to voice mail, which must mean he's asleep. I leave him a message to call Timber, and then I think about calling my house, but I don't want to wake my parents yet. By then we're back at the club.

"Wait here," I tell the driver.

Timber looks at me. "He's going off duty, Zeph."

"He'll wait," I say.

"I'll wait," the guy says.

"Wow," says Timber as we pile out of the car and go running for the club door.

Inside is more jam-packed than when we left. Now the place is totally jumping, wall-to-wall kids on the dance floor grooving to the ear-blowing music. The flashing red, blue, and green lights immediately give me a headache, and I have no idea how we'll find anyone in here. Timber's punching in a message to Kenji as we push through the crowd looking for anyone familiar.

I spot Chelsea's flame-red hair where she's sitting on the couches chatting up some guy in a blue jumpsuit. "Have you seen Kenji or my cousin?" I lean down and shout in her ear.

She shoots me a nasty look but says, "No!" then ignores us.

We work our way through the crowd until we see Bella and Gunther at the bar. Bella's sitting on a stool nursing another Diet Coke. As soon as she sees us, she opens her arms and squeals, "Oh the happy couple!" Then she slaps Gunther on the arm and snorts. From what Timber has said, I'm guessing that Diet Coke has some secret ingredients.

Timber sidles close to her and shouts into her ear. I do the same to Gunther. Bella shakes her head but Gunther nods. He points toward the back. "I saw her go with those two nut jobs who run the place about an hour ago."

"What about Kenji?" I ask.

"You mean the little Japanese dude with the hair?" Gunther asks. I nod. He shrugs. "Dude's whipped over that girl. He's probably with her."

I don't have time to explain or to take issue with how rude Gunther is, so I yell thanks and yank Timber away from Bella, who's taking this opportunity to talk to him way too long, way too close to his face.

I push through all the bodies to the back room, where another crowd gathers around a large flat-screen TV. Levi stands on a platform playing an electric guitar while everyone else chants and shouts at his avatar. I don't see Briar, Clay, or Dawn, but I do see a beaded curtain leading to another door in the back of the room. I squeeze past the bodies, pulling Timber along behind me. I part the curtain and see a short, dark hallway with a door at either end. Both doors are marked EMPLOYEES ONLY. I head toward one door, but Timber pulls me back and points to the sign. I don't care. If Briar's in there, I want to find her.

I turn the knob. The door pops open. Inside is an office. A large, green metal desk sits against one wall cluttered with a computer and three small TVs showing different parts of the club. Grainy black-and-white images rotate around the screens. First the dance floor, then the bar, the back room, outside the front of the club, an empty stairwell, a small storage room where I see lots of boxes and a small kennel cage, the back parking lot of the club where a group of people are smoking glowing cigarettes, then another room with a couch and two chairs. I see a shadow move toward the couch, but then the image changes to the dance floor. I keep watching those screens, trying to catch a glimpse of Briar or Clay or Dawn as the images rotate. I see the storage room again and look closely at the kennel. It looks like a small animal is in the cage, but I can't make it out, then the image switches to the parking lot. I look closely for anyone we know, but all the people are strangers. The images switch. We both watch carefully.

Then the room with the couches comes back around. I see someone slumped on a sofa. I press my face close to the screen, but the pictures switch again. I scan the other screens until that couch comes back. "I think that's Briar!" I say, pointing at the person who's wearing a skirt and has long hair like her.

"But where is that?" Timber asks.

"We have to find out." I leave the office and jog down the hall to the other door. At first the door sticks and I'm afraid it's locked, but when I push, it pops open to reveal the empty stairwell that was on the screens. Timber and I run down the stairs, trying to stay quiet, but the sounds of our footsteps bounce around the blank walls as we descend into a basement hallway. Timber opens the first door and we find a storage room full of boxes marked CUPS, STRAWS, and ID BANDS. He's about to close the door again, but I step around him and look for that kennel.

"She's not in here," he whispers to me. "And we shouldn't be in here either."

I tiptoe around the boxes and come face-to-face with two shining eyes. I jump back and gasp.

"What is it?" Timber's at my side.

I take a closer look at the cage and see a small, reddish-brown animal curled into a ball. "It's the fox," I say.

"What fox?" he asks.

"Grove and Briar saw it before," I explain. The fox looks at me, panting with pleading eyes, and I feel terrible for it. No animal, least of all a wild animal like a fox, should be in a cage in a storage room. Now I know Clay and Dawn are weird and that Dawn was lying when she said they had a cat. As much as I'd like to take that fox home to Bramble so he could care for it then release it in the woods, I know we have to leave it for now so we can find Briar. "Sorry," I tell the fox.

We back out of the storage room and tiptoe down the hall. We can hear the muffled music from above and the ceiling shakes where people jump on the dance floor. No wonder that fox is uneasy with all the noise and shaking. We find another door. Timber steps in front of me. He grabs the handle and turns it slowly. My heart beats quickly, half afraid of what we might find. He pushes the door open and we both peer in to see the room with the couch and two chairs. There, asleep on the couch, covered with a blanket, is Briar.

"Oh, thank the stars!" I say, and rush toward my snoozing cousin. "Bri!" I shake her. "Bri, wake up! You okay?"

Slowly she opens her eyes. "Hey, Zeph," she says, but her words come out thick and slurred, and her eyes immediately close again.

"Briar, wake up," I insist, shaking her arm. "What's wrong with you?"
I look to Timber.

"She seems stoned," he says.

"What do you mean, like drugs?"

"Or booze. Maybe she was drinking and she passed out."

"No way," I say, still trying to rouse her.

"It's possible," Timber says. "Maybe Clay and Dawn put her down here to let her sleep it off so she wouldn't get in trouble going home."

"But why wouldn't Kenji be with her?" I ask.

Timber shrugs. "Maybe she needed a break from him."

"None of this makes sense," I say. "We need to get her home. This is creeping me out."

That's when the door opens behind us. We all jump. Timber and I, and Dawn, who stands in the doorway. "What the hell?" she yells. "How'd you get down here?" I see anger flash across her face, and her eyes seem to darken.

"Hey, Dawn," Timber says. "Kenji got upset because he couldn't find Briar so we came looking for her."

Dawn pulls in a breath as if to calm down, but I see fury behind her eyes and in her fists balled at her sides.

"What happened?" I ask, pointing to my cousin.

Dawn licks her lips and looks over her shoulder into the hallway. I wonder if Clay is coming. I don't want to find out. I want to get out of here as fast as I can. "She had too much to drink," she says.

Timber laughs. "That's what I said happened."

"She doesn't drink," I say.

Timber goes on. "I said you probably let her crash down here to cool out so she didn't go home messed up."

"That's right," Dawn says, but I think she's lying. Something about the way she holds her body, as if she's on the defense of an attack, and how she licks her lips. I don't trust her.

"We need to get her home," I say.

Dawn's face brightens. "Clay can take you. He's getting his car right now. He was going to drive her home."

"No thanks." I pat Briar's hand, trying to rouse her. "We have a car outside."

Dawn blocks the door. "You can't take her through the club like this. I could lose my license. She was drinking illegally. I don't know where she got the stuff. Maybe her boyfriend. We were trying to do her a favor."

I look at Timber. "Kenji didn't give her anything," I say. "He's been looking for her."

"Whatever, but you can't take her up through the club like this," Dawn says again.

"We'll go out the back. Through that parking lot," I say.

She narrows her eyes at me. "What parking lot?"

"Where a bunch of people are smoking," I say, and level my gaze at her. "Where's the door?"

Dawn shifts uncomfortably. "Look, Clay will be here in a minute. Just wait for him and he'll help you get her out without a problem."

There's no way I'm waiting on creepy Clay. I turn back to my cousin. "Briar!" I bark and shake her. "Wake up. What's going on? You have to get up now."

She rolls her head back and forth. "Do you know the U.P.?" she asks, and holds up two limp hands to look like Michigan. "Here by the knuckle." She points to her pinky knuckle of her left hand as if she's showing us where Alverland is, then she slumps back down and closes her eyes.

I whip my head back toward Dawn. "What has she been telling you?" I demand, remembering all the strange things Dawn knows about my dad and all the questions she asks me every time I see her. I don't know who she is, but this doesn't feel right to me. That's when I see Dawn's left hand rise up. I notice the way she's turning her wrist, inward, and I see her lips begin to move.

Before I can think, I zap her. "Limp fish!" I call out, and point. Her arm falls to her side. "Mute newt," I call, and zap her throat. Timber looks at me, bewildered, but I don't have time to explain my reaction or why Dawn's mouth is moving but no sound comes out or why her arm hangs useless by her side. It comes from years of my brothers and sisters and cousins and me casting spells against one another. I know that flick of the wrist. I know the way we move our lips as we conjure. I don't know if that's what Dawn was doing. It makes no sense, but her movements were too familiar for me to wait and see.

"Grab Briar's other arm," I command Timber. He does what I say. We hoist Briar up and sling her arms across our shoulders. She moans. "Stand up," I tell her. "Now!"

Briar comes to a bit. "Zephy," she coos at me.

"You're in big trouble," I grumble at her. "Let's go," I tell Timber.

He helps me almost drag Zephyr toward the door, past Dawn, who's still trying to find her voice and the use of her arm. In the hallway, I see one more doorway. It's silver with a panic bar in the center. "That's got to be an exit," I say. "Maybe it goes to the parking lot."

We head that way, Briar heavy between us. We turn backward to push against the door just as Dawn comes into the hall. Her voice is hoarse and her arm isn't moving correctly yet, but it looks to me like she's trying to cast another spell.

"Go! Go! Go!" I yell as I bang against the door. An alarm shrieks as we push through. There's a steep, dark staircase behind us, but it's freezing, so I guess that we're heading outside. Above us are trapdoors. We lift them over our heads and crawl up into the cold air of the parking lot. The smokers congregated by a staircase behind the club watch us with their mouths hanging open while the alarm continues to shriek. The door at the top of the steps flies open and people spill out into the night.

"Pick her up!" I shout at Timber. He scoops Briar into his arms and we run through the parking lot. I look over my shoulder to see Dawn emerging from the trapdoors. I yank Timber into the crowd and we disappear from Dawn's sight.

We round the side of the building and cut through an alley to the front of the club. People pour out the front door, too, and now I hear sirens. The car service guy still waits by the curb, which is lucky because very soon my spell will wear off him and he'll wonder why in the world he's sitting here. As I run for the car with Timber carrying Briar behind me, someone grabs my arm. I turn, ready to zap Clay or Dawn or whoever it is, but my brother Grove catches my wrist. "What's going on?"

"Grove!" I throw my arms around his neck. "Thank thunder. We've got to get Briar out of here."

Kenji steps around from behind Grove and throws himself at Briar, who's still limp in Timber's arms. "Is she okay?" he wails.

"Did you drive?" I ask Grove. "Where's the car?"

"This way," he says, and we head for the van that's across the street.

chapter 17

WE SCRAMBLE INTO the van, pushing Briar's half-limp body into the back and looking over our shoulders as fire trucks and police cars converge at the club. I buckle into the front seat and Timber slams the side door closed just as Clay and Dawn pop out from the alleyway beside the building. Luckily the chaos of all the kids on the sidewalks and firemen yelling into bullhorns stops them in their tracks, but I see the way Clay points at us with vengeance flashing in his green eyes.

"Get out of here," I hiss at Grove.

He shoves the van in gear and takes a sharp right around a corner, away from all the flashing sirens. "What the hell happened?" he yells.

In the back I hear Briar half moaning, half singing and Kenji nearly keening, "I couldn't find you! Where did you go?" Glancing over my shoulder, I see that Briar is sprawled over the backseat with Kenji draped over her body.

"Did you give her alcohol?" I yell at Kenji.

He whips his head toward me. "No! Where would I get it? I don't even drink. She disappeared with that goon who runs the club."

I look at Grove negotiating the bumps and potholes of the old, half-paved streets. We pass by empty docks and parking lots full of weeds. I can tell Grove is furious by the way his hands are tight around the wheel and his jaw is clenched. "You guys better be able to explain this," he barks at me.

"Grove," I whisper harshly. "Something's not right back there."

"No kidding, Zephyr," he says. "Kenji wakes me up and drags me out of the house at midnight. There are cops, firefighters, Briar half in the bag. What the hell?"

I lean over close to him and squeeze his forearm. "No, listen," I say as quietly as I can. "Clay and Dawn. Something's weird."

Grove looks at me with his eyebrows flexed and his mouth tense. "What?"

I glance over my shoulder. Kenji is absorbed in stroking Briar's hair and babbling to her, but Timber leans forward, trying to hear my conversation with Grove. I sigh, frustrated, but I know what I have to do. "Sorry, Timb," I mutter. "Waterfall!" I flick my fingers toward him and instantly he shakes his head and pokes a finger into each of his ears, which are temporarily blocked by the sound of a roaring waterfall inside his head. I turn back to Grove and start talking fast.

"I think Dawn was trying to cast a spell on us. I zapped her, but Timber saw me. It was the only way we could get Briar out of there."

Grove frowns at me. "You have an overactive imagination."

"No, listen. I saw the fox in a cage in a storage room."

His face clouds over but then he shakes his head. "So what? Erdlers are weird. There could be a logical explanation for why they have a fox . . ."

I sneak a peek at Timber, who bangs his hand against the side of his head and opens and closes his jaw, trying to get back his hearing, which will return in about five seconds.

"I think they're dark elves," I say quickly.

Grove's eyes flash at me and the van swerves. A truck blares its horn at us and Grove careens the van the other way. I grab the door handle and we all sway left to right and left again. "Whoa! Whoopee!" Briar yells from the backseat, then she laughs.

Grove gets the car in the right lane again, and we stop at a red light.

"Jeez," Timber says, working his jaw side to side. "What the hell is going on? My head is all plugged up."

Grove jams the gearshift into neutral and turns to look at me. "What are you talking about?"

I look from him to Timber and back to Kenji and Briar. "I think they drugged her or something."

"Who?" Timber asks.

"Briar," I call to the back.

"Thass me!" she says, giggling.

I roll my eyes because drugged or not, she's annoying. "Why were you down in the basement with Clay and Dawn?"

"Who?" she asks, then hiccups.

I shake my head. "We have to get her home and let Fawna take a look at her," I tell Grove.

"Dude, don't tell your parents!" Timber says. "They'll never let you out of the house again. So Briar got a little tipsy. Obviously Dawn had a few too many herself. Did you see her stumbling around down there in the basement? She couldn't even talk. Briar will feel like hell tomorrow and she won't do it again. At least not for a while. It's just normal teenage crap." Then he laughs. "I can't believe you set off the fire alarm, Zeph!"

"Oh crikey," Grove says, then he puts the car in gear and peals out on the green light.

* * *

First we drop Timber at home. He still thinks the whole thing is a big joke, but at least he didn't see me zap Dawn and he thinks she was tipsy and not under the influence of my magic. In fact, I can't get him to leave. He hangs by my open window. "I'll call you first thing in the morning," he says, all moony-eyed.

"Great," I tell him. "Good night."

He leans in. "Just one more kiss, please?"

I lean forward and peck him on the lips.

"No, a real one." He reaches in and pulls the back of my head forward, then plants a long, luscious kiss on my lips. Not that I don't like kissing Timber, but I've had enough for tonight.

I pull back. "Okay, thanks. Good night. Talk to you in the morning," I say, but he won't leave. He grabs my hand and presses it to his cheek.

"I'll miss you," he says, and kisses my palm.

I wriggle my hand free. "Yeah, um, miss you, too. Gotta go."

"You're so pretty." He strokes my face.

"Good granite," Grove mumbles. "Can we get out of here already?"

I look over my shoulder at him. "I'm trying!"

"What time will you get up?" Timber asks.

"I don't know. I'll call you, okay?" I push the button to roll up the window, but Timber keeps his hands on top of the glass.

"But what time? I'll set my alarm," he calls through the shrinking space between me and him.

"Good night!" I pry his fingers one by one away off the window.

He presses his palms flat against the glass. "Don't go!"

"What's wrong with him?" Grove asks.

I ignore his question because I'm not sure I want to know the answer. I wave and smile at Timber, who stands on the curb with his hand pressed against his chest until we turn the corner.

We drop Kenji off next and it's nearly the same scene prying him off

Briar, only Briar's snoring happily now, so at least she can't prolong it. I manage to get Kenji out of the van by promising him that Briar will call him first thing in the morning, too.

Once we're driving back to our neighborhood, I open my mouth to explain things to Grove, but he holds up his hand. "Save it for Mom and Dad."

"But . . ." I say.

"Nope," he tells me. "I don't want to hear it. You guys got yourselves into a big mess and you have to clean it up."

"But . . ." I try again.

He raises his hand and flicks his wrist. "Mute!" he says, but I'm quick enough to deflect him. "Backfire," I say. He shakes his head with disbelief. "When did you get so fast?" he asks.

I shrug. "Don't know, but it saved my tail tonight. Truce?"

"Truce," he says. "As long as you shut up."

"Deal," I say, and lay my head back against the seat. My body feels as heavy as a dead tree, but my mind races, trying to fit all the pieces together. I know I need to talk to Grandma Fawna before any of this will make sense.

"It can all wait until morning," Grove says as we carry Briar into the house.

"No," I whisper back to him. "I'm waking Fawna. She'll be able to tell if Briar is just drunk or if Clay and Dawn did something to her."

Grove shakes his head. "I'll help you up the stairs, but then I'm done."

"You're such a jerk. Just put her on the couch and I'll take care of it myself."

"Fine," he says.

We sling Briar to the couch, where she curls into a little ball and murmurs. "Near Ironweed."

"See!" I whisper.

"What?" Grove asks.

"She's been muttering about Alverland on and off."

"So what?"

"So that's weird."

"No, it's not," he says. "She's loopy right now. Of course she'd talk about something she knows really well."

He might have a point, but I'm still creeped out by how Dawn was acting. "Just go to bed then."

"I'd love to." He turns to go but then he stops at the bottom of the steps. "Oh, and you're welcome, by the way, for getting up in the middle of the night to save your butt."

I soften. He's right. I walk toward him. "I'm sorry," I say. "Thanks for helping us. You didn't have to do that but you did."

"Of course I did," he says, then slowly climbs the stairs.

I tiptoe to Fawna's room, which is in the back of the house on the first floor. I tap on her door then open it slowly. She sleeps peacefully on her back with her long, white hair spread out on the pillow like a butterfly in flight. I see that she holds an amulet shaped like a six-point buck while she sleeps, and I wonder if that's how she keeps Grandpa close to her heart.

Gently I touch her shoulder. "Grandma," I whisper. "Grandma Fawna."

Fawna pops upright and I hop back. "What is it?" she says clearly.

"Dang, you wake up fast," I say, my hand pressed over my racing heart.

"What's wrong? What happened?" she asks. "Is everyone okay?"

"I need your help," I tell her. "Something's wrong with Briar."

Fawna tosses her covers back and slips the amulet around her neck. "Hand me my robe," she says, pointing to the rocking chair as she puts on her slippers. "Where is she? Does she have a fever?"

I lead Grandma to the living room while she ties the robe. "I don't know how to explain it all but I'll try . . ."

As Grandma touches Briar and listens to her breathe, I recount the night, leaving out the part about going to Timber's apartment by myself. When I get to the part about the fox, Fawna's head snaps up and she stares at me.

"You saw it, too?"

"Yes," I say.

"Are you sure?"

"I know what a fox looks like."

"But why would erdlers keep a fox?" she asks more to herself than to me.

When I tell her about Dawn, Grandma puts her hand over her mouth and sits in silence for a moment. Then she says, "Go to the kitchen and put on the kettle, then go into the pantry and get your mother's small kit of infusions."

I hurry off and do as she says. A few minutes later I watch her concoct a potion. She steeps several different dried plants from Mom's tiny glass bottles with little cork stoppers.

"What are you making?" I ask from a kitchen stool, where I sip a mug of warm chamomile tea.

"This will tell me what Briar has ingested over the past several hours," Grandma says as she mixes precise amounts with a small silver spoon she wears around her neck. "Bring me some honey. We want it to taste good so Briar will drink it all."

When the potion has steeped and cooled, I carry it into the living room. We sit Briar up and call her name until her eyes flutter open. "Drink this," Grandma instructs her, and tilts the cup up to Briar's lips. Briar must be parched because she quickly and easily downs the entire cup, which smells like lavender and honey and strangely of butterscotch with just a hint of dandelion greens. Grandma sets the cup on the end table and waits. After a few seconds Briar begins to hiccup, then she groans and holds the sides of her stomach as she slumps over onto the pillows.

"It's working," Grandma says.

I step back. "Is she going to barf?" I'm grossed out that I might have to pick through puke to see what was in her stomach.

"No, no," Grandma says gently. "Nothing so horrible as that."

Briar moans and writhes, then she squirms herself upright and opens her eyes wide. She looks slightly terrified as she opens her mouth. I see a line of spit between her parted lips that grows to fill her mouth. Her eyes dart back and forth from Grandma to me as a bubble inflates her cheeks, pushes her lips out, and then escapes her mouth. I hear her stomach gurgling as the iridescent bubble expands. Swirls of colors cover the surface of the bubble, which is big enough to hide Briar's entire face now. Grandma waits patiently with her hand on Briar's knee. I stand back fascinated and sort of horrified. The bubble grows and grows while Briar gags and her stomach grumbles angrily until finally she jerks forward and closes her mouth, and the bubble floats away from her.

"Ah," Grandma says, catching the bubble lightly between her hands. Briar slumps back against the couch with her eyes closed again as if she never woke up. Grandma stands and carries the beautiful, shimmering bubble close to the yellow light from the lamp beside the couch. "Come," she says. "Have a look."

When I peer inside the bubble, I see floating visions of liquids and solids.

"You'll have to help me interpret some of these things," Grandma says. "I have no idea what you kids eat these days from all those bags and boxes."

"That's probably Vitamin Water," I say, pointing to an orange pool.

"And that looks like french fries over there. I see some salad greens and tomatoes and a chocolate bar. There's a chocolate chip cookie and a red apple."

"Do you see anything that you don't recognize?" Grandma asks. "Anything strange?"

I look carefully at each little floating item, but there's nothing out of the ordinary. "It all looks like stuff we usually eat," I tell her.

"Hmm," says Grandma. "Well then, I don't think she was drinking alcohol or taking some kind of illicit substance. If she did, it would show up here." She turns to me. "Take this into the kitchen and pop it over the sink." She holds the bubble out to me.

Even though I'm totally grossed out by touching something that came out of Briar's stomach, I take the bubble between my fingers and carry it to the kitchen. It's more firm than I would have thought, but still, yuck! I set the bubble in the sink, then poke it with a paring knife. It pops with a little burp sound, then swirls around the sink and into the drain in a weirdly pretty, shimmering puddle.

When I get back into the living room, Grandma is bent over Briar, rubbing two polished stones over her temples, down the sides of her neck, across her chest, and onto her belly. She frowns as she works, occasionally slowing down and breathing deeply. I don't interrupt as she works her magic.

"Tsk, tsk, tsk," she says as she moves the stones back up Briar's body. She stops below her chin and gently circles them across the front of Briar's neck. "Here," she says. "I've found you. Interesting. Very, very strange." She sits up and puts her rocks into the pocket of her robe. Then she looks at me. "Sit," she says, patting the couch beside her. I do as she says. "Now then." She turns to me and lays her hand on my knee. "I want you to tell me very slowly and carefully everything that happened.

And don't leave out any details. I need to understand everything. Do you understand? Absolutely everything."

I take a deep breath before I start because I know I have to spill my guts this time, and it ain't going to be as pretty as Briar's tummy bubble.

"We need to leave now!" This is the closest my mother has ever come to yelling, and I flinch where I'm curled in a kitchen chair.

"But we have to figure this out before we can leave," Dad says.

"We should just go," says Mom. "Pack the kids up and get out." She looks at me, and for the fifteen thousandth time she shakes her head. All morning she's gone from being angry at Briar and me to hugging us tightly because she's relieved that we're all right. "They could have been hurt!" she says again, her eyes filling with tears.

My dad reaches out and pulls her close to his body. "But they weren't. Zephyr did the right thing. There was no way they could've known."

"Known what?" I ask again, because no one will answer any of my questions.

"Do you think it's Iris?" Grove asks.

"Aunt Iris?" I ask.

Grandma leans against the counter with a mug of tea. "There's no way of knowing unless we go there."

"Go where?" I demand, slapping the table.

My mom shakes her head. "No one is going back there. Ever!"

"We need to hear what Briar has to say first," Dad says. He holds Mom's shoulders and he takes a step back to look down into her face. "Is it ready?"

Mom nods. She wipes the back of her hand across her eyes, then she goes to the stove and lifts the lid on a small copper pot. A cloying smell of rotten berries and pine bark fills the room. "I just need to cool it and sweeten it," she says. "Zephyr, would you go see how Briar's doing?"

Poor Briar finally came out of her stupor around seven o'clock this morning. She can't remember much, so Mom's cooking up some strong herbs to help her piece things together. Now she lies on the couch with a cold compress over her eyes and forehead to alleviate her massive headache. She's wrapped in two blankets and the fire's going because she can't get over the chills. I kneel beside her and hold her hand.

"Poor bunny," I say. "What did they do to you?"

Briar lifts the compress and peeks out at me. "Hiya," she says.

"Any better?"

"A little," she says.

"Mom has the potion."

"Do you think it'll be gross?" she asks.

"Smells gross," I tell her.

She nods. "I'm ready, though. I want to do this."

Mom carries in a steaming mug. She sits on one side of Briar, and Grandma sits on the other. They prop her up between them and wrap their arms around her shoulders. My dad stands by the fire while I stay on the floor, rubbing Briar's feet and legs through the layers of blankets. Grove took the little kids sledding to keep them out of the way, but there's only so long they can be gone, so we all know this has to work fast. Dutifully, Briar gags down the concoction, then we all wait for it to take effect.

"Zephyr," Mom whispers to me, "you'll have to ask her the questions because we don't know anything that happened. Just be calm and gentle and try to lead her through last night."

I nod. "Remember last night when we went to Clay and Dawn's club?"

"Mm-hm." Briar nods with her eyes closed.

"And remember how I was sad because Timber and I had a fight?" Mom's mouth opens in surprise.

"Yes," says Briar. "You were so sad."

"Remember that I wanted to dance when Timber came to the club?"

"I asked Dawn if we could dance onstage," Briar says.

"Yes, that's right!" I tell her happily.

Briar smiles, then with her eyes still closed she starts the chant. "*Sha we no, hallenschor, um triden fayre la dolly.*" I join her and we both move our arms just slightly to the rhythm of our words. My mom's eyes widen. She looks over Briar's head at Grandma, who looks equally stricken. They both look over at my dad, as do I. He stares up at the ceiling with his mouth open and his head shaking back and forth, as if he can't believe what he's hearing. I trail off the chanting and think, *Moose crap, I don't know exactly what we did, but we're really in trouble now.*

Briar laughs. "And then you dove off the stage. Do you remember that? Right into Timber's arms. It was awesome. And everyone exploded into applause. Except for Bella. She was p.o.'d. Serves her right. I should've dropped a light on her head. And then you guys left," Briar says. "Where'd you go?"

I grimace. I really don't want to admit it, but I can't lie, so I take a breath and say quickly, "To Timber's, and you stayed behind. I remember you were with Dawn and Clay. What happened then?"

Briar is quiet for a moment while she thinks. "Well, I know I wanted to thank them for letting us dance because it won Timber's heart for you. And they said they were happy to do it, but they wanted to know more about the dance so they could book some gigs for us."

I glance up at my mom and Grandma, who exchange looks.

"So they asked me to go into the back of the club where it's more quiet and they could video me dancing. I said I wanted Kenji to come with me, but they said he was in the bathroom and they would tell the bartender where I was, so we went downstairs."

"Did you do the dance for them?" Mom asks.

Briar thinks about this. "I don't think I did," she says. "I remember going into a little room with couches and chairs."

"That's where I found her," I whisper.

"And behind the couch there's another door to a dark room with a bed and a video camera," she says.

"What!" My dad steps forward. His eyes flash.

I shake my head. "I don't remember seeing another room." I think back to the security camera screens. "It must be hidden."

Then Briar rolls her head on the couch. "And the strangest thing," she says. "There was a little animal on the bed in there. A little, cute, furry animal. But not a cat. Maybe a dog, but no, that's not it—"

"Was it a fox?" I ask eagerly.

"Yeah," she says dreamily. "It was a fox." Mom, Grandma, Dad, and I all look at one another while Briar tries to remember. "And Dawn scooped it up. She stroked its fur. Clay told her to take it out and she was mad because she loved cuddling it. I wanted to hold it, but they said no. Dawn put it in a cage and took it out of the room." Then Briar stops and she whimpers.

Mom and Grandma tighten their arms around her shoulders, and I wrap my arms around her legs. "What, honey?" Mom asks. "What happened?"

Tears leak out of Briar's eyes. "I was alone with Clay."

My dad takes another step forward. I see anger in his eyes and his fists come together in front of his chest. "What did he do?"

"I don't know," says Briar. "I can't explain. He had a little bag with dust. He took it out and said it would make me laugh and feel good. I said no, I don't do drugs, but he sprinkled it into his palm and blew it over me. I felt like I was floating. I wanted to dance for them. Dawn came back and I asked her to dance with me. They told me they just wanted to talk. They asked me lots of questions while I danced around the floor. I felt so light and free and like I could tell them anything."

"What did they ask?" Grandma says.

"Questions about our family. Where we live," she says.

"Did they ask you about Alverland?" I ask.

"Yes," Briar says. "They wanted to know where Alverland is."

Mom gasps.

"Did you tell them?" Grandma asks calmly.

"I don't know," Briar says. "It's all so murky. I guess I probably did." She opens her eyes, and tears stream down her face. "I shouldn't have told them, should I?"

Mom hugs her tight. "You couldn't help it. They gave you a truth dust. Your magic's not strong enough to combat it."

"Are they dark elves?" I ask.

Mom and Dad look at each other, but Fawna nods. "I believe they might be," she says, rubbing her amulets.

"But what do they want with us?" I ask, and everyone is quiet.

"We have to go," Mom says.

Briar sleeps for the rest of the morning while I ask questions that nobody will answer. After Grove and the kids come back, he and Dad drive to Red Hook. I beg to go, but they won't let me, which is so unfair. Timber and Kenji both call a zillion times, but we let everything go to voice mail so we don't tie up the phone lines in case Grove and Dad need to call. They get back around eleven, but there's not much for them to tell us.

Dad looks like he does when he comes back from a hunt empty-handed.

"We went in through the back," says Grove. "Those basement doors you told us about, Zeph."

"Everything is cleared out," says Dad. "Looks like they're long gone."

"They could be on their way to Alverland," Mom says.

"We'll leave tomorrow morning," Dad says.

"No," Mom tells him. "Now."

"I have a gig tonight," says Dad.

"And we have school and rehearsals," I say, but I shut up when Mom flashes me the look of death.

Fawna stands up. "I'll fly."

"No!" Mom says firmly. "It took too much out of you when you shape-shifted before." I remember how sick Grandma was last fall after she shifted into a hawk and flew back and forth from Alverland to Brooklyn to check on us. Mom turns to my dad. "You have to cancel," she tells him.

"I can't," he says.

"I'll go," Grandma says. "It's the quickest way. Then you can bring the children in the van tomorrow."

"Mother," says Mom, but Grandma shakes her head.

Mom turns to Dad, helpless. Dad takes a deep breath and nods. "I'll cancel," he says.

"That doesn't change my decision," says Fawna, then she leaves us all in stunned silence.

There's not much to do at this point except exactly what Mom and Dad tell us to do. We pack our clothes, gather food, and get the little kids into the van as quickly as we can. I don't know what I'm going to do about school, about the performance, or about Timber, but there's nothing I can do, because just like that, without so much as good-bye, we leave Brooklyn.

chapter 18

I WAKE UP to the sound of silence and wonder, *Where are the buses and honking cars barreling down Prospect Park Southwest?* Then I remember we're in Alverland. Dad and Grove drove us straight to Ironweed yesterday, only stopping so we could pile into skeevy truck-stop bathrooms and rest areas to pee every few hours. We got to Ironweed, the closest town to Alverland, at five this morning and had to hike through a two-foot blanket of snow to get to our house. We all fell into our cold beds, hunkered under thick, goose-down comforters to sleep off the stupor of a long, tense van ride.

Now I sit up and rub the sleeve of my flannel pajamas against the frosty windowpane. The world outside is white, green, and brown—snow, pines, and barren oak trees. I forgot how pretty it is, and my heart fills with excitement as I think about seeing my sister Willow, my grandfather Buck, and all my aunts, uncles, and cousins very soon.

My sibs are still sacked out under their covers, so I quietly slip into my thick indoor booties, robe, and hat, then head downstairs where I can smell the fires blazing and hot tea perking up the morning. I find Mom curled on Dad's lap in an easy chair by the kitchen fireplace. They both sip giant mugs of tea and look more relaxed than I've seen them in months.

When I join them in the rocker by the fire, Mom points to a covered basket on the table and says, "Aunt Flora brought over some dried-huckleberry muffins and venison jerky if you're hungry. Plus, there's tea."

"Was Flora beside herself when Briar showed up this morning?" I ask.

Mom grins. "I doubt that she's stopped hugging her. Poor Briar was dead tired and Flora just couldn't let go of her. I'm sure the word is out by now. Flora said everybody started cooking the minute Fawna showed up last night. They're probably letting us get our rest, but pretty soon we'll have a whole line out the door."

I take a mug out of the cupboard and pour myself some steaming mint and lavender tea, then I twirl a thick line of golden honey into my mug. "Has Willow been by yet?"

Mom shakes her head, but she smiles. "She's off at Ash's mother's house, so I'll have to hike over there in a bit to let her know we're home. Although, who knows, word might have gotten that far already. You want to go with me?"

"I'd like that," I say, but then I stop. "The only thing is, I need to let someone in Brooklyn know we're gone."

"Someone named Timber?" Dad says.

Uh, yeah, not that I'll admit it, though I'm sure I blush. "I have to tell Mr. Padgett that I'm going to miss rehearsals and the performance this week."

Dad smacks his forehead. "We didn't even think about that." He looks at me. "Are you really upset that you're going to miss it?"

What I'll miss is Timber, but I don't say that either. Instead, I grab a warm muffin from the basket and shrug because I realized something during all those grueling rehearsals and the Rockefeller gig. "I'm not sure acting in musicals is my thing," I admit. "I like being with my friends and I like performing, but Mr. Padgett sucks all the joy out it. Maybe singing with a band to a smaller crowd is more me."

"Well," says Mom. "I'm sure that you can do whatever you put your mind to."

"Thanks, Mom," I say. "I'll remind you of that the next time I want to try something new."

"Oh dear," she says. "I should learn to keep my mouth shut."

"Regardless," Dad says, "you're right that you have to contact someone. Why don't you and Briar walk into Ironweed in a bit and use the library computers."

I don't mention that the last time Briar and I used the library computers, the librarians threatened to ban us from ever stepping foot in there again.

"Do you think it's safe for them to be out in the woods?" Mom asks.

"The men have been combing the woods since Fawna showed up yesterday, and they haven't seen anything," Dad says. "I seriously doubt Clay and Dawn, or whoever they are, would show up here."

"But Iris is still missing," Mom says.

"Do you think Clay and Dawn have something to do with Iris?" I ask, trying to make my grandmother's sister and those weirdos from Red Hook fit together in my mind.

"I wish I knew," Mom says. "But until we do, I don't like the idea of your going out into the woods alone."

"Mom," I say, "we've been walking there alone since we were twelve. We'll be fine."

"Even if Clay and Dawn are out there," Dad says. "The girls can handle themselves."

"Yeah," I say. "Those big, blond doofuses would be no match for us in the woods."

* * *

Briar and I bundle up in our thick tunics, leggings, deerskin boots and cloaks, and long woolen hats to walk to Ironweed. We traipse through the forest on our well-worn path like fairy-tale characters with five-foot birch walking sticks. We keep our eyes and ears open for anything strange, but everything is calm, quiet, and normal. When we get to Ironweed, the only signs of life are the few parked cars, the blinking OPEN sign in the bait shop window, and the lights in the library at the end of the road.

Briar cracks up when we step out onto the empty narrow street. "This place used to seem so big and scary to me."

Somewhere in the distance I hear a snowblower, but other than that, it's as if the whole town has been deserted. "Now it seems like the most podunk place in the universe," I say.

Inside the library, the old biddy at the desk stares meanly at us, but she lets us pass. There's no one else here, so we get online right away. As soon as I open my e-mail, I find twenty-two messages from Timber.

"Great granite!" I say, and turn to Briar, but she's got the same stuffed in-box from Kenji. We both burst out laughing, which makes the librarian scowl more. We try to stifle our amusement over our crazy boyfriends so we don't get tossed out into a snowbank.

I scroll through the messages, which started yesterday around noon after we left Brooklyn. We wanted to call them or text them from the car, but we knew better than to ask for Dad's or Grove's phone because everybody was so freaked out. I open the most recent message first, figuring the other twenty-one are outdated by now. It's from ten o'clock this morning and says,

> From New York City to Mackinaw
> Across the country
> I've seen it all

> but nothing takes the place of you
> It's you I've got to find

"What the . . ." I mutter to myself. I open the message before that one. It's from eight o'clock this morning.

> I pass the lakes as big as seas
> I haven't seen anything but trees
> and miles and miles of corn and beans
> but still you haunt my dreams

"Check this out." I tap Briar's arm for her to read it, but her mouth is hanging open and her eyes are wide.

She grabs my leg and leans close to look at my screen. "Oh my God," she says, then she whispers, "They're coming here."

"No way." My face is screwed up tight. "They don't even know we're gone."

"Click on the first message from Timber," Briar says.

I open it to find this:

> Came by your house today. No answer. No lights.
> Drake canceled his show 2nite. Where r u?

"Were they spying on us?" I ask.

"What's the next one say?" Briar asks.

I open it:

> Crossing the GW, leaving NYC far behind, it's you
> I've got to find

"See?" says Briar. "They left New York."

"They wouldn't. The performance is this week." Then I open each message from yesterday and today. The last one says,

> I'll fly after you. I'm a crane. I'll come for you. I'm
> insane. I'll dance and sing and flap my wings, 'cause
> baby, it's you I've got to find.

"Snakes and adders, he's lost his mind!" I laugh out of sheer disbelief. "Do you really think?" I start to ask. His words are insanely sweet, but my stomach churns because if Timber's really trying to find me, it's not good. "What are we going to do?" I whisper.

"Quick," she says. "E-mail Timber. He's got his iPhone."

"No," I say. "Let's think about this. There's no way they could find us. They must have turned back." Just then a new message pops up. We both jump.

> I'm sitting here in Ironweed, eating eggs and ham
> without a lead. You disappeared among the pines.
> It's you I've got to find.

My stomach drops, my heart revs, and suddenly I'm sweating like it's a hundred degrees in July.

"How the frog did they find us?" Briar says way too loud. The librarian hisses at us to quiet down, but we don't care. We bolt from our chairs and run for the door, because if they're here, they're nearby. We grab our walking sticks and throw on our cloaks as we run down the street with our scarves and hats flying behind us.

"There's only one place they could be." I point across the street at the only place that's open. Part of me wants to run inside and find him. To open my arms and hug him because what could be cooler than your boyfriend driving eight hundred miles to find you? Then again, I'm kind of freaked out because my boyfriend drove eight hundred miles to find me! But if he's here, I've got to find him before he finds me.

A clanging bell above the grocery/bait shop/restaurant door announces our arrival when we explode into the musty, overheated store. The guy behind the counter looks up from his newspaper and splatters his coffee onto the cash register. We run through the aisle and back toward the little coffee shop, and true as the noses on our faces, Kenji and Timber sit by the fishing rods, mopping up egg yolks with toast. When they see us, they both jump out of their seats and start yelling.

"We found you!"

"I can't believe it!"

"It's really you!"

Briar and I rush to them, half laughing, half scared out of our wits about what we're going to do next.

It doesn't take long to piece together the whole story over cups of hot cocoa with marshmallows, but I still can't believe these guys are so possessed.

"We just had to find you," Timber explains again.

"But how did you know we left?" I ask.

Kenji's face turns red. "You didn't call in the morning."

"So we went to your house in the afternoon," Timber adds.

"Somebody's always home," says Kenji.

"Your neighbor said you packed up the van and left," Timber says.

"But how did you know we came here?" I ask.

"Where else would your whole family go?" Timber asks, which is a good point.

"Then I remembered that VH1 interview your dad did in the fall," Kenji tells us. "We looked it up on YouTube and found the part where he's standing by the sign for this town."

"We put Ironweed in the GPS and here we are," says Timber.

"Whose car are you driving?" I ask.

"My dad's," Kenji says. "My parents are in Japan for some lame wedding of some distant cousins."

"Do you even have a license?" I ask them.

Kenji shakes his head no, but Timber says, "I have a learner's permit. I just haven't gotten around to taking the test yet."

"What about the performance?" I ask.

Timber shrugs. "What about it?"

My jaw drops. A few days ago he wouldn't even blow off a Friday night rehearsal! "Does your mom know you're gone?" I ask him.

"Well," Timber hesitates. "She does now."

I groan. "We're all going to be in so much trouble."

Timber reaches out and grabs my hand. "Aren't you happy to see me?"

I look into his eyes, those gorgeous gray-blue windows, and I melt a little. "Of course, I am . . . " I say. Then I shake my head. "But you don't understand. You can't be here."

"Why not?" he asks, confused and hurt.

I look to Briar. There's no way to explain this. "What are we going to do?" I ask her.

After lots of discussion in the bathroom, Briar and I come up with a plan. We know that we can't stick around Ironweed for too long, or the erdlers here will get suspicious and start asking questions. So we decide that I'll hike the guys up to Barnaby Bluff while she goes back to Alverland and gets my dad, who won't flip out on Briar like he would on me, and who'll likely be cooler about this whole fiasco than our moms would be.

We convince Kenji and Timber to leave their backpacks in Timber's car because we know they'll never be able to make the hike carrying heavy packs. I tell them we'll come back with a sled to get all the gear later. They have no idea what we're doing, and we've decided it's best to keep them in the dark as long as possible. We all walk down the main road of Ironweed and duck into the woods. We follow the path together for a few miles, Kenji and Timber exclaiming about how beautiful this place is every five seconds and being amazed every time they see a squirrel or a chickadee.

"City boys," Briar says, and we both giggle.

At the huge hemlock where the trail splits, we stop. "Listen," I tell Kenji and Timber, "we can't take you to our homes just yet."

"We have to let our families know you're here first," Briar explains.

"What, do you live in some weird gated community?" Timber asks.

Briar and I look at each other. "Sort of," I say, which obviously isn't true, but what else am I going to say? "I'm going to take you on a little hike while Briar gets my dad."

"I want to come with you," Kenji says to Briar.

She hugs him and kisses his cheek. "I'll just be gone for a little bit."

"We could get in a lot of trouble if we show up with you guys. You're not supposed to be here," I remind them.

Kenji lets go of Briar and steps back. "Okay, but hurry."

I have to stop myself from rolling my eyes, because I realize that my boyfriend is acting just as nutty driving twenty hours to find me. "Come on, guys," I say, leading them away from Alverland and toward the bluffs. "You're going to love this. We'll probably see lots of hawks and maybe even some deer and moose."

"Will you shoot one for me?" Timber asks, grabbing me around the waist. "I'm starving."

I push him away. "Do I look like I'm carrying a bow and arrow?" I ask, kind of annoyed.

"Maybe you could club one to death with this big stick." He laughs, which really ticks me off.

"It's a walking stick," I tell him. "My grandfather carved it for me." I hand him the stick so he can see the intricate designs of flowers and leaves, totem animals, and old elfin words worked around the birch.

Timber turns the stick around and around in his hands. "This is beautiful," he says as he studies the wood. "I've never seen anything like it."

"Buck makes one for each of his grandkids. And he has a lot of grandkids," I say.

Timber nods and hands the stick back to me. "It's amazing. I'm sorry I made fun of it."

I smile. "That's okay. Would you like to use it?"

Timber's eyes widen. "Really? You'd let me?"

"You'll need it more than I will." I point up to the top of the bluff.

"We're going up there?" Timber asks.

Briar laughs as she gives Kenji a little nudge down the path toward Timber and me. "That's right, city boys," she tells them. "And you better get a move on."

It takes nearly an hour to get to the top of the bluff, and I feel kind of badly for Kenji and Timber. Even though they both play soccer and run at home, they're clearly not in hiking shape. At least my walking stick helps Timber tromp through the snow. I find a branch for Kenji to use, but because they haven't slept in twenty-four hours, the hike is especially grueling for them. By the time we get to the edge of the cliffs to look out over the miles and miles of pine forests and lakes, both of them are red, wheezing, and totally exhausted. They flop down on a clear rock and groan.

"Dang, Zeph," Timber says between gasps for air. "You're like a freakin' mountain goat."

"Oh my God," Kenji huffs and puffs. "I think my lungs are going to explode. How do you walk so fast in those boots? Aren't your feet freezing? Even my Gore-Tex isn't keeping my toes warm enough."

"Poor little urban boys." I pull some venison jerky and dried blueberries from deep in my pockets. "Here. Have some of this. It'll make you feel better."

As they devour the snack, I shade my eyes and scan the forest below. Alverland is perfectly hidden in a small valley beneath the canopy of trees, but if you know what to look for, you can find it and all the other elfin settlements in this area. I know where each one of my great-grand-mothers lives by the depressions in the land and proximity to the rivers and lakes that I can see from up here. To the east is Mother Hortense's land. Straight north is Mother Jonquil. Over to the west is Great-grandmother Lily. And six miles south of Alverland is where Willow will live after Mama Ivy passes on. Beyond that is where Willow's fiancé Ash's family lives. My mom is probably there now. I get goose bumps thinking about seeing my sister again. I've missed her.

As I scan the world below I catch a shadow moving through the trees at the base of the bluff. Thinking it must be Briar and my dad, I lift my arms and wave. "Hoi!" They don't answer, so I start to call out again. When I look more closely I realize that it's not my dad and Briar. These people are not in deerskin cloaks. In fact, they don't look elfin at all. I crouch down and squint.

"What's wrong?" Timber asks.

"Shhhh," I hiss at him. I shade my eyes and watch the two people pick their way over rocks and through the trees. I need to get a better look to decide if we should stay here or get inside one of the caves so we don't arouse any suspicion. "Wait here," I whisper to Kenji and Timber as I move to the other side of the bluff. When both of them start to follow me, I get mad. "I mean it. Wait here and stay quiet," I bark at them.

I stay close to the ground and move between the trees silently until I find a good sassafras tree with low-hanging branches. I scurry up half-way so I can get a better look down below. At first I can't find the people and I think they're probably just hikers who've gone off on another trail. It's rare, but sometimes hard-core camping erdlers come this way. Usually not in the dead of winter, though. I keep scanning the woods until I catch sight of them again. That's when I realize why they've been hard to spot. They're wearing white so they nearly blend into the snow.

They're picking their way through the trails pretty easily, except one of them is carrying something cumbersome. It doesn't look like a back-pack, but I can't get a good look because they're too far away. I glance toward the bluff where I left Kenji and Timber. I can see them lying down, resting on the rock, so I decide it's safe to cast a spell. "Hawk's eye," I say, and zap myself.

My eyes zero in on the man and a woman, both blond, in white coats and hats, carrying a cage. "Thunder and lightning!" I gasp, and lose my grip, sending me crashing backward through the branches of the tree, grabbing for anything to slow me down, but every twig slides through my mittened hands. I see a hawk circling above me in the sky as I thud onto a bed of pine needles. Timber runs up the path and throws himself down on hands and knees beside me.

"Oh my God. Are you okay? Are you hurt? Did you just fall out of a tree?"

The fall knocked the wind out of me, so I sputter for a few seconds while grabbing at his coat. "It's them." I say, my voice raspy.

"Who?" Timber asks, cradling my head.

The red-tailed hawk above screeches and veers sharply to the right, then dives straight for the sassafras tree. She swoops up again and spreads her wings, thrusting her talons forward.

"What the . . ." Timber ducks and covers his head, but I'm not afraid as she lands on the branch above us.

I look the hawk in the eye. My voice comes back to me. "It's Clay and Dawn," I say. "And they've got the fox!"

"Who? What? Where?" Timber looks all around.

The hawk spreads her wings and alights, screeching as she goes. I push myself up onto my elbows. "But it's okay," I tell Timber. "My grandmother knows they're here."

chapter 19

"COME ON. We have to go faster," I tell Timber and Kenji as I lead them through heavy snowdrifts and pine trees to a cave around the back of Barnaby Bluff.

"Zephyr," Timber says, grabbing my hand to slow me down. His face is bright red and he's huffing, but at least he's keeping up. Kenji's lagging twenty feet behind. "You're not making any sense. What's the big deal?"

I whip around to face him. At first I think I'll just zap a mute hex on him, but then I decide that I'm tired of zapping people whenever a problem comes up, because I just end up causing myself another problem. But obviously I don't have time to explain, so I talk over my shoulder as I push forward up a steep hill. "This is my home," I tell him. "Not Brooklyn. Clay and Dawn are not safe." I stop and reach out for his shoulder. "You have to trust that I know what I'm doing."

Timber shakes his head. "But hiding? Why do we have to hide?"

Kenji has caught up with us now. He bends over, hands on knees, and pants like a dog. "If . . . I . . . had . . . known . . . this . . . is . . . what . . . you . . . guys . . . do . . . for . . . fun . . ."

"You're hiding," I say to Timber and Kenji as I point to the opening in the cave's mouth. "I'm going for help."

"You want us to go in there?" Kenji asks, his face screwed up like I just told him to walk down a dark alley in Newark at night.

"It's perfectly safe," I say, grabbing them each by the hand and tugging.

"What if there's a bear?" Kenji asks.

"We come up here all the time. There aren't any bears!" I plunge my hands back into my pockets. "Here, have some more jerky." I shove dried venison meat at them, which they each take.

"But why can't we come with you?" Timber asks.

"No offense," I say, shoving them toward the cave's mouth. "But you're slow and loud in the forest. I can go more quickly and quietly on my own. Plus, I'll know exactly where you are."

"But you said that your grandmother already knows they're here, so why don't you stay with us?" Timber asks, dragging his feet as I push him forward.

This is seriously trying my patience. I consider a hibernation spell to knock them out in the cave for a few hours, but I stop myself. The more time I spend with Timber and the deeper my feelings grow for him, the harder it is to zap him. "Please," I plead. "Please just do this for me and I'll try to explain things later. I don't have much time."

"I don't like it," Timber says, but he ducks his head and enters the cave anyway.

"Do you have a flashlight?" Kenji asks.

"No I don't have a flipping flashlight!" I say. "Just go in there and take a nap, for thunder's sake."

The guys crouch down and enter the cave, but then just as I'm ready to run off into the woods so I can track Clay and Dawn, Timber pops out and grabs my arm. "Zeph!" he says.

"What now?" I ask.

He pulls me into his body. Warmth emanates from beneath his coat collar, and for just a moment it's wonderful being snug in his arms. He bends down and kisses me. "I love you," he says.

I'm so startled that I feel like I'm falling out of the tree again. I stumble backward over a rock, stammering, "I . . . I . . . I . . ." I regain my balance and look up into his smiling but worried face. "I have to go!" I grab my walking stick from the side of the cave, then turn and run into the woods.

I circle back around the bluffs and slip up into the branches of a tall, slender birch tree. It doesn't take me long to spot Clay and Dawn. They're clearly lost because they've hiked in a huge circle for the past hour and are now standing, arguing, on an outcropping of rocks on the north side of the bluffs. They've set the cage down and the fox paces.

My mind is reeling. Timber said he loves me! My family could be in trouble. No one knows where I am. Why are Clay and Dawn here? What should I do? Does he really love me? Should I make a run for Alverland to get help or stay here and keep an eye on Dawn and Clay until someone else finds us? Do I love him? And how in the honey did everybody find us?

Clay and Dawn pick up the fox's cage and start moving again, this time south, toward Alverland, but I doubt that they know this. I wish I had a good hearing spell so I could listen in on their conversation, but I haven't learned one yet. Which reminds me that I'm a sucky elf. By now, my magic should be so much stronger, and if it were, I could probably figure out what to do. Since I don't know what to do, I decide I should at least follow them so if they get close to Alverland before someone else finds them, I can warn everybody. I climb down the tree and move stealthily on the hills, being sure to stay hidden by the trees.

When I catch up with Clay and Dawn, they're obviously lost again because they're making another big circle, this time heading back up toward the bluff. This is good, I decide, because at least it's buying time and wearing them out. By now Briar should have reached my dad, and soon they'll be up on the bluff looking for Timber, Kenji, and me. Dad will know what to do. I decide to take a shortcut up through the steep gash in the side of the cliffs, which will put me out on top where I'll be able to watch Clay and Dawn without exhausting myself tracking them. I head up through a rocky path, keeping low so they don't catch a glimpse of me.

As much as I've made fun of Kenji and Timber for being lightweights up here, I realize now that I'm out of shape, too. I used to be able to run all over these cliffs and woods without ever losing my footing or running out of breath, but I'm starting to tire. I'm also hungry, but I gave all of my food to the city boys.

As I hike alone, picking my way over the rocks and ice, I have to smile at the thought of Kenji and Timber in the Ironweed Bait Shop eating eggs. What were they thinking? I can't believe they followed us. In a way it's very sweet, but it's also pretty deranged. I don't know how we'll explain this to our mothers, especially because, deep down inside, I know that Briar and I caused this. I don't know exactly how, but we did something in that dance that made these boys go gaga.

I scramble more quickly up the rocky path, hoping to reach the top before Clay and Dawn round the other side. But in my hurry, I misstep on the ice and slide. I grab for rocks or tree roots to stop myself, but the loose rocks on top of the ice begin to tumble along with me. I let out a shriek, then clamp my mouth closed, shoving my walking stick into the ground. But everything is frozen solid and the stick slips out from under me, sending me flat on my belly. Kicking and grabbing only makes it worse. Now rocks slide, picking up speed, tumbling over my splayed arms and legs as I try to get a toehold or roll to the side, but it's too slippery to stop. I careen down the path like it's a giant slide until I land in a heap at the bottom, curled up against the base of a huge, red pine tree.

"Fancy meeting you here," a voice says.

I look up to see Clay standing ten feet away from me, a sick grin on his face. As I scramble to my feet, Dawn steps around from behind another red pine, holding the cage.

"Zephyr!" she says with a loud, fake laugh. "You left in such a rush the other night."

I'm barely steady on my feet after the fall, and I can't make sense of what's happening.

"We knew if we just kept walking around we'd find someone sooner or later," Clay says, taking slow steps toward me.

I search for my walking stick. It's fallen three feet from me to the right. "What are you doing here?" I demand.

"Briar told us all about Alverland," Clay says. "We thought it sounded like a perfect vacation destination, didn't we, Dawn?"

Dawn laughs her stupid, fake, girly laugh again. "Any good skiing up here?" she asks. "Or only ice sliding?"

I move slowly to my right, inching toward my stick, which is thick and heavy and will give me at least a little protection from these two creeps. "Who are you? What do you want?"

"Actually, we're just here visiting our grandmother," Clay says, and snorts at his joke. He continues toward me, slowly and carefully, as if he's not sure what I'll do. I wish I knew what to do. I don't think my magic is strong enough to take on both of them.

"Your grandmother?" I ask, and reach down for my stick.

"You don't know?" He narrows his vibrant green eyes and studies me. "You haven't figured it out?"

I crouch and lay my hand on my stick. "You're dark elves," I say, standing up straight with the stick at my side. Clay is only about four feet from me now, and my heart pounds while I try to steady my breath and figure out how to protect myself.

He snorts again and rolls his eyes. "Took you long enough, duh."

"Why are you here?" I ask. "What do you want from us?"

He steps forward. "We just need you to show us the way to Alverland. Can you do that for us?"

I see his left wrist begin the inward twirl. I jab my stick into the ground by the base of the tree and jump, kicking my legs up so his spell will miss me. When I land, I spin around and yell, "Limp fish!" zapping in his direction.

But Clay is fast. His right arm comes up. "Backfire!" he shouts and deflects my spell.

I look toward Dawn, to make sure she's not about to zap me, but she stands still, cradling the cage in her arms while the fox crouches and hisses. Then a snarl erupts from the tree line. We all whip around as a dark shadow leaps from the rocks above. I don't know if it's a coyote, a mountain cat, or a wolf, but I don't wait to find out. I crouch with my stick over my head while the thing tackles Clay and brings him to the ground. As they wrestle, I whip around on Dawn again. I run as fast as I can toward her, twirling my wrist and yelling, "Stone still!" I zap her and she freezes.

Behind me I hear the grunts and yelps of Clay wrestling the animal. With my stick in front of me and my knees bent I turn toward them, ready to protect myself from either one, when I see what has Clay pinned down. "Timber!" I scream.

Timber crouches on top of Clay, his back curved into the arch of an angry animal and his teeth bared. When I call his name, he flashes at me with wild eyes. "I've got him! You get the fox!" I yell.

Timber leaps off Clay's body and runs across the forest floor faster than I've ever seen him move. I lunge toward Clay and zap. "Stone still!" I yell, freezing him in an awkward half stoop, one arm on the ground, one moving toward me with his wrist turned inward, midspell. I have no idea how long my spells will last, so I spin around and dart toward Timber, who's pushed frozen Dawn to the ground and grabbed the cage. "Run!" I scream. "Run! Run! Run!"

We tear through the forest. This time Timber's close at my heels. I lead him deep into the woods, dodging branches, hurdling roots, side-stepping snow-covered rocks and stumps. We sprint for at least five full minutes until I'm sure Clay and Dawn won't be able to follow us. Ahead I see an old sugar shack and I immediately know where I am. We're only a fifteen-minute run to Alverland, but I know we both need rest. I grab Timber's arm and pull him into the dark hut.

We collapse onto the soft dirt ground, both struggling to catch our breath. As our eyes adjust to the rays of sun slanting into the shack through the slatted roof, we look at each other and dissolve into hysterical laughter.

"Shhh! Shhh!" I try to hush as we roll, clutching our sides, but I can't stop it either.

"What the . . . ?" Timber says over and over between guffaws. "What the hell just happened?"

I'm laughing so hard that I'm crying, but not because this is funny. "I don't know, I don't know!" I say. I can't explain how any of this happened or why I'm in our sugar shack with a small, frightened fox and Timber, who can run like a wolf. And when we finally both calm down enough to catch our breath, we clutch each other and I begin to cry.

"It's okay," Timber says, stroking my hair. "We're fine. We got away."

I try to fight back the tears, but I'm so confused and overwhelmed that the tears keep on coming. Timber holds me tight and lets me cry until I'm all cried out and I can talk again.

"You were amazing," I say, stroking his soft hair.

"Me? You're like some crazy woodland ninja girl. Oh my God! You were flipping and spinning and I don't know what you were doing, but it was freaking badass . . ."

"What were you doing out of the cave?" I ask him.

"I heard you shriek, then I heard rocks falling. I was worried about you. Kenji fell asleep, so I came alone. I saw you at the bottom of that hill. I tried to call to you, but you didn't hear. So I followed you. That's when I saw Clay and Dawn going after you."

I let go of Timber and sit up. "Oh no," I say. "Kenji's still up there and Clay and Dawn will start moving again." I scramble to my feet. "I have to get help. You have to stay here. This time you have to promise me you'll stay because I need you to take care of this fox. It's very important."

Timber starts to stand up. "I can't let you go out there by yourself again."

"No." I hold out my hand to stop him. "I can take care of myself. We're really close to my house and I can go faster alone. No one will find you here if you're quiet. I need you to take care of this little guy." I look over at the fox, who's curled in a ball, hiding its snout in his tail.

Timber frowns but he says, "Okay. I will, but . . ."

"I'll be back as soon as I can." I step forward and kiss him. "And Timber," I say as I push open the door.

"Yes?" he says.

"I love you, too!" Then I bolt.

By the time I get to Alverland fifteen minutes later, it's clear that everyone knows something's wrong. My uncles and oldest male cousins gather in the clearing in front of Grandma Fawna's with their bows and arrows. The older girl cousins hurry the little kids into Grandma and Grandpa's house. I see Aunt Flora scurrying across the clearing with an armload of dried herbs. "Where's my dad?" I yell to her.

When Flora sees me, she drops the herbs and runs toward me. "Thank Mother Earth. You're safe!" She wraps me in a hug. "Where are the others?"

My uncles, aunts, and grandfather gather around me. I try to explain everything as quickly and as clearly as I can. In an instant, the men fan out, forming search parties. Some are already tracking Clay and Dawn. Others will bring Timber and the fox back to Alverland. My dad, Briar, and Grove have gone to Barnaby Bluff to get Kenji. The oldest girls bundle up and are sent in twos with their bows and arrows and small bags of signal herbs to the other settlements to warn everyone that we've been infiltrated. If they see Clay and Dawn along the way, they're to light the bags and throw them in the air to signal where they are, then they're to disappear into the woods and hide. My grandfather gives them permission to use their bows and arrows to defend themselves. Then Flora leads me inside Grandma's house.

Fawna presides over a huge cauldron where my aunts mumble chants and toss in herbs. "You're back," she says calmly as I charge into the kitchen.

"Are Mom and Willow here?" I ask.

Fawna smiles gently at me. "Let's get you out of those wet clothes." Aunt Flora pulls off my cloak, soaking now from the melting snow.

"But I have to warn them," I say, trying to get out the door again.

Fawna holds up her hand. "They can take care of themselves. Your mother's magic is very powerful, my dear."

"I'll get you a dry tunic," Flora says.

"My friends," I say to Fawna. "I shouldn't have left them. I should have . . ."

Fawna lays her hands on my quivering shoulders. "You did the right thing. I'm very proud of you. Your friends will be found."

I bury my face in my hands. "I don't understand any of this."

Grandma comes to my side and rubs my back. "None of us do yet."

I peer up through my wet, tangled hair. "It's my fault, isn't it?"

"No," she says simply.

I struggle with this. "They followed us."

"You can't control what other people do."

I drop into a chair, exhausted. "We got the fox," I say. Everyone stops what they're doing and looks at me.

My grandmother smiles. "Excellent!"

"It's with Timber in the sugar shack," I tell them.

Fawna's face falls. She scowls. "How could you leave it with him?"

"Timber saved me . . ." I say. "He's the only reason I was able to get the fox from Clay and Dawn."

Grandma Fawna sighs, then she rubs the polished stone amulet around her neck. "This is unexpected," she says. She leans down and studies my face. "Tell me everything that happened again."

The whole story floods out of me, in more detail this time. How we took Kenji and Timber to the bluff. How I left them, and how I fell. How Clay and Dawn tried to zap me. How Timber leaped out of the trees.

"I see," says Fawna when I'm done. She thinks this over for quite a while. "I think I've underestimated your friend Timber."

"I knew you didn't like him," I tell her.

"You're right, but there's a reason."

"Just because he's an erdler . . ." I say, and sniffle.

"No, Zephyr, that's not why," Grandma Fawna says. Flora comes back with a dry tunic and leggings for me. "Put these on," Fawna says as she rises to put the kettle over the fire. "Then we'll have a nice, long talk over a cup of tea."

chapter 20

I CURL UP in Grandma's rocking chair under a heavy blanket with the fire roaring in front of me. Fawna sits across from me in Grandpa's matching rocker. As usual, she looks as calm as a clear blue sky, even though all around us everything is falling apart. I can't muster any interest in the lady slipper tea with honey or the dried-blueberry rusk she's put on my lap. I should be famished after all the running and zapping I did, but my appetite is gone. I'm too worried about Briar, my mom, Willow, Kenji, and especially Timber.

"Worrying yourself sick won't help," Grandma tells me for the millionth time when she sees me frowning into the steam coming off my tea.

"But what if . . . ?" I start to say.

"What-ifs never help."

"Grandma!" I set my tea down. "You're killing me. How can you be so calm? What is it that you need to tell me about Timber."

"I think it's time you know the truth about him." Grandma leans forward and rests her hands on her knees. I lean forward and hold my breath. "He carries a troubling mark, but before I can explain, I have to back up."

"Argh!" I moan and flop back in my seat. Everything has to be a history lesson with her. But I know that the quicker I shut up and listen, the quicker she'll get to the point.

She absently rubs one of her amulets between her thumb and forefinger as she explains. "You see, a very long time ago all the magical creatures of the world and the erdlers intermingled quite easily. If you listen to any of the old erdler stories, they even talk about it. The wolf in 'Little Red Riding Hood.' The troll in 'Three Billy Goats Gruff.' The giant in 'Jack and the Beanstalk.' Nowadays, erdlers think those stories are only children's play. But they aren't. They're true, or as true as any old story can be." She sits back and rocks easily as she talks. "They've probably been changed over time, but as you know, things such as gnomes and pixies and fairies really did exist."

"What's this have to do with Timber?" I ask, impatient for her to get on with it.

She holds up her hand and, as usual, is in no hurry. "Erdlers can be quite an aggressive bunch when they feel threatened," Grandma says with a sigh. "It's one of their worst traits. So the erdlers of old simply eradicated the beasts they didn't like. Some of the more peaceful creatures, like elves, well, we just slipped away and formed our own quiet communities out of the erdlers' way. But then some creatures decided they liked the erdler world better with all its gadgetry and motion. They decided to pass."

"Pass what?" I ask.

"Pass as erdlers," she explains. "So some fairies, pixies, ogres, shapeshifters, what have you, slowly drifted away into erdler life. They didn't use their magic anymore, so no one suspected them."

"Elves, too?" I ask.

"Oh sure," she says. "Many elves have done that over the centuries. They've walked away from our settlements to live among the erdlers.

Like your family did. The difference is that no one ever came back. Until you, of course."

"Like your cousin Hyacinth?" I ask.

Grandma nods, but she looks uncertain. "Not everyone who left turned dark, though."

I shift uncomfortably. "After all the trouble we've caused today, I think I know why the others never came back."

Grandma nods. "Mixing together can certainly complicate the world." She sips her tea then continues. "Eventually those who walked away intermarried with the erdlers and had children and never let on that they had another side. Their children were half magical, then the next generation was a quarter magical, and so on until their natural ability for magic became so diluted that erdlers carrying any of these marks wouldn't know they had it."

I sit up straight with my heart revving. "Are you saying Timber is part elf?" I ask hopefully.

She shakes her head. "No, dear, I'm not."

I slump back. "Then what is he, Grandma?"

"A *hamrammer*," she says.

I look at her blankly. "I don't know what that is."

"It's a kind of shifter," she says slowly. "One who takes an animal form. They could take many different forms—bears, dogs, boars . . ."

"So what's Timber?" I ask, sitting now on the edge of my chair.

"Wolf," she says.

I fall back, making the chair rock as I think about his eyes, his smile, the way I've felt he wanted to devour me. "But . . . but . . . but . . ." I sputter.

"There's a very contentious history between elves and the *hamrammers*, especially the wolf people, or werewolves as erdlers like to call them, but that sounds a bit silly to me. Like something out of those vampire stories everyone goes on about."

"Were vampires real?" I ask, creeped out now.

"Heavens no!" she says with a snort. "That's just erdler fantasy made up to sell lots of books."

I shake my head. "How do you know all this?"

"I'm not as clueless as you think, Zephyr. I watch that TV contraption in your house and I sometimes even read the newspaper."

"Whoa." I shake my head at the thought of my grandmother watching *Entertainment Tonight* and reading the *Daily News*. "But what I mean is, how do you know this about Timber? How can you be sure?"

"I can see the mark he carries," she says. "I don't know how to explain it to you beyond that. It's part of my power, I suppose."

Still skeptical, I ask, "Do you see marks on other erdlers?"

This cracks my grandma up. "Yes, all the time! I find it quite funny all these erdlers walking around part fairy, part gnome, part ogre, and they don't even know it." Her laugh is light and happy, but I'm freaking out because my grandmother is telling me I'm dating Teen Wolf.

"Are any of my other friends, you know, marked?"

She nods. "But I'm not going to tell you who. I don't think it's good for you to know because really, in the end, you must keep it a secret from them." The smile disappears from her face. "Same is true for Timber. He mustn't know."

"And today in the woods . . ." I start to say.

"It came out in him because he was protecting something he cares a great deal about."

"Me?" I ask, feeling my eyes sting with the memory of Clay advancing on me.

"I misjudged him because of my feelings about wolf people from the past. They used to ransack elfin villages and carry off babies to devour. They were a violent and nasty bunch. But I was wrong about Timber. I should have gotten to know him, then I would have seen that despite—

or even perhaps because of—his family history, he is a good person. What's more, he and I have something in common."

I blink at her, trying to figure out what Timber and Fawna could possibly have in common.

"We both care about you," she says.

"Do Mom and Dad see Timber's mark?" I ask.

Grandma shakes her head. "Probably only a few of the older elves can see it. It's a subtle thing."

"But what about Clay and Dawn?" I ask. "Why are they here?"

Grandma rubs the amulet around her neck. "I don't know, but I suspect when Timber gets here with the fox, we'll figure out some answers."

Outside we hear a commotion. I run to the window to see half the men in my family coming into the clearing behind my grandparents' house, and there, in the midst of them, is Timber. I head for the door.

My aunts and cousins flood out into the clearing. Briar's mom, Flora, throws her arms around Uncle River's neck. "For thunder's sake, what took you so long? We've been worried sick!"

I hop over the rail of the porch and run toward the group. Timber sees me and breaks away from the crowd. "You're safe!" I yell, jumping into his arms. "I was so worried Clay and Dawn would come back or that you wouldn't know the search party was there to help you and . . ." I bury my face in his shoulder.

He pats my back. "But it's okay. I'm fine. And I'm here now. And whoa," he says, looking all around.

We part from our hug and I see that everyone has gathered in a half circle around us. All of my cousins have piled out of my grandmother's house and stand staring at the strange erdler in Alverland. Poppy, Bramble, and Persimmon push their way to the front of the group and wave. Timber waves back then turns to me, wide-eyed. "It's like seeing a hundred different versions of you," he says, and I have to laugh because he's right.

"There's a bit of a family resemblance," I say.

Grandma Fawna and Grandpa Buck stride up through the group and hold out their arms. Timber steps back when he sees Fawna coming toward him, but when he realizes she's about to hug him, he relaxes. My grandfather takes Timber's hand in his. "You have done a great service for our people," he says. "And for that we are grateful."

"Oh, I, um, I didn't really . . ." Timber stammers.

Buck turns to all of my relatives. "Hup ba!" they yell in unison. "Hup ba! Hup ba! Hup ba!"

"So that's where that comes from," Timber says.

"It's sort of like a high five around here," I tell him.

"Cool," he says, smiling.

"Come." Grandma Fawna takes him by the arm. "Flora will find you dry clothes and nourishment." She stops and lays her hands on his shoulders, looks into his face, and says, "But first, I want to thank you for helping us." She leans down and kisses his forehead. Timber stands there blinking, unsure what to do. Then Fawna turns back toward the search party. "Now I must attend to this fox."

As Flora leads us into the house, Timber whispers to me, "I thought your grandma didn't like me."

"Not anymore," I tell him. "She thinks you're awesome."

"What changed her mind?" he asks.

"Well, um," I stammer and hesitate, trying to figure out how to say it. "She looked deep inside of you and liked what she saw."

"My spleen?" he asks, laughing.

"No." I smack his arm.

"My liver?"

"Stop," I say, but I'm giggling.

"My kidneys?"

"No," I tell him. "Same thing I see when I look at you." Then I pat him on the chest and say, "Your heart."

Not long after Timber is settled in some of Grove's clothes with a plate of smoked fish, bread, roasted nuts, and dried fruit, we hear my father's voice in the clearing. I run for the door with Timber close behind. We find my dad, Briar, and Kenji with Poppy, Bramble, and Persimmon hanging off their arms. They're surrounded by the same wide-eyed group as Timber was a short while ago, only I don't know who's more surprised—my family to see someone who looks like Kenji or Kenji to see a bunch of people who look just like us.

"There's no sign of them that I can find," my father's saying as we break into the circle surrounding them.

Kenji throws his arms around Timber. "Dude, am I glad to see you!"

"You have a nice nap up there?" Timber jokes.

Kenji runs his hands through his blue-tipped hair. "Actually," he says. "I did. I woke up to Briar and Drake shaking me."

This cracks me up. "He slept through everything!"

"We were so worried about Timber," Briar says. "Where'd you go?"

"Long story." I sling my arm around her shoulders. "I'll tell you over some tea."

Over the next hour, all the search parties come back to the clearing. There have been no signs of Clay and Dawn anywhere in the woods. It's as if they vanished into thin air. Briar and I tell our stories over and over again to our aunts and uncles, while they try to piece together who Clay and Dawn are and what they want in Alverland. The one missing piece, of course, is the fox. Fawna says we can't figure that out until my mother returns, which has everyone worried because she's been gone all day. So for now, the fox is left happily feasting on dried rabbit meat by the fire in Grandma's kitchen.

"I'm worried about Mom and Willow," I tell my dad as we make a bed for Timber. He and Kenji are off at the bathhouse before everyone feasts together.

Dad hands me two down comforters and pillows, which I fluff. "Your mother and Willow, more than anyone here, can take care of themselves. They'll be along when the time is right."

"But they have no idea Clay and Dawn are out there," I argue.

He unrolls a large, thin pallet on the floor of our central room. "All the settlements have been warned, and so far no one has seen hide nor hair of Clay and Dawn, so it's pretty likely they took off after that whooping you gave them." Dad laughs.

I look around the room to make sure we're alone. I lean in and whisper to my dad. "There's something you should know about Timber."

He leans closer to me. "What?" he whispers back with a silly grin on his face.

"Fawna says he's a *hamrammer*."

My dad rears back and stumbles over a bedroll, landing on his back on the floor. "Crikey, Zeph! I thought you were going to say he's your boyfriend."

"But don't worry." I reach out for my dad's hand and help pull him to his feet. "He saved me in the woods."

Dad shakes his head. "I don't think so."

"No, it's true," I plead. "He's not the bad kind."

Dad looks at me for a moment. "I don't have a problem with him being a *hamrammer*, honey. Or your boyfriend. I was surprised, but I know he's a good guy, that's clear. I'll tell you one thing, though: my daughter doesn't need anybody to save her butt. Whatever you two did in the woods to get rid of Clay and Dawn was a joint effort." Then he laughs. "I wish I could have seen it."

"What?" Grove asks, carrying in a set of sheets for the bed.

"Your sister kicking dark-elf bootie," Dad says.

Grove bumps me on the shoulder. "Way to go, little sis. I thought you were crazy saying they were dark elves."

Poppy, Bramble, and Persimmon rush into the room, yelling, "Dinner's ready!"

"Hey there." My father scoops them all three up into his arms. "What are we having?"

"The usual," Bramble says.

"Pizza and hot dogs?" my dad asks.

"No silly!" Poppy says. "That's erdler food."

Grove and I follow them out the door, grabbing our cloaks on the way back to Grandma's for dinner.

I just about lose it when I see both Kenji and Timber dressed in elfin tunics. They look so out of place, like they're dressed for Halloween. Especially Kenji because his clothes are two sizes too large, so he's had to roll up the pant legs and sleeves four times. He turns around to show off his new duds.

"Man, I've got to say this whole tunic thing is working for me," he says. "I wish someone had told me how comfortable these things are. I'm giving up my jeans and hoodies for a whole new vibe."

I can't contain myself, and I burst into a fit of giggles.

"It's not half bad," Timber says, striking a pose as if he's about to shoot a bow and arrow. "But I think I'd like one in teal."

Briar and I lead them to the kitchen, where we all fill our plates with corn bread, roasted potatoes, squash, fried apples, and rabbit stew. We find a place to sit among my many cousins. The littlest ones are fascinated by Kenji and Timber, even reaching out to touch Kenji's dark, blue-tipped hair. But because there are erdlers in our presence, everyone else is subdued.

Kenji and Timber are both great sports about everything, and to their credit they're not asking many questions yet. I don't know how we'll answer anyway, so I'm glad that for now the novelty of this situation is sidetracking everyone. After people finish eating and the dishes are cleared away, my aunts, uncles, and cousins bring out their lutes, flutes, guitars, and mandolins, and everyone begins to sing and dance. Timber grabs my hand and taps his toes. I can tell by his goofy smile that he's enthralled by the music, and if I weren't so worried about my mom and Willow, I would be, too.

Then, in the middle of the third song, while my cousins are dancing a four-hand partner jig, Grandma Fawna's door swings open and there's my mother, bundled in her cloak, with Willow and Ash by her side. Everyone rushes for them, talking at once. I push through the crowd and find my mother's arms.

"I was so worried about you!" I say as I throw myself at her.

She kisses my forehead and rubs my back. "We're fine, honey," she says. "Just fine."

Then I turn to Willow. As soon as I see her beautiful face and sparkling green eyes, I grab her. We cling to each other, rocking back and forth. "I've missed you so much!" we say over and over to each other.

As my mother steps into the room, she shrieks. Everyone stops talking. We all turn to see what's upset her. "Great horned owl!" she says with her hand pressed against her chest. "What are they doing here?"

"Hi, Mrs. Adler," Timber says, weakly waving.

"Hey there," Kenji says with a grimace.

Mom turns to me. "Zephyr?" she says. "Would you like to explain what's going on?"

chapter 21

AFTER THE LITTLE ones are packed off to bed and I've told the whole story (again) to my mom, I find Timber and Grove by the fire. Timber's noodling around on my father's guitar as Grove plucks a mandolin. They're riffing on an old elfin melody called "Green Glen Ladies," and I'm surprised by how well Timber can keep up.

I hate to interrupt them, but I have my marching order. "Mom wants you guys to go to our house now."

"We're having too much fun," Timber tells me as he strums. "Your dad's guitar is amazing. I could play it all night."

"Take it with you," I say.

"Are you coming, too?"

"I have to help my mom and the other women. I'll see you in the morning."

Grove stops playing and packs up his instruments, but Timber doesn't move. "I don't want to go. I want to stay with you," he pleads like a child clinging to his mommy, which annoys me.

"Come on, Timb," I say. "You must be exhausted. Plus, you and Grove can play music back at our house."

"What about Kenji?" he asks.

"He's staying at Briar's house." I glance over and see that Briar is having as much trouble disentangling herself from Kenji as I am from Timber.

"But . . ." Timber stands up and lays his hand on my shoulder. "There are so many questions I have and so much I want to talk about with you. Plus . . ." He leans in close. "I've barely been able to touch you, everything has been so crazy around here."

I move away from his reach. "I can't really talk to you about it all now. I have to help my family. Please go with Grove."

He hangs his head as if I've wounded him. I step toward him again and kiss him on the cheek. "I know it's weird for you to be here, but it's been a really long day, and I need to help my mom."

"Okay," he says reluctantly, but before he lets go, he wraps his arms around me tighter.

Embarrassed that my aunts and cousins may see, I pull away. "Enough, really. I'll see you in the morning."

The moon is huge and round and yellow over the clearing behind Fawna's house. The men have organized watch parties for the night— four men, one at each corner of the settlement, taking two-hour shifts until daybreak. It's the same at all the settlements in the forest, my mom told us when she returned. For extra protection, Grandma Fawna and all the other matriarchs in their own settlements have cooked up barrier spells and spread them around the houses. There's no way Clay and Dawn will get to anyone tonight.

With Kenji and Timber safely inside the houses, my mother, grandmother, and aunts are ready to look at the poor little fox Clay and Dawn have been lugging around. It sits perkily on a stump in the center of the clearing surrounded by all the women in our clan.

"He looks a little happier," I say, cooing over the cute little fur ball.

"She," Mom says.

We all turn to Mom, who stands behind the fox, gently rubbing it between the ears. "Willow and I spent most of the day tending to Grandmother Ivy, who is fading very quickly now." Everyone murmurs their regrets about losing Ivy, but my mother smiles gently. "She's comfortable, though, and ready to move on when her time comes, but one thing does trouble her."

We all get quiet. "Iris has been missing for quite a while now. Ivy still has enough strength to sense that Iris's youngest girl, Hyacinth, is not well."

At the name Hyacinth, all of my aunts gasp.

"Who?" Briar asks.

"She was the youngest," Grandma adds. "A youngest-youngest in fact. She married a man from another clan and they turned dark. They left Alverland before you girls were born. Of course, as is tradition, we've not communicated with Hyacinth, and her husband, Orphys Corrigan, since they departed."

"But Iris had," Mom says, and my aunts begin to murmur again. Mom gives them a stern look. "Each one of you is a mother," she says. "And you know our love for our children never leaves, even if that child takes a path that we don't approve of." The murmuring quiets as my aunts nod their heads. "Iris never stopped loving Hyacinth as none of us would ever stop loving our daughters."

"But she's dark!" Briar says.

Flora reaches out to touch Briar's shoulder. "Oh, but my darling, there's nothing you could ever do that would make me not love you. Nothing. Even turning dark. The same is true of Iris's love for Hyacinth."

When Flora says this, I know it's true, and I relax a bit about Timber and Kenji showing up here. My parents might love me forever, no matter what I do wrong, but I know I'll be in a heap of trouble as soon as this crisis is over. If Briar and I hadn't danced an elf circle for them, none of this would have happened.

"Mama Ivy believes that Iris knew Hyacinth was ill and she shifted in order to find her," Mom says.

"Iris's totem is a fox," Grandma Fawna says.

We all catch our breath and look at the little fur ball panting happily in the center of us. "And that's . . ." I start to ask.

Mom nods. "We believe it might be Iris. But we think she's stuck. Maybe Clay and Dawn cast a spell on her or perhaps she's so low on energy after her journey that she can't shift back."

"But why did they want her?" Briar asks.

"Well," Mom says slowly, "there's no way of knowing for sure, but we think perhaps Clay and Dawn are Hyacinth's children."

I think back to what Clay said about his grandmother and coming to Alverland. "You mean, we're related to them?" I ask, feeling sick to my stomach.

Mom nods. "Perhaps."

"So what do we do?" I ask.

Mom bites her lip. "Well, first things first." She looks at us. "We have to deal with the erdlers." Briar and I shrink back a little. "Then," Mom says, "we have to take the fox to Mama Ivy. She's the only one powerful enough to bring Iris back."

Late that night, when all of Alverland is quiet and the only light comes from the yellow moon and the crackling fires of the sentries standing watch, I'm awake in my bed and I'm starving. What I really want is a gooey slice from Pizza Plus on Seventh Avenue near Ari's house, but obviously, I can't go skipping into the woods for pizza. Instead, I pad quietly to the kitchen and search for something to calm my growling tummy. I settle on a giant bowl of granola, then curl up in a chair by the dying embers of the fire. A board squeaks behind me. I turn, expecting to find my mother, up pacing, worried about the fox. I realize that it's Timber, standing in the doorway, watching me.

"Hey," I whisper, turning around in my chair.

"Hey." He comes quietly in the room, so cute and cuddly in his elfy jammies. I almost have to laugh to see him in a long, linen nightshirt and cap.

I pat the chair next to me for him to sit. He wraps his arms around himself.

"You cold?" I pick up the poker to stir the fire. When the flames don't come back, instead of zapping the logs with a fire hex, I load on some small pieces of kindling, then more logs, then pump the bellows until the fire perks to life.

"Wow," Timber says with a small, uneasy laugh. "You're magic."

I laugh at the irony of his statement. "What's the matter, city boy, you never built a fire?" I tease, then I blast him with a pump from the bellows.

Rather than laugh or try to get me back, Timber sits quietly.

"You okay?"

"I couldn't sleep. I can't get my brain to shut up. Too much has happened in the past few days." He looks at me. "There are so many things I don't understand."

I'm quiet because I'm afraid of what his questions might be and how I'll answer, or really, how I'll avoid answering them. We both watch the fire as it cracks and pops. "You've seen some pretty weird stuff here, haven't you?" I finally say.

He nods.

"Alverland is different from Brooklyn," I say, then I think, *Duh, understatement of the year.* "Are you freaked out by all of this?" I wonder if seeing this side of me has changed his mind about being my boyfriend. Which would be strange, since I've seen another side of him, too. A side he doesn't even know about.

Timber slowly shakes his head. "No, not really. I mean, actually I think it's pretty cool. I thought it'd be really boring here, but dang . . ."

I laugh. "It's not usually like this."

"I figured, but still." He leans forward and warms his hands by the now blazing fire. "I loved sitting around singing with everyone in your family and the way everyone eats together. I wish there was more of that in Brooklyn."

"I didn't appreciate it until I moved and saw how other people live, all alone in their little bubbles with TVs and computers and headphones on all the time. I used to think eating with a big group and singing every night was boring, but now I think it's amazing."

"Plus," Timber says, "it's what made you a great singer."

I can feel myself blushing. "I'm not great, though."

"Yes, you are," he says. "I think you're the best singer at BAPAHS."

"What about Bella or Mercedes?" I ask.

"Bella is Bella," Timber says. "She has something, some star quality, that people love for no good reason. Plus, she's ruthless. She'll get what she wants and step on anyone who gets in her way. She'll be famous someday, but she'll never be happy. And Mercedes has a big voice. People like that. It gets them excited. But you have more range. Your talent is more subtle."

"Then why didn't I get the lead in the musical?" I ask.

"Politics and popularity," he says. "It's never only about talent."

"Anyway, doesn't matter. It's not like I'm going to perform anyway, but you . . ." I look at him. "You have to go back, Timb. You *are* the lead. Without you, there's no performance."

He shakes his head. "I don't even want to do it. It's not fun anymore. And I want you to be there."

We hold hands in front of the fire for a few minutes, and I realize that this is probably what Willow and Ash or my mom and dad feel like when they sit together in the evenings. I used to think I never wanted a life so boring as sitting in front of a fire, holding hands. After today, I realize that having some quiet, simple happiness ain't half bad sometimes.

"Zeph," Timber says after a while.

"Yeah?"

He drops my hand and turns to look at me. "What did you do to Clay and Dawn in the woods?"

It's the question I've been dreading. So long, quiet, calm happiness. Hello, stomach-squinching anxiety. "You mean after you jumped out of the trees like some crazy kung fu fighter?" I ask, just to stall.

Timber rubs his forehead. "That, too. I remember following the sound of your voice. I remember seeing Clay coming after you and then I remember being on top of him, but I don't get what happened." He looks to me.

"It was just adrenaline," I tell him. "You were pumped up."

"But something happened because when I went to take the fox from Dawn, she was . . ." He looks troubled. "Stiff. It was weird. And then Clay, curled half on his side, stuck. And then I was thinking about at the club in Red Hook when Dawn surprised us and we were trying to get out the door. I thought she was drunk. But . . . I don't know what it was. You said something and she backed off and went limp."

"Wow, Timber," I say, trying to laugh light and easy, but I can hear the strain in my voice. "I don't remember it that way at all."

"What do you remember then?" he asks.

"I think it was just the moment, you know? There was a lot happening and we were both scared and . . . and . . ."

The back door off the kitchen squeaks open. We both whip around to find my mom wrapped in her cloak, carrying a small candle through the door. "Hello, you two," she says, lowering her hood.

"How's the fox?" I ask.

Mom sets her candle on the table then fills the kettle with water. "Better," she says. "I think she's getting her strength back. How are you, Timber?"

"Good, thanks," he says.

I take a long pair of tongs and pluck a glowing ember from the fire, then drop it into the stove with some kindling to heat mom's water for tea.

"Tea for you?" she asks us. We both nod. "The sun will be up soon," she says as she pulls down a tin and measures dried leaves into a pot. "Are you talking about what happened in the woods?" she asks, calmly, smoothly, evenly, betraying no concern as she busies herself in the kitchen.

"Uh, um, yeah, he uh . . ." I stammer, wondering how much she heard.

"I really love it here," he says.

"That's so very nice," says Mom, "but you can't stay." Mom cocks her head to the side and smiles at us. "Come," she says, pulling two chairs away from the table. "Flora is bringing Kenji and Briar, and we'll talk about what we're going to do."

Timber and I sit quietly as my mom slices thick slabs of bread and slathers them with wild strawberry preserves. She sets out six cups, the honey jar, and the steaming teapot, all the while taking her time, humming. I want to ask her what she's up to, but I know I should just wait until she's good and ready to spill it. Soon, the door opens again and in walks Flora followed by Kenji and Briar, who look as sleepless as Timber and I.

We all sit around the table, but none of us touch the tea or the bread. Mom leans forward and asks, "Zephyr, Briar, did you know what you were doing when you danced in the park, at the skating rink, and at the club?"

Briar sits back in her chair and crosses her arms. "We were just dancing," she says. I don't say anything because I don't want to admit that I knew we weren't just dancing.

"You were dancing an elf circle," Flora says. At the word *elf*, Briar and I suddenly straighten up and gulp in air.

"Elf circles can be very powerful, especially over erdler men," Mom adds.

"Mom!" I look from Kenji to Timber, who both wrinkle their brows in bewilderment.

"Well, they should know," Mom says.

"You did enchant them," Flora points out.

"We did?" Briar asks.

"You did?" Kenji asks.

"You what?" asks Timber.

"Oh no," I say, beginning to realize that Mom and Flora know more about what we did than we do.

"It's an ancient spell," Mom says, and my mouth drops open. "It's harmless fun among the elves, but it can be very harmful to humans who get in the way."

"Dark elves have used those dances for centuries to drive erdlers out of their minds with love," Flora adds.

"What are they talking about?" Timber asks me.

"Why are you saying all of this in front of them?" I want to know.

"We told you no magic in Brooklyn," Mom says, stirring her tea.

"But we didn't exactly know," I plead.

Flora and Mom look at us hard and they wait. I shrink back.

"We didn't," Briar says in a small voice.

They continue to stare at us.

"So maybe we sort of suspected," I admit and cringe.

"But honestly," Briar says, "we didn't really know what we were doing."

"You were doing magic," Mom says calmly but sternly.

"And now they know," I say, pointing to our friends, who both sit rigid and pale.

"It's important for them to know the truth," says Mom.

"It is?" Briar asks.

Flora leans forward and lays her hand on top of Kenji's. "Kenji, dear, it's been so very nice to meet you. I know you've been a wonderful friend to my daughter."

"Uh thanks," he mumbles, and tries to withdraw his hand.

"But there's something you should know about her," Flora continues.

"Mother!" Briar snaps.

"She's an elf," Flora says, pointing to Briar.

"So is she," Mom says, looking at Timber but pointing to me.

"So are we," Flora says.

"All of us," Mom adds.

Laughter bubbles up from Timber. "This is whacked."

"I'm sorry," Kenji says. "I'm too tired for all of this." He rubs his eyes with the backs of his hands and looks weary.

"It's true," Mom says. "We're all magic. Want to see?" Timber and Kenji stare at my mom like she's crazy and they'd like to be on their way home about now. I'm flabbergasted by what's gotten into my mother and Flora. "Do some magic," Mom says to me.

"Mom," I beg. "Enough."

"Don't be shy. Show Timber what you can do." She looks around the room. "Zap the fire," she says.

I shake my head.

"Go ahead," Mom prods.

"No," I say, feeling anger rising at my mom. "I'm not doing that. He'll think I'm a freak."

"Can you really?" Timber asks.

"This is ridiculous!" I say.

"Go on, Zephyr," Mom prods. "Zap the fire."

"Why are you doing this?" I plead.

"Don't you think they deserve to know the truth?" Mom asks.

"I'm glad you like them well enough to trust them, but after everything that's happened with Clay and Dawn, don't you think . . ." I rant.

"Zap the fire!" Mom commands.

Out of fury, I zap the fire with all my might, yelling "Burn!" Giant flames leap in the hearth.

Timber and Kenji jump back in their seats. "Whoa, what the . . ." Timber says.

"How'd you do that?" Kenji asks.

"Your turn, Bri," Flora says. "Change this rock into water." She pulls a smooth river stone out of her tunic pocket and plunks it on the table in front of us and I realize that they've been planning this.

"Fine," Briar says. "Liquid." She lazily zaps the rock, which melts into a small pool.

"This is starting to freak me out," Kenji says, his voice a little shaky.

"I don't understand what you're doing." I pull at my own hair, frustrated. "They have to go back to Brooklyn and you're trusting them with too much information—"

"Once you started casting spells," my mom says, angry now, "you set this all in motion."

"But we didn't know what we were doing," Briar says again.

"Exactly," says Flora, her voice tight. "So the next time you better make sure you know what you're doing before you start mucking around with magic in front of your erdler friends!"

"So what are we supposed to do?" I ask, pissed off at my mom and aunt and a little bit scared for Kenji and Timber. "Tell them everything now? Should I tell Timber he's got a *hamrammer* mark?"

"A what?" Timber asks.

"You're a werewolf," I say, just to spite my mom. "Or really, someone in your family a long, long time ago was. You carry a mark. My grandmother can see it. And yesterday when you jumped out of the woods, it was the wolf coming out in you." I watch my mother as I spill all of this, but she doesn't react. "Happy?" I ask her.

"What kind of crazy . . ." Timber says, half under his breath.

"Is that true?" Briar asks me.

"Fawna says it is," I tell her.

"I'm feeling very uncomfortable." Kenji slowly scoots back from the table.

"Do you want to go back to Brooklyn yet?" my mom asks.

Kenji looks from Mom to Flora to Briar, then he hesitates.

"What about you?" Mom asks Timber.

His eyes rest on me and he doesn't answer.

"Can you leave these girls?" Flora asks.

"Do they have to willingly leave in order for us to break the elf circle spell?" I ask, starting to catch on. "What if they say no?"

My mom nods at me. Now I understand. I turn to Timber. "I cast a spell on Dawn in the club. She's an elf, too. A dark elf, which is bad, and she was going to zap us. And in the woods, I froze them stiff so they couldn't chase us," I admit, but as I say it my eyes fill with tears because I know exposing myself will push Timber away. "And I zapped you once, too. In the van. Remember when your ears clogged up? That was me."

His face clouds over and he looks perplexed, as if he can't decide if I'm being serious, and if I am, if he wants to be near me anymore.

"Did you ever cast a spell on me?" Kenji asks Briar.

She hangs her head. "Just the one," she says, chagrined.

"So?" Mom asks. "Do you guys want to stay?"

Timber's jaw is set and his eyes are cold, hard blue disks. "I'd like to go home now."

I bury my head in my arms and try to swallow the sobs I feel coming.

"Kenji?" Flora asks.

"I don't know," Kenji says.

"What's going to happen to them?" Briar asks.

"We'll take them back to Ironweed," Mom says. "And take away their memories from here."

"Come on, man," Timber says, pushing away from the table. "This place is nuts."

Kenji looks torn, turning from Timber to Briar, back to Timber.

"She's not like you," Flora says and dips her finger into the little puddle on the table. Then she flicks the water, turning the droplets into tiny pebbles, which rain down on the table with a soft clatter.

Kenji jumps back from the table. "I'm ready to get out of here."

Briar runs from the room wailing.

"It's time," my mother says. She pulls her cloak hood over her head.

Kenji and Timber stand at the trail head, awkward and unhappy in their own clothes, which have been washed and dried for them.

"I know it's hard." Flora hugs Briar tightly on Grandma's front porch later that morning.

"You're ruining my life!" Briar yells at her mother and struggles away.

Flora steps back and crosses her arms. "Oh, my love. I'm so sorry it hurts you, but this is what has to happen."

"Come," Mom says, so Briar and I reluctantly follow.

Dad and Grove come with us, too. We all carry our walking sticks with our bow and arrows slung over our backs. We move quickly and quietly through the forest, keeping our eyes and ears open for Clay and Dawn. The search parties were out all night scanning the woods, but no one found a trace of them anywhere.

"You're sure they won't remember any of this?" I whisper to my mom.

"Nothing except coming to Ironweed to look for you," she says.

"But what about what he saw in Brooklyn?" I ask. "Like when I zapped Dawn?"

"I don't know, honey," she says. "Erdlers have a way of integrating weird occurrences so they seem logical. I think the idea of magic is very scary to them, so they explain those things away."

"Like when he thought Dawn was drunk when I gave her the limp fish hex?" I ask.

She nods. "Like that."

I sigh as I watch Timber walking. "Now I know more about him than he knows about himself, but he'll never be able to truly know me."

Mom puts her arm around my shoulders. "I'm afraid that's right."

All of this seems horribly unfair, but the funny thing is, it doesn't change how I feel about Timber. Werewolf or not, I love the essence of who he is. I can only hope that's the way he feels about me, spell or no spell.

I hurry up to where he plods through the snow. He looks over his shoulder at me with those cold blue eyes, and my chest aches as if someone has dunked my heart into freezing water. I want so badly to reach out and weave my fingers into his, because this might be the last time I ever get to hold his hand, but I know that I can't. Instead, I hold my walking stick out to him. "Here," I say. "This will help."

Reluctantly, he takes it from me. As our hands brush against each other, I wish there was something I could say to make him understand that I really do care about him and that when I said I loved him, it was true. "Timber, I . . ."

"Don't," he growls at me.

I stumble back on the path and let him walk ahead. My mom catches me in her arms and huddles me close to her side as I walk through the quiet forest with tears streaming down my cheeks.

In Ironweed, Briar and I take Kenji and Timber into the bait shop as planned. We order them ham and eggs even though no one's hungry. We wait in awkward silence until their food comes. Then my mom and dad come in while Grove keeps watch outside. Dad chats with the guy behind the counter, asking him for advice on deer rifles. When Mom walks back to our table, Dad zaps the man with a paralyzing spell, then he reaches over, turns the OPEN sign to CLOSED, and locks the door. Briar and I stand up and join hands with Mom. We whisper the reversal chant, circling Kenji and Timber, who stare at us, worried but strangely trusting. "*Sha we no, dally per, um vaden sim la folly. For shaden bing um fladen fling, um vaden sim la folly.*"

Like the other times I've been in an elf circle, I lose my sense of time and place, but this time my heart remains heavy. We chant and chant and chant until my mom tugs on our hands. I open my eyes to see Kenji and Timber slack-jawed and frozen, eyes wide but unseeing as we back out of the bait shop slowly and quietly. When we're on the porch, Dad brings the man back to his senses. "Thanks for the advice," he says. "I'll be back if I want to buy a gun." We all slip off the porch and around the back of the shop, where we disappear among the trees to where Grove has been keeping watch.

We wait. Ten minutes later, Kenji and Timber walk into the lightly falling snow. Timber messes with his phone. "I think my battery died," he says.

"This was such a stupid idea," Kenji says as they head down the street away from us.

"It was your idea to try to find them." Timber pockets his phone.

"My idea?" Kenji says. "I don't think so." We watch them walking, leaving footprints in the snow to their car parked across the street. "You just had to see her."

"What was that all about?" Timber asks with a snort.

"I don't know, bro. You're whipped."

A little stab goes through my chest. Now that the spell has been reversed, I know that Timber's feelings for me have changed, but I won't know where we stand until I get back to Brooklyn. If I get back. But as Kenji brushes snow from the windshield, Timber leans against the roof of the car and takes in a deep breath. "Yeah," he says. "She's pretty awesome."

My heart swells and I hug my walking stick to my chest because that's the last thing he touched.

Then he fishes the keys out of his pocket and I hear him say, "But I'm not going to drive all over the country trying to find her."

I nearly laugh at the folly of it all.

"Yeah," says Kenji as he opens his door. "This place gives me the creeps. Let's get back to New York."

Timber climbs into the car. Before he shuts his door, he says, "My mom is going to kill me."

chapter 22

THE MOON WILL rise early tonight, and long before the sun begins to set, we see its faint outline peeking through the branches of snow-covered pines. Usually we would be getting ready for a three-day solstice celebration, one of the biggest festivals of the year. Instead, when we get back from Ironweed, everyone is tense and glum. For one thing, there's still been no sign of Clay and Dawn, despite the fact that search parties have continued combing the woods and standing guard outside each settlement. I'm beginning to feel like I made them up because I'm the only one who's ever seen their dark elves side in action (except for Timber, and we wiped away his memory, so that's no help). For another thing, the fox has been fighting off a fever, so we have to get her to Mama Ivy as soon as possible.

I curl in a chair by the fire to pout because everything seems 100 percent sucky right now, but as usual, my mom and dad have something up their sleeves. "Come on," Mom says, bustling into the kitchen and pulling me out of the chair. "Bundle up and pack a bag. We're heading out."

"Are we going back to Brooklyn?" I ask, shocked.

Mom levels her gaze at me. "Are you seriously asking me that?"

"Right," I say. "Didn't think so."

Poppy tears through the room and zips up the stairs, yelling, "We're going to Grandma Ivy's! We're going to Grandma Ivy's!"

"Is that true?" I ask.

"We're taking this show on the road," Dad says as he sweeps through the kitchen.

"Is everybody coming?" I ask.

Mom nods. "An exodus," she says. "Now go help the little ones pack."

"We haven't done this in so long!" I say happily from the trail among my entire extended family.

We look like one long weirdo parade in our long, hooded cloaks, our walking sticks, and our soft boots that make no sound on the freshly fallen snow. We're each carrying a rucksack filled with clothes or food, plus small gifts for our faraway family. In the back of our long line, Grove and three of my cousins pull a sled with the fox, wrapped in blankets and cloaks. My mother walks beside her, chattering away as if the fox understands everything she says.

The hike is ten miles, so the little ones take turns riding on long sleds that we pull, or we carry them on our shoulders. Sometimes they scurry around, picking up sticks and rocks, antlers and bones, or other treasures they find scattered on the forest floor. As I watch my little sisters and brother and all my younger cousins playing, singing, laughing, zapping one another with harmless spells, I miss being a little kid when I never had to worry about things like, *Is my erdler boyfriend really a werewolf, and did I just cause my entire world to collapse by leading dark elves to Alverland?* No pressure here. Just an ordinary teenage life.

Good granite, life is rough sometimes. Except for now, when despite all the problems swirling like a blizzard around me, I'm happy to be on our way to the solstice celebration.

We come out of the woods into Mama Ivy's clearing just as the sun fades to pink above the pine trees. I grab Willow's hand. "I forgot how beautiful this place is," I say.

We stand on the crest of a small hill. Ivy's house sits in a hollow that is filled with wildflowers in the spring. Now the hill makes the perfect sledding slope for the little ones, who climb up and swish down on their birch bark toboggans. Below, wisps of gray smoke swirl out of Ivy's stone chimney. Her house is an old-style Alverland house, one of the earliest built by our first mother, Aster. It's made of logs, stuffed with moss, and covered by a thick thatched roof. Behind it is the gathering place, much like Fawna's, with tree stump chairs, long tables filled with food, a cooking pit, and a small platform decorated for the coming solstice performances.

"This will be yours soon," I say to Willow.

She bites her lip. "I can't imagine it yet."

"But aren't you excited?" I ask.

"Sort of, but I don't know. It's sad, too, because that means Ivy is going to pass."

"Right," I say quietly. "That part is weird."

"And," Willow says. "I feel too young for all this. It's a lot of responsibility."

"But it's not like you'll be the matriarch," I point out. "Grandma Hortense will still be in charge. You'll just have this amazing house!"

"But I'll be so far away from Mom and Grandma Fawna . . ." Willow shakes her head. I'd never thought that she might be scared about her new life.

I squeeze her hand in mine. "You and Ash will be great together."

When I mention Ash, she smiles. "It's funny, when I'm with him I feel like I can do anything. Like he complements me, you know? What I'm bad at, he's good at."

I sigh, wondering if Timber and I will still be together when I get back to Brooklyn. If I get back to Brooklyn. Everything in my life feels uncertain right now, and I don't dare ask my mom and dad when, or if, we're going back.

"Come on," Willow says. "Let's go help unpack."

That night, after we feast, the women gather in the center of a circle of torches in Mama Ivy's clearing. In the center of our circle, on a stump, is the fox, looking more alert now, but still shivering from the fever. And sitting by the stump in a chair is Mama Ivy. She is shrunken down after nearly two hundred years of living, but her eyes still twinkle and her cheeks radiate a light that rivals the moon.

"It will take all of our magic," Mama Ivy tells us, "to bring Iris back—if this is, in fact, Iris. But if we're wrong . . ." She hangs her head. "I'm afraid this fine fox will perish under the power."

"You mean she'll die?" Briar asks, her hand pressed against her lips.

Mama Ivy nods. Everyone is quiet for a moment, but of course, we all know what we have to do. A fox is a fox, but if this fox is Aunt Iris, we have to bring her back.

"Gather," Mama Ivy says.

Everyone moves forward and links hands. This is the first time Briar and I have been allowed to join a group spell, and despite the circumstances I'm kind of excited. I squeeze Briar's hand and she squeezes mine back. Grandma Fawna brings over a small blue bottle of potion that's been cooking down for the past two days. My mom turns the fox onto her back. As first she struggles, but Mom strokes her belly and whispers in its ear a language I don't understand. The fox relaxes.

Fawna moves around the circle, dabbing potion into the center of each of our foreheads, where our totem animals reside. I don't know yet what my totem will be. It's a journey I have to take when my magic's strong enough, but it's inside of me waiting, just like Timber's wolf is deep inside of him. Next Fawna takes the potion to my mother, who dabs it on Mama Ivy's forehead, then her own, then she rubs it on the fox's belly.

Mama Ivy begins the chant, "*Sham, sham quin quin. La dor mi vin. Sham, sham du forse di tee shu.*" She looks up to us and we all join in as we're able.

I close my eyes and say the words, allowing my consciousness to be lost in the flow of the strange language. Each syllable travels up from our mouths into the night sky, carried away on the wings of owls to circle the moon. As we chant, a vision of Aunt Iris forms inside my mind. I see her standing before me, faint at first, and then more clearly. The chanting grows louder, more intense, and the image in my mind becomes more vibrant. I see Iris now, strong and healthy with dancing eyes and glowing skin.

I feel a deep tug in my heart for the love I have for each of my relatives. They are each a part of me and I a part of them. Without these bonds, who are we? I wonder. Nothing but a lone cougar. How did Hyacinth walk away from such love?

We chant and chant until I am lost, no longer here beneath the sky but only in the loving embrace of my family, and then we hear the yipping of the fox grow louder and morph into something deeper, fuller, more vocal. The voice of a human gasping and panting for air.

I come back into the world, to the circle, to Briar's hand and Willow's hand in my own. I open my eyes and see, lying on the stump in the center of the circle, Aunt Iris, naked, shivering, but alive.

Quickly, Mom and Grandma cover her with cloaks and blankets. The women scoop her up and carry her into the house, where they can minister her back to health.

* * *

A few hours later when the moon is in the center of the night sky, Hortense opens Mama Ivy's door and ushers the women in. "We're ready," she says. "Come, come."

The kitchen is packed with all the female relatives from several clans. Briar and I sit on the floor by the fire. At the front of the room is Mama Ivy, sitting in a rocker by the huge stone hearth. She is beautiful in the warm light of the fire, illuminating her long, white braids twisted around her head. "Come in, children. You are welcome."

Next to Ivy is Iris, looking stronger now. I can only imagine that this house gives her strength with its open rafters hung with dried herbs, flowers, and pine boughs. The long table and soft chairs are worn from hundreds of feasts over the centuries. The ever-present smell of honey, lavender, wood smoke, and tea fills the air. This will be my sister's soon, and now I understand what she means. It will be a lot of responsibility to keep it up so that the next generation of daughters and granddaughters and great-granddaughters can come here and find the same warmth by this fire someday.

The first-firsts gather behind Ivy and Iris. This includes Willow, my mother, and Fawna, plus all my great-grandmothers back to Ivy.

Ivy lifts a rough-hewn wood cup with mulled cider and says the invocation. "In the name of Aster, the first mother who settled Alverland after the great migration, and all the first daughters, we welcome you." She sips from the cup and hands it to her oldest daughter, Hortense, who drinks, and passes it on to her oldest daughter, Apricot, then to Laurel and Jonquil, then to my great-grandmother Lily, who hands it to her daughter (my grandmother), Fawna. Mom takes it from Fawna, sips the cider, and hands it on to Willow, who takes the final drink and sets the cup back on the mantel, where it stays until the next gathering of women.

Grandma Fawna steps forward. "Grandmother Ivy's asked me to preside since my clan has been most involved with these troubles." She reaches out and puts her hand on Iris's shoulder. Grandma takes a few moments to explain to everyone how we found Iris in fox form and what happened up at the bluff. Murmurs and small cries of surprise and anguish carry through the women because nothing in recent memory has happened like this. Then Fawna says, "And now Iris will tell us her story."

Iris sits up straighter and draws in a deep breath. She begins, "For a long time I have felt a pull from my youngest daughter, Hyacinth." She pauses to let everyone get over the shock of speaking a shunned elf's name. "She has come to me in dreams. Her voice has visited me on the wind. I have seen her reflection in pools of rainwater and always she did not look well. Soon I came to realize that my daughter is . . ." She bows her head and tries to speak, but no words come out. Ivy reaches for her hand. My mother, Fawna, Willow, and the other great-grandmothers surround her and lay their hands on her shoulders. Iris slowly looks up at all of us. "She is dying."

We all gasp, including Briar and me. This is unheard of. Elves live for nearly two hundred years, but Hyacinth is my mother's age, not yet fifty.

"I know the rules of shunning and that Hyacinth made her choice when she married Orphys Corrigan and left. But I felt my daughter was calling to me and that she perhaps had regrets." She holds her hands out and pleads. "How could I not go to her?"

I hear the whispers behind me.

"How could she not?"

"I would go."

"Nothing could stop me."

"And so I called to her and then I shifted so I could travel unnoticed," Iris explains. "It took me weeks to find her. She is far away near the coast in a city with many buildings. At first I visited secretly, watching her daily life. I learned she has two children. My grandchildren. By watching them tend to their ailing mother, I grew to love them." She bows her head again. "I didn't realize they had called me there."

Briar and I clasp hands. "Clay and Dawn," I whisper to her, and she nods.

"The children have known for some time that Hyacinth was ill. An erdler disease that afflicts those who go dark. They had been waiting for the right moment. They drew me in and when the time was right, they pounced."

Then Iris looks down at Briar and me. "I don't know how they found you," she explains. "I don't know if it was a coincidence or if they knew where to look. But they came for you, too. There was nothing you could have done to stop it."

"But Iris," Mom says thoughtfully. "Why? What do they want with all of us?"

"It's not us that they want." Iris shakes her head and looks down at her hands. "It's something here." She looks all around the kitchen. "On this land handed down from first-firsts. Something that they believe will cure Hyacinth."

"Ahhh," says Mama Ivy from her rocking chair. "Now this is beginning to make some sense." Then she laughs softly. "I should have guessed, but I'm getting too old and feeble, I suppose."

"What is it, Grandmother Ivy?" Fawna asks.

Ivy shakes her head. "Not something I can reveal to everyone, I'm afraid," she says. "Only first-firsts may know."

All but the first-firsts leave Mama Ivy's kitchen, including Briar and me. Though we protest and try to argue that we deserve to know what's going on since we're the ones who found the fox, Grandma Fawna tells us firmly to leave and we do. When we come back out to the clearing, the little ones have been sent to bed. I see my older cousins sitting around the slowly dying bonfire to play games. The uncles are gathered at the edge of the woods to strum their guitars, drink hot cider, and tell hunting stories.

Briar and I join our cousins by the fire, but we're not much interested in their games and stories. We huddle together on a pallet with thick blankets over us. Since there are so many people here, most of us will sleep outside near the fires tonight. The snow has stopped for now, and for the first time lying here, I feel the exhaustion of the past two days settling into my body. "What do you think they're talking about?" I ask Briar as we gaze at Mama Ivy's house where the first-firsts' walking sticks have been arranged in Xs across the door, barring any entry.

"I don't know," she says. "But if whatever Clay and Dawn want is in that house, it will be up to your sister to protect it soon."

I wake to a faint purple sky with a few morning stars blinking down at me. The sun's not yet up but the moon has gone to bed. Tomorrow a new year will start in Alverland, though in Brooklyn, there's still ten days until New Year's Eve. I stretch and sit up, pushing the blankets back. Briar and many of my other cousins snooze around me. I'm thirsty and I have to pee, so I slip out of the pallet and head toward Ivy's house.

The walking sticks have been moved, and clearly the first-firsts have finished their meeting. I knock softly. When there's no answer, I tiptoe into the big, empty kitchen. Only a few embers smolder in the cold hearth, but the room is still warm from all the activity into the wee hours of this morning. After I go to the bathroom, I help myself to water and find some leftover slices of bread and cold roasted chestnuts in the kitchen cupboard.

As I sit down at the long table to eat my snack, Willow comes to the kitchen door. Her hair is wild down around her shoulders. Her eyes are pink-rimmed and the delicate edges of her nostrils are raw. "Oh Zeph," she says, and flings herself at me, tears streaming down her face.

I catch her in my arms. "What happened? What is it?" I ask, stroking her hair. "Is it Ivy?"

Willow looks up at me. "They want me to take over Mama Ivy's house now."

I smile, despite how upset she is. "But Willow, that's great, isn't it? Don't you want to?"

She pulls back and wipes her sleeve across her nose as she settles into a chair next to me. "I don't know if I'm ready. I don't know if I'm strong enough to protect"—she stops and motions all around—"*this* from the dark elves."

I lean forward and whisper. "What is it, Willow? What are they after?"

She shakes her head. "Can't tell."

I roll my eyes and slump back. "Yeah, yeah," I say, annoyed. "First-firsts only."

"Hey," Willow says. "I'd gladly trade you. I don't want all this responsibility. I didn't ask for it. Sleet and hailstones, Zephyr, I don't even know if I can handle it with Mom and Fawna off in Brooklyn taking care of all you guys. You always make fun of me for being traditional and sticking around Alverland, but what else am I supposed to do? I was born first. You weren't!"

Now I feel like a big jerk. "Sorry, Willy," I say. "Maybe if I knew what Clay and Dawn want, I could help you protect it so you wouldn't feel so much pressure, because this is my fault."

Willow shakes her head. "It's not your fault. They played you, Zeph. "

"But I, well, Briar and I, fell for it."

Willow shrugs. "They sucked Aunt Iris in, too."

"Can you imagine?" I say. "Tricking your own grandmother!"

"I know. Evil, right?" she says. We're both quiet for a while, then Willow sighs. "I guess I have to go through with it. It's the only way to keep things safe."

I reach out and wrap my arms around her neck. "It'll be okay," I tell her.

Later that morning, Mama Ivy calls me into her bedroom. "I need your help," she says from her rocking chair. "Be a dear and open up that cedar chest over there beside the cupboard." She points a gnarled finger across the room.

The chest smells like the fresh spring forest when I lift the lid.

"You'll find some old tunics in there. Just put them on the bed," she instructs.

I lay them carefully across the bedspread. Each one is more beautiful than the next. One is deep blue like a midnight sky with red embroidery around the cuffs and collar. The next is rose colored with green stitching. Another is mossy green with burnt-orange cuffs and collar. The final one is off-white, the color of trillium flowers, with tiny gold stitches swirling down the bodice and around the hem.

"I inherited these from Aster," Ivy explains.

"The first mother?" I ask.

Ivy nods. "She brought them from the old country. You see all that fine embroidery? No one does it like that anymore. We're all in such a hurry nowadays."

This almost makes me laugh, the thought of elves in a hurry. Obviously Ivy's never been to Manhattan!

"Now, take this blanket and put it over the tunics and then go get your sister Willow."

I do as she says even though I have no idea why we're playing hide-and-seek with tunics.

When I bring Willow back to the room, Mama Ivy has her eyes closed. The skin on her face and hands resembles bark with all its intricate lines and gullies. "Mama Ivy?" Willow whispers, touching her hand. I'm relieved when Ivy's eyes flutter open.

"Now then," she says, as if we're in the middle of a conversation already. "Since the clearing out back is now yours, you'll preside over the solstice celebration tonight," Mama Ivy tells my sister.

"No," says Willow, shaking her head. "I couldn't, I—"

"Hush, now," Ivy says with a laugh. "Of course you can. I wouldn't ask you if you couldn't. But you can't wear that old tunic. We have to find the right garments for you."

Willow looks around the room, confused.

"Close your eyes," Mama Ivy tells her. "That's the best way for you to see."

Willow closes her eyes.

"Let the tunic choose you."

Willow stands quietly for a moment and then she moves across the floor, as if drawn to the bed. She hesitates, then reaches out her hand to hover over the blanket. Her arm moves back and forth, left and right, then suddenly stops. She reaches down and places her palm firmly on top of the blanket.

"Ah!" says Ivy. "I love that one, too. Pull the blanket back," she tells me.

When Willow sees what she's chosen, she presses her palm against her cheek. "I don't think I could wear this," she says, lifting the gorgeous off-white tunic. "It's far too beautiful. What if something happened to it?"

"Oh drivel dravel," says Ivy. "This is meant to be worn. By you."

Willow picks it up very carefully and holds it against her body.

"But you'll need a cloak, too," Mama Ivy says. She points to the trunk again. "See what's down there at the bottom, Zephyr."

I reach deep into the trunk and sure enough, at the very bottom, wrapped in a layer of linen cloth, is a heavy deep-red cloak with white fur trim around the hood and cuffs. Gold braid, small gold coins, and intricate blue, yellow, and green embroidery form a crest across the back. Willow gasps when I pull it out.

"This was Aster's cloak that she wore when she made the long walk from the old country. Some believe that just by being worn by the first mother it is imbued with magic." Ivy's eyes twinkle.

"Oh Grandma Ivy!" Willow drops down and lays her head in Ivy's lap. "Thank you."

"No, my dear," Ivy says, stroking Willow's long, golden hair. "Thank you for doing your duty and taking on this huge responsibility when you're so young." Ivy pats her back. "We're all in good hands with you, Willow," she says. "That I know for certain."

That night more clans arrive for the solstice celebration in Mama Ivy's— no, Willow's—clearing. The moon is large and bright, so even beyond the bonfires into the edges of the forest, the woods feel lit up. As is the custom, Willow, wearing the beautiful tunic and cloak, greets everyone, including Ash's family (which is a distant part of my father's clan).

We have a huge bonfire under the bright full moon and a terrific feast of smoked venison and trout, baked potatoes, butternut squash stew, fried rabbit, fresh bread, corn and beans, dried-berry cobblers, and roasted chestnuts. Then, as is our tradition on the solstice, each family takes a turn entertaining everyone else.

My family hasn't had time to prepare, so it takes us a few minutes to get ourselves together. Willow and I have our lutes, Grove has his mandolin, Dad has his guitar, Mom plays the flute, and the little ones play pennywhistles and hand drums.

"What do you want to sing?" Dad asks, as he plucks his A string and we all twist our tuning pegs to match him.

"How about some of your songs?" Willow asks.

My dad looks surprised. Willow doesn't usually want to sing my dad's songs. She's more of a traditionalist, going for folky elf stuff that's been sung around these fires for centuries.

"I miss hearing your music," Willow admits, which makes my dad beam with pride.

"All right then, Miss Willow. What would you like to hear first?" Dad asks.

"Mom's song," Willow says.

"'Aurora Dawn' it is," Dad says, then counts us all in.

As we play, everyone else dances or sings along, or at very least sits and taps their toes to the music. Even Iris and Ivy, both bundled up in rocking chairs by the fire, nod to the beat, smiling as if everything in the world is okay. And that's the way it should be, I think as I strum my lute and harmonize with my dad. Music should make people feel happy and welcome and part of something larger than themselves.

This is what I missed at the BAPAHS musical. It was all about Mr. Padgett and nothing about us or the audience. I think in some ways, it's the reason Briar and I started doing the elf circles, to connect with our crowd again. Only we didn't realize just how strong that connection could be.

When we're done with "Aurora Dawn," everyone claps, hollers, and whistles. Briar stands in front of the stage with my other cousins and jumps around screaming like a loon. "Addlers rock!" she yells, which makes us all laugh.

"Zephyr," Dad says. "Why don't you sing 'Flying Dancer'?"

"No," I say. "It's your song."

"But you sing it so well," Dad says.

Briar overhears Dad and she starts to chant, "'Flying Dancer,' 'Flying Dancer,' 'Flying Dancer'!"

"Come on." Dad tugs me by his side. "We'll sing it together. You take the verses and I'll come in on the chorus."

I set down my lute and walk to center stage. I plant my feet like Dad taught me before the *Idle America* audition, then I face the crowd, only this time I'm not nervous. I feel at peace when I see the familiar and loving faces of my aunts, uncles, cousins, and grandparents watching me. There's no teacher I'm trying to impress or mean girl I'm trying to beat out for the lead or people who will make fun of me mercilessly if I mess up. This time I'm singing for people who love me and care about me, and I want to bring them joy.

My family plays the intro. The notes blend together beautifully and swirl gently into the swaying trees. The music mixes with large, soft snowflakes that cascade down on us. No matter what's gone wrong the past few days or what might happen tomorrow, right now it's all good. I draw in a deep breath and begin to sing.

> Flying dancer, cold air flows
> you're leaving again
> when the north wind blows
> But you'll be back
> in early spring
> for the one you love,
> you'll return to sing

As the words leave me, I see Briar absorb them. She throws her head back, bows, and jumps, spreads her long arms and dances in near perfect imitation of a sandhill crane looking for its mate. She even picks up sticks and tosses them in the air like the cranes will do in the frenzy of their mating dance.

A passionate dancing duet
a song you haven't sung yet
you'll find the one, don't fret
to sing your song in spring

I sing for Timber now, wondering if I'll ever have a chance to sing my passionate dancing duet with him, wondering if he's my other sandhill crane? My other cousins dance with Briar until they're all flailing like the giant birds, then we all sing the chorus together,

Fly dancer, fly
Don't let life pass you by
Spread your wings and soar
To find the one you adore

When the entertainment is done, we all go back to feasting and mingling, getting reacquainted with our long-lost cousins from different clans. Ash's family is lots of fun. They've brought their instruments and games. They have tricksters and contortionists in their clan who entertain everyone with their acrobatics and elfin pyramids. Even Ash's littlest brothers and cousins join in, standing on top of their fathers' heads or balancing on one leg in the palm of Ash's hand.

I'll be the first to admit that Ash has some superfine cousins, but I don't feel much like mingling. I don't know exactly what it is, maybe seeing Willow and Ash so happy together or watching everyone have so much fun, but something makes me miss Timber more than I ever have.

I know he wasn't supposed to be in Alverland and I know that he won't remember it, but I wish he could be here with me now. He'd love all this. The music, the games, the people entertaining one another. More than any other erdler I know, Timber would get this. So, rather than join in, I sit on a log with my plate of little maple cakes and watch, feeling melancholy.

"Persimmon! Percy darling!" I hear my mother calling for my little sister. "Have you seen Percy?" she asks me.

I crane my neck to look around, scanning the groups of little kids playing hoops and rings, dancing to the music, and watching Ash's cousins put on shows. "No," I tell her. "Want me to help you look?"

"No," Mom says. "It's all right. She asked me for some elderberry juice but now I can't find her."

I set my cake aside and stand up. "I'll help you."

"I'm sure she's curled up asleep on someone's lap by now," Mom says. "I got sidetracked talking to Ash's mother about the wedding, so it's been a while since she asked me for the juice."

Mom doesn't seem at all worried, but I have an uneasy feeling. "I can get Briar and Grove and we'll find her."

Mom smiles at me and pats my shoulder. "No, honey. Enjoy yourself. It's a glorious night and Percy's fine. I'll find her sooner or later." She walks off calling my sister's name but is immediately waylaid by another well-wisher, hugging her and exclaiming how amazing Willow is as Mama Ivy's replacement.

I don't know if it's because I'm sad about Timber or if I'm really worried about my sister, but suddenly I don't want to be in the middle of all this fun. I want some space and room to think and be alone. So I leave my cake on the log and slip off into the woods. I know I shouldn't be gone long because my family's going to sing again soon, but if I'm going to be any good in front of everyone, I need to get my head on straight. While I'm walking a big circle around the wooded outskirts of the clearing, I call Percy's name, just in case she's wandered too far and can't find her way back, which is pretty unlikely.

"Percy," I call quietly. "Where are you, little chipmunk?"

As I crunch over the snow, I wonder what Timber's doing. He and Kenji should have made it back to Brooklyn by now. I wonder if his mother was furious. If Kenji got in trouble or if his parents didn't realize he was gone? If Bella roped Timber into more private rehearsals to make up for the time that he was AWOL? The performance is tomorrow night and in true showbiz fashion, it will go on without me. Mostly, I wonder if I still have a boyfriend.

"Looking for something?" a deep voice says. I whip around, expecting one of Ash's cute cousins to be behind me, but there's no one there.

"Huh?" I say aloud. "Is someone there?" I peer into the darker spaces between two large pines.

"I said, looking for something?" the voice comes from above me. I feel a deep panic rising inside of my chest. I recognize that voice. It's coming from a branch of a stately old pin oak tree. I raise my arm, ready to zap Clay if I could see him in the midst of dark branches.

"I wouldn't if I were you," he says, and then I spot him on a large branch low in the tree. He lifts his arm and points to a higher branch above my head. "I've got something you want." I look up and see my little sister suspended from the branch.

"Percy!" I scream. "Get her down now," I command, and wind up my wrist.

"Not so fast," he says, and lifts his right arm while still pointing at my sister with his left. "You cast a spell and I drop her."

I let my arm fall to my side. "What do you want? Let her go!" I yell.

"Hush now, Zephyr," he says, smooth as snail snot. "You're just the person I was hoping would come this way. Not some silly cousin of yours skipping off into the forest to kiss new boys from faraway clans. Gads, elves are boring."

"What do you want?" I demand again.

"Oh, but don't you know by now?"

"No," I admit. "I don't."

"Come on," he says. "You expect me to believe that you don't know what we're after? If that's the case, then you're all boring and stupid."

It takes all my will not to zap this pile of badger poop, but I don't because I know he'll hurt my sister. "Only the first-firsts know what you're after."

"Leave it to the elves to make things complicated," he says, clearly annoyed.

"If you tell me what you want, I'll get it for you," I say.

"Oh really?"

"Yes, but only if you let Percy go."

"Sure thing," he says, then he laughs, making the branches quiver. I lift my arms to catch her if she drops. "As if. The minute you go back into that camp you'll have all those arrow-happy uncles of yours out here shooting us up. They've been crawling all over these woods like maggots on a dead skunk."

"I won't tell them," I say. "Why would I? You've got Persimmon."

My eyes have adjusted fully to the dim light, and I can see him smile. Oh how I hate him. "That's right," he says, and rocks my sister back and forth until the branch squeaks.

"Stop! Stop it!" I yell, trying to keep my body directly below hers.

"Don't worry about it, Zephyr. I won't let her fall. She's my bargaining chip. I thought that little foxy would get me what I wanted, but that didn't work, did it?" He pauses. "Because of you and that weirdo half-erdler boyfriend of yours. He should really come and see me back in Brooklyn," Clay says. "I could turn those hidden powers into something awesome."

"You leave Timber out of this," I say.

"Bossy, bossy," Clay tells me. "That's why you're not fun. Now your cousin Briar, on the other hand. She's a good-time girl."

"Shut up," I tell him.

"Oh sissy," Clay calls. "You can come out to play now."

Dawn steps out from behind the tree and immediately zaps me before I even have a chance to react. "Slow as sap," she says, and I feel her spell enter my blood. My arms and legs are heavy, my mouth feels as if it's full of cotton, and it takes all of my energy to move. "Didn't think I had it in me, did you?" Dawn teases. Then her voice turns cruel. "I should lay you down and stomp you."

"Now, now, play nice, li'l sis. We're going to need her to call on Willow," Clay says.

"Later," Dawn threatens.

"Now listen up, cuz," Clay says. "You're going to call Willow out here so we can get what we need from that house. Once we have what we want, we'll give you back this rotten piece of fruit dangling from the tree." He rocks Percy again and I have to force myself not to react.

"She . . . won't . . . come . . ." I say slowly and thickly.

"What's that?" he asks.

"Willllllllllloooooooow," I mumble, as if I'm caught on a slow-motion reel.

"Oh for crap's sake," Clay says. "Let her go, Dawn. I can't take listening to her voice like that. She's not going anywhere."

"Fine!" Dawn says. She undoes the spell, then crosses her arms and pouts.

I stumble. "Willow," I tell them. "She won't leave the clearing. She's presiding over the celebration. It's better if you tell me what you want. I'll go get it."

"How do we know you'll come back?" Clay asks.

"Send her with me." I point to Dawn. "She can wear my cloak. There are so many people here, everyone will think you're someone else's cousin. We'll just walk in and get what you need, then come back."

Dawn looks up at Clay. He thinks about my plan for a moment. "Not half bad, elfy girl. You should consider coming over to our side. It's so much more fun."

I bite my tongue so I don't spit at him in the tree. "I would never ever become a dark elf. I'd rather die."

"You might get your wish, yet," Clay says, and laughs meanly.

I stand my ground.

"Oh all right," Clay says. "Give her your cloak."

"But I don't know what we're after," I tell them as I slip off my cloak and hold it out for Dawn.

"Aster's spring," Clay says.

I look at him blankly.

"Seriously, you don't know?" he asks.

"For real," I say as Dawn takes off her puffy white parka and puts on my cloak.

"The spring runs beneath Ivy's house. It was dug by Aster when she first got here and made eternal by her magic. You'll have to find it somewhere below the floor." Dawn reaches into the pockets of her coat that's on the ground and takes out two small glass bottles with corks in the tops. "Fill the bottles."

"Will that heal your mother?" I ask.

Clay flinches. "What do you care?"

"I wouldn't want my mother to die," I say.

"Yeah, yeah, pity party for the dark elves," Clay says. "When you bring the water back, I'll let this one go."

"Promise?" I ask.

"Sure," he says. "Why not? You have my word."

I realize that taking the word of a lying dirtbag dark elf is like trusting a snake not to bite you, but it's the best I've got right now.

"Come on," I tell Dawn, and march forward to rob my ancestral home.

chapter 23

DAWN FOLLOWS ME silently through the woods. In the distance, we can hear music and laughter at the party, which makes me want to run screaming straight to the clearing for help. But I know I can't do that, so instead, I take her the long way around, toward the front of the house, so that we don't meet any revelers. We pass my uncle Reed in the woods and I look to him hopefully, but he just raises his hand and waves because my cloak is an excellent disguise for Dawn. He keeps right on walking without so much as a second glance.

Going this way also gives me time to think. I know I have to fill those bottles and take them back to Clay in order to get Persimmon, but I also know that I shouldn't let Clay and Dawn take the water with them. Then, part of me wonders what would be so bad about letting them have it.

I look over my shoulder at Dawn, who scans the woods around us as we walk. "I meant what I said back there, you know." She looks at me and cocks her head to one side. "That I wouldn't want my mother to die either, so I understand why you want the water." She stays quiet. "But why didn't you just ask us for help?"

Dawn snorts and raises an eyebrow at me. "My mom and dad were shunned, dumb ass. We can't just waltz in here and be welcomed with open arms."

"You could if you came back," I say. "This wasn't your choice. You were born into it."

"Yeah, that's not going to happen," she says.

I slow down so we're walking side by side. "Why not?"

"Listen, Goody Two-shoes, it's not that easy," she says, but I see a flicker of uncertainty in her eyes beneath the hood of the cloak.

"What would be so hard?"

"I think my mom would have, but . . ." She trails off.

"You could. You can make your own choice." I want to reach out and touch her arm, but I don't.

"What? And give up all this?" she says with a mean little laugh. Then she levels her gaze at me. "Look, this isn't some stupid movie where everything's going to turn out the way you want it to. It's more complicated than that, so stop your yapping and get us to the house."

"You remind me of Bella," I mutter, as I walk faster.

"What'd you say?" she asks.

"You're worse than a mean erdler," I say, then I hurry along the path, ready to get this over with.

For some reason, elves rarely use their front doors (seems too formal, I guess). We all go around the back. So the front of Ivy's house is dark, but we can hear the party going full force on the other side, plus there are voices all around us coming from the woods, where small groups have broken off to play music and games or talk. We sneak up on the porch, my heart pounding, wishing I could think of something clever to stop this from happening, but I can't.

"I don't have a problem giving you this water for your mom," I whisper to Dawn, standing in the shadows of the porch. "Like I said before, I wouldn't want my mom to die. But before I do it, I need to know that Clay will let Persimmon go."

Dawn stands close to me. I see her eyebrows knitted together and the line of her jaw tight. She looks scared and I almost feel sorry for her, only I've learned my lesson with Bella many times before. The minute you're nice to a mean girl, she'll turn around and snap at you. "We're not all evil, you know," she says. "We just use our magic for different purposes."

"Trying to convert me?" I ask.

"Hardly," she says. "You'd make a crappy dark elf."

I'm not sure whether to be insulted or flattered.

"I don't want to hurt anyone," she tells me.

"Is the water really for your mother?"

She hesitates, but then she says, "Yes."

I figure that's as much of a promise as I'm going to get tonight, so I nod and head for the door.

We pause in the entryway and listen. The front room of Ivy's house (or should I say Willow's) is quiet except for the ticking of a grandmother clock with carved wooden owls. The hearth has a few glowing embers, but the place is cold since the fire hasn't been tended to while everyone's been outside for hours.

"I don't know where the spring is," I whisper to Dawn.

"Beneath the floor in the kitchen," she says. "We have to find a stone and move it."

As we tiptoe through the rooms toward the kitchen in the back, I feel a strange tingling all over my skin. It's not an itchy or tickly feeling, it's more like the sensation I get right before I cast a spell, only I'm not thinking of any spells, so it can't be that. I also can't stop thinking about Willow, and this is the worst part. The image of her in the cloak blazes in my mind. I want to pull her to me, and I have to stop myself from calling out her name. I feel terrible as we creep slowly toward the kitchen because I know that I'm about to steal from my sister.

A dim light from the hearth and a low lantern on the table give the kitchen an eerie glow. "Help me look," Dawn says, getting down on her hands and knees. "One of these stones will move."

"There's probably a spell on it so we can't lift it up," I tell her, but she ignores me.

As I crawl around the floor, trying to move stones, the tingling on my skin gets stronger, almost like a surge of power coursing through my blood, and the image of Willow never leaves me. I crawl toward the far wall and the sensation dissipates a bit, but when I turn around and crawl back toward the center, the feeling grows. Once I cross the centerline and head toward the other wall, the feeling wanes again. Dawn has started at the other end of the room and methodically moves from stone to stone, trying to lift each one by working her fingernails into the grout, but nothing budges. I go back to the middle of the room where the tingling is the strongest and I'm almost blinded by Willow in my mind. I close my eyes to concentrate and crawl down the center of the room toward Dawn.

The feeling grows until I'm squirming, then a flash hits me and I bolt upright on my knees. I open my eyes. I'm in the exact center of the floor. Below me is a twelve-sided stone from which all others radiate out. Willow pulsates behind my eyes and I have to slap my hands over my temples to keep my head from exploding with her image. "Here!" I call to Dawn.

She scrambles over to me like a skunk scurrying to a garbage can. We both work our fingers into the grout around the stone, but it won't budge.

"Move back," she says.

She pulls out a small pouch. As she unties the knotted leather thongs holding it closed, I hear myself muttering, "Willow, Willow, Willow, Willow."

"Shut up," she hisses at me while she sprinkles a line of the powder from the pouch around the outline of the stone. The powder sizzles and smokes, eating away at the grout. "Help me," she says. We each pry up our side of the stone.

It comes loose with a loud pop, sending us both back on our butts, me with the stone on my chest. For a split second I consider heaving the big rock at Dawn to knock her out, and I know by the strong pulsation across my skin that I could do it, but then I remember Percy hanging from that tree and I stop. We crawl back toward the hole and peer down inside.

Cool air wafts up and the scent of the cold, fresh spring floods the room. I can hear the faint tinkling of running water coming from the dark hole.

"Get the lantern," Dawn says.

I hurry to the table, then raise the wick as I bring the lantern close to the hole. The reflection of the light sparkles on the water below like a midnight sky full of stars. Dawn rummages beneath the cloak and pulls out the bottles and a small rope. She uncorks one bottle, ties the rope around the neck, and lowers it down. I hear the gentle splash as it reaches Aster's spring and I want to cry. They could do anything with this precious resource blessed by the magic of our first mother. I'm sure it's more powerful than they're letting on, and they certainly wouldn't need so much to heal their mother. But what can I do to stop them with my little sister suspended from the branches of an oak tree?

"You don't have to do this," I say one more time.

"I have no choice," Dawn says. "And neither do you. Cork it." She hands me the bottle. Then she lowers the next one.

When I take the bottle in my hand, the water roils and bubbles up to the top.

"Stop it!" she hisses at me.

"I'm not doing anything . . ." I say, trying to shove the cork on top, but the water flows over the top of the bottle and back into the spring below.

"Give me that!" She swipes the bottle from me while holding the rope steady with her other hand. "Do you think I'm an idiot?"

"I wasn't doing it," I tell her again.

"Right, it just jumped out of the bottle by itself."

"It did!" I nearly laugh because it sounds so ridiculous, but it's true. "Aster's magic is strong."

Dawn sets the bottle on the floor and pulls the other one up. She gets both corks in the bottles and tucks them beneath her cloak. "Put the stone back," she tells me.

I push it across the floor and fit it in place. Before I stand, I pat the stone and whisper, "I'm sorry."

As we leave the room, the tingling on my skin lessens, but the image of Willow remains in my mind. When we get to the porch the feeling's nearly gone, but Willow stays, and as we duck into the woods, the tingling evaporates, yet Willow's still with me. I almost wish she'd go. I feel so guilty. Dawn and I both run. I don't know why. It's not like anyone is after us. Perhaps I'm trying to run away from the horrible feeling I have. *I'm sorry, I'm sorry, I'm sorry*, I chant in rhythm with my running feet, but it does no good. Willow haunts me.

A few times I think I hear rustling behind us, but when I glance over my shoulder, I see nothing but the dark shadows of trees. No one even noticed that we snuck into Ivy's house and took the most precious possession of my people. Still, we move through the woods like two deer being chased by a mountain lion.

When we reach the tree, Clay's still perched near Percy, who rocks gently in a midnight breeze. His white coat glimmers in the moonlight and he sneers at us. "What took you so long?"

"Shut up," Dawn tells him. "We got it, now let's get out of here."

"Let my sister go," I say, and I feel like Willow's saying it, too, from inside my brain.

Clay hops down from the branch, which is at least twenty feet high, but he lands with no problem. "Let me see it first."

Dawn takes the bottles out of her cloak and hands them to him. He holds each one up to the moonlight and studies the water as a snide smile creeps across his lips. "This will do wonders for Mommy," he says. "And for all the little converts."

"What converts?" I ask, my heart pounding.

"Didn't you just love watching Bella sing?" Clay asks. "Funny how mesmerizing she can be, isn't it?"

I shake with fury as I remember the strange smell wafting through the club when Bella performed and how entranced everyone was.

"We could never quite perfect it, though," he says.

"Is it enough?" Dawn asks.

"Let her down now," the phantom Willow and I say again. I position myself below Percy in case he cuts her loose and lets her drop.

"Only takes a drop," he says.

I whip my head around. "What do you mean?"

"That's for me to know." Clay bobs his head like a bratty little kid. "And you to find out."

"Now!" Willow screams from inside my head, and without thinking I whip around and zap Clay in the chest. "Wind gone!" I shout, taking his breath away.

Then, as if from nowhere, Willow appears, twirling in Aster's cloak. She is a blur of blue in the shining moon, and for a second I wonder if she's really here or if she's only in my mind, but then I see Dawn flinch and try to cast a spell, but Willow is too fast, too strong. She whirls, knees bent, arms arcing over her head. She catches Dawn in her magic, tossing her aside like a twig in a tornado, then she zaps Clay, who rises in the air like a broken bough. The bottles slip from his hands as he lands crumpled in a snowdrift.

I spin around, shouting, "Percy!" and lift my arms to the sky, searching for her tiny falling body, but when I look up into the tree, I stop. Ivy hovers there, surrounding Percy with her arms. She is beautiful with her silver hair flowing into the moonbeams cast down among the dark, empty branches. But she is iridescent. The light shines through her skin, and I know then that she's not really here. Percy awakes and stretches. She laughs at being up so high. "Hi, Fephyr!" she calls and waves, but I can't move from the sight of Ivy's apparition cradling my sister.

A great shout goes up from the distance. Willow and I both turn toward the clearing. We hear chaos and shouting, running and cries. "What is it?" I say.

"Catch her!" Willow yells.

Automatically, I lift my arms ready for impact, but Persimmon floats to me and lands lightly in my grasp. I hold her tight against my chest to protect her. When I look up, Ivy is gone.

Willow has broken the spell by turning away, and Clay stumbles to his feet. "Willow!" I scream, but it's too late. In a flash he morphs. The white of his coat splits as his skin turns to woolly hair across his broad back. His nose and mouth elongate into a bearded muzzle and his ears shift to horns circling his head, but angry green eyes still flash from the center of his face. He rears up on his hind legs, then crashes down and lowers his head. He is a mountain goat preparing to ram my sisters and me. Willow spins and gathers Percy and me beneath her cloak. We jump and some power lifts us over Clay as he charges. We land and spin around to find him, but he's gone, charging through the forest in a clattering of hoofbeats against the crackling snow and ice.

"Dawn!" I say. We turn around to find her, but all that's left is my cloak wilted on the ground. Willow steps forward and plucks at it. A small mouse scurries out. We both jump back, but I yell, "It's her." Willow slams the cloak onto the ground, trying to stop her, but the mouse darts away into the underbrush of the trees.

We both drop to our knees, scrambling on all fours. "We'll never find her," Willow says. "She's gone."

Percy looks at us. "Why was I up there in that tree?"

I gather Percy in my arms while Willow searches for the bottles in the snow. "Shhh now," I say to Percy and I wrap her in my cloak. "Mom has some elderberry juice for you."

"Grandma Ivy rocked me," she says.

I kiss her head. "Yes," I say, still trying to understand. "She did."

Willow comes to us, carrying the bottles.

"I'm so sorry," I say to Willow, reaching for her arm.

She tucks the bottles into a pocket inside her cloak, then she takes my hand. "For what?"

Her skin feels good against mine, but I'm not sure I deserve her touch right now. "For leading Dawn to the spring," I say, my head hanging low. "For letting her take the water."

Willow pulls me close to her side beneath the warmth of her cloak. "Didn't you feel me with you?"

I draw in a quick breath. "I thought you were haunting me because I was doing something so bad."

Willow almost laughs as she begins to walk. I match her steps to stay tucked beneath her arm. "I led you there."

"The tingling?" I ask.

She nods.

"But how did you know?"

Willow shrugs. "You're in my heart," she says. "I could tell that you were troubled."

"I thought it was the magic of the water making me tingle, but it was you all along."

She kisses the top of my head. "It was us together."

I look around the forest. "Do you think they're really gone?"

"For now," Willow says. "But we should warn the others."

As we begin to walk toward the clearing, Willow raises her head. "Do you hear that?"

"What?" I ask, straining my ears, but I hear nothing.

"Something's wrong," Willow says. "It's too quiet."

"They probably noticed that you're missing," I say.

"No," she says. "It's Ivy."

"She was in the tree," Persimmon says again.

"Come on," I say, grabbing Willow's hand, and we run.

When we get back to the clearing, there is no music, no acrobats, nobody eating or drinking or playing games. Everyone stands in hushed circles, holding hands, hugging, and crying.

"What is it?" Willow demands, rushing into the center near the dying bonfire. "What's happened? Where's Ivy?"

My father runs over and takes Persimmon from me and starts asking me the same questions. "What happened? Where were you?"

We're immediately mobbed by cousins and aunts, everyone talking at once so that I can't understand anything until Grandmother Hortense, Ivy's oldest daughter, comes to the center of the clearing and raises her hands. Everyone hushes. The first-firsts line up alongside Hortense: Apricot, Laurel, Jonquil, Lily, Grandma Fawna, and my mother, who reaches out and calls to Willow. Slowly, Willow walks to the center.

"Ivy has left us," Hortense says.

"But I saw her!" I shout, and everyone turns to me.

"Zephyr?" Mom asks. "What did you see?"

I step forward, toward the first-firsts. "She saved Persimmon."

Everyone turns to look at Percy, who's snuggled in my father's arms. Percy nods. "She held me tight. I was swinging from a branch."

As I explain what happened in the woods, I realize that Ivy sacrificed herself to save Percy and now she's gone.

Willow and I tell the story of what happened in the woods and how Clay and Dawn shifted. Hortense bows her head when we're done. "We are safe," she says. Then she lifts her face to the sky. "Grandmother Ivy has seen to that."

"Hup ba! Hup ba! Hup ba!" we elves all yell, and somewhere in the ether, where Ivy's magic swirls, I'm certain that she hears.

chapter 24

WE STAY AT Willow's for Grandmother Ivy's funeral. It's a natural extension of the solstice celebration because elfin funerals are celebrations of life, not sad occasions. Sure, we miss Ivy terribly, but we know that she lived a good, long life and that her magic will always be with us, so we choose to celebrate what she gave us rather than mourn what we've lost.

I can't help but think of Dawn and Clay, though, and how a funeral for their mother, my aunt Hyacinth, will be different. Maybe it's because we elves live so long that we find death less threatening or because our deaths are almost always peaceful that we're not scared of dying like erdlers seem to be.

The day after the funeral, my family stands on Willow's back porch watching the long exodus of elves in cloaks and silent boots pulling sleds with exhausted children into the trees surrounding Willow's clearing. We can hear the quiet singing of each family as they disappear into the forest, radiating out from this land to populate the small settlements surrounding the first ancestral home that my sister now protects.

"It's going to feel so empty around here," Willow says with a sigh.

Ash pulls her into a hug and kisses the top of her head. The next time I see them will be for their wedding in the spring.

I drop down into a rocking chair by the door with a loud *oomph*! "Thunder and lightning, I feel like I lived an entire century in one week." I stretch my arms above my head and yawn long and loud. "I'm going to need to sleep for a month to recover from all the shape-shifting, solstice celebrating, and dark-elf battling!" I let out a laugh from the ridiculousness of it all, then I close my eyes. There's been no word about Clay and Dawn, but everyone thinks they've run away for good. Even so, Willow and the other first-firsts are on alert.

Someone smacks the bottom of my boot, which is resting on the porch rail while I try to drift to sleep. I open one eye to see Briar standing in front of the porch. "You guys heading back?" I ask.

She nods, but then I see that she's upset. I pop up from the chair and hop over the rail. "What's wrong?" I ask, wrapping my arms around her. "Why are you sad?"

Briar buries her face into my shoulder. "Mom and Dad said I have to go back to Alverland."

"But Bri," I laugh at my cousin, who never wants to leave a party. "Everyone's leaving today except for us. We're going to help Willow get settled and then we'll be back in a day or two . . ."

"No, Zeph." She looks up at me. "For good."

I blink. "You mean . . . ?"

She nods. "They don't want me to go back to Brooklyn."

"Ever?"

"Ever," she says, and I see the tears sparkling on her lashes.

"Oh, Bri!"

"I'll never see Kenji again. I'll never dance on an erdler stage. I'll never go back to Galaxy for hot chocolate or hear Mercedes laugh."

"Yes, you will," I say. "We both will." But then it occurs to me that I might not be going back either.

We hug each other tightly. As frustrated as I've been with Briar in Brooklyn, I can't imagine going back without her. Then again, I can't imagine not going back at all.

"Briar!" Aunt Flora calls. We turn to see Aunt Flora and Uncle River with their other kids Camilla, Sorrel, Lake, and Storm, hugging Mom, Dad, Grandma Fawna, and Grandpa Buck by the clearing. "It's time to go now."

"It'll be okay," I whisper to her. "I'll talk to my dad."

She nods. "Beg him, please."

"I will."

We stay two more days to help Willow set up house, and I'm on my very best elfy behavior the whole time. I help as much as I possibly can and I never mention Brooklyn once, hoping that if I'm supergood, Mom and Dad will realize that living in Brooklyn hasn't changed me too much and it's okay for us to go back.

On the last day at Willow's, Grandma and I help her put away the cloak and the tunic until the next celebration. Willow and I spread them on the bed on top of long linen shrouds.

"I never thought I'd own something so beautiful," Willow says as she smoothes the fabric.

"They are exquisite," Grandma says.

"I think I'll wear one for my wedding," Willow says.

"But what about the dress you and Flora have been making?" I ask.

Willow shrugs. "Plans change."

"Wow," I say. "That's a new attitude from you. You usually hate for things to change."

"I do," she admits. "But I realized that you can't do anything about it, so it's better to embrace change when it happens."

"Very wise of you my dear," Grandma says. She carries her bundle to the chest. "So many treasures in here," she says quietly as she peers inside.

"Does that mean you feel okay about taking over this house?" I ask Willow.

Willow and I carry our bundles to the chest. "No," she says, and closes the lid. "Not at all." She sits on top of the chest and wraps her arms around her knees. Maybe it's because she's tired or maybe it's because she owns this house now, but my sister looks older to me. Something in her face has shifted. She's still beautiful, but her jawline appears stronger and her eyes sharper.

"You're strong, Willow," I say, remembering her in the woods kicking Clay's sorry butt.

"What if I'm not strong enough? What if Clay and Dawn come back? Now that Ivy's not here . . . what if Mom's not here?" She looks from me to Fawna.

Grandma reaches out and lays a hand on Willow's shoulder. "You would like to have your mother near, wouldn't you?"

"Of course," says Willow.

"What do you think?" Fawna asks me.

"Me?" I sputter. "I . . . I . . . I don't know. How would I know?"

Fawna stares at me with kind and patient eyes. She always asks a question for a reason, and I know she won't let me off the hook without an answer. I look away from my sister and my grandmother to a spot of sunlight filtering through the window. "I guess we should stay to help Willow," I mutter.

"Zephyr," Grandma says. I glance at her but I can't look straight into her eyes. "When someone asks your opinion, you should do them the honor of telling the truth about what you feel; otherwise, people will stop asking."

"But what if what I want makes everybody else mad?" I ask.

"Is it the worst thing in the world to have others mad at you?"

"Yes!" I say. "It's terrible."

She smiles kindly at me. "But isn't it worse to hide your true feelings?"

"But Grandma!" I whine then I stop myself, remembering my best elf self. "I'm trying not to be selfish."

Grandma laughs gently. "Why is it selfish to say what you want?"

"Because what I want will take away what Willow wants," I explain. "And I don't want everyone to hate me for that."

"Oh but my dear," Grandma says, holding her arms open to me, but I don't budge. "We all love you for who you are, even if that means you want things that we don't want. Besides," she says with a little shrug, "is the only solution for your mother to be here or there?"

"I guess it is," I say. "No matter how strong Mom's magic is, she can't be in two places at once."

"But perhaps instead of your mother, Willow could have me," Fawna says.

Willow's face lights up, but my face falls. "You mean you'd stay here?" we ask at the same time.

Fawna nods. "I could, if it allowed more people to have what they want and need."

"So wait . . . does that mean Mom and Dad are planning to go back to Brooklyn?" I ask cautiously.

"I don't know," Fawna says. "But perhaps they'll be more easily convinced to go if I stay here."

"Oh Grandma!" I say, and fall into her arms. "Would you do that for us?"

"Of course," she says with a happy laugh. "Anything for you."

* * *

The next day, as my family packs up for Alverland, Poppy, Bramble, and Persimmon run around the clearing in crazy circles like dogs chasing their tails. They haven't had this much fun in months, and again I feel selfish for wishing we'd go back to Brooklyn.

"All right, you wily badgers," my father calls to my littler sisters and brother. "Come over here and say good-bye to Willow."

They scramble up the porch steps and attack my sister.

"We'll miss you sooooo much!" Poppy exclaims.

"I'll miss you, too," Willow says as she hugs the three of them close to her body.

"When are we going to see Willow again?" Bramble asks.

"At her wedding!" Dad says.

"Oh my, I can't believe you'll be getting married so soon!" Mom says, and then she throws her arms around Willow again.

If you ask me, elf good-byes take far too long with all the hugging and kissing and declarations of never-ending love. I like the erdler high five and see ya' later version better. But when it's my turn to say good-bye to Willow, I almost lose it. I clutch my sister and don't want to let her go. "Thank you," I whisper into her ear.

"For what?" she asks.

"Just . . . for . . . I don't know . . ." I look up into her face. "For loving me no matter how badly I screw up." Then before I start blubbering like a baby, I let go and run for the woods.

An hour later, on the path back to Alverland, I can't take it anymore. I hang back, letting my brothers and sisters pass me so I can walk with Dad, who's bringing up the rear. He smiles at me as I fall into step with him. "Dad," I say, "what are we doing?"

He looks around at the trees and snow-covered ground. "I think we're heading back to Alverland, if I'm not mistaken."

I hold his wrist and slow down so the rest of my family gets out of earshot. "No, I mean, are we going back to Brooklyn or are we staying here?"

Dad looks up into the canopy of trees above our heads. The sky is brilliant blue today and the air is clear. "It's nice here, isn't it?"

I nod, but a heaviness comes over me.

"What do you want to do?" Dad asks me.

I shrug, reluctant to tell him my true feelings, so I ask a question instead. "What's Mom want to do?"

Dad is quiet for a moment. "Mom feels torn. She's needed in both places, and no matter what she does, it leaves someone vulnerable."

"Not if we all stay together," I say. "In Alverland."

"Is that what you want?"

I remember what Fawna said to me about being honest when someone asks my opinion. "You really want to know?"

Dad nods.

I take a big breath. "I love it here." I motion to the snow-covered pines, the hawks circling overhead, the squirrel tracks across the ground. "And I hate to see my family threatened." I think back to Clay holding Persimmon prisoner in the tree. "But," I say and cross my arms, "I'm selfish enough to want to go back to Brooklyn for myself and for Briar, because we both love it there, too."

"I don't know that that's so selfish," Dad says.

"Not everyone feels that way."

"Yes, but . . ." Dad sighs, sending out a plume of white air. "I don't know that we have a choice anymore."

I look up at him, bewildered.

"Someone has to keep an eye on those dark elves running loose around New York," Dad says.

"I think they have bigger plans than we know," I tell him.

"You're probably right."

"But if they come back to Willow's . . . ?"

Dad lays a hand on my shoulder. "Your sister can take care of herself, and she's got Fawna and all the other first-firsts to help, too."

"Does that mean we're going back to Brooklyn?"

He nods. "For now I think we will."

Even though I'm happy, I can't quite smile and feel relieved yet. "What about Briar?"

Dad shakes his head. "I don't know," he admits. "Flora is very upset."

I stamp my foot into the snow. "It wasn't Briar's fault any more than it was my fault, though."

"No one thinks it was."

"Then why can't she come back with us?"

Dad sighs. He loops his arm through mine as we walk down the path. "Briar is a youngest-youngest, so her mother worries that she's more susceptible than you because of her birth order."

"Susceptible to what?" I try to work it all out as we move through the woods, which suddenly seem bigger and more mysterious to me than they ever have.

"To trouble," Dad says. "I don't know why, but youngest-youngests tend toward darkness. You see how Dawn is, and her mother, Hyacinth. It runs in the blood."

"But that's not fair," I say. "Briar's a good person."

He nods. "We all know that, but we have to do our best to keep her that way. And even you can see that she takes more risks and makes poorer choices than you do sometimes."

I can't argue that one, but still the thought of going back to Brooklyn without Fawna and Briar is too much. "She has to come back with us."

"We have to leave that up to Aunt Flora and Uncle River." Dad hugs me to his side. "But I'll do my best to convince them."

chapter 25

I HAVE MORE butterflies in my stomach than I've ever had. Well, maybe not as many as when I was battling Clay and Dawn in the forest, or when I was waiting for Aunt Flora and Uncle River to decide if Briar could come back to Brooklyn, but other than that, I'm pretty well freaked out.

"What are you going to wear?" I turn to Briar, who studies our shared closet as we get ready for Chelsea's New Year's Eve party.

"I don't know." She scoots hangers over the bar. "I'm thinking about skinny jeans, yellow Uniqlo sweater, and boots. What about you?"

"Can't decide." I flop back on the bed and close my eyes. "Isn't it funny to be back in the erdler world worrying about what we're going to wear?"

"I really thought they weren't going to let me come back," Briar says for the six hundredth time since we got to Brooklyn last night. It took a lot of convincing, but Flora and River finally agreed that Briar could return on the condition that she never cast another spell on an erdler and that she has to go back to Alverland for Willow's wedding and for the whole summer.

"Maybe I should wear my orange T-shirt with the manga girl," she says. "Kenji likes that."

"What if they don't want to see us?" I ask, sitting up now.

"I keep having the same thought. What if we walk in and they're like, 'Ho-hum who are you?'"

"At least Bella won't be there tonight."

"You sure about that?" She holds up a short skirt and the manga top in front of her body, studying herself in the mirror.

"Are you joking? Chelsea and Bella hate each other."

Briar shakes her head. "That never stops erdlers from pretending to be friends."

"True," I say. "It's not like dark elves and light elves, is it? Erdlers can be both good and bad, sometimes at the same time."

"You don't think elves are that way?" She shoves the skirt back into the closet and takes out a pair of black cords instead.

"Just seems more cut and dried with us. You're either dark or you're light. Good or bad."

Briar shakes her head and puts the pants and shirt back in the closet. She flops down on the bed beside me. "I'm not so sure about that anymore."

I turn over and prop myself up on my elbow so we're face-to-face. "You're a good person, Briar." I reach out and squeeze her shoulder. "Doesn't matter if you're a youngest-youngest or a first-first or a middle like me."

"But what if it does matter?" she asks, biting her lower lip. "What if that's the reason I do things like let Clay and Dawn cast a spell on me?"

"You had no control over that. You had no way of knowing what they were up to."

"But you knew right away that something was wrong with them."

I'm quiet because it's true, but then I say, "They would've found a way in, Briar. Whether it was through you or not."

"I just made it easy."

I hug her. "I love you for who you are."

"Thanks." She pulls away. "I hope Kenji does, too."

I draw in a deep breath. "There's only one way to find out." I hoist myself off the bed. "And we'd better get ourselves together. We have to meet Ari and Mercedes in twenty minutes."

At nine-thirty sharp, Ari and Mercedes are waiting for us on the train platform so we can ride the subway together to Carroll Gardens, where Chelsea lives.

"So?" I ask as soon as the doors close and we pile into seats. "How was it? How was the performance?"

"Oh honey," Mercedes says, slapping my leg. "You don't even want to know."

"I'm dying to know," I tell her. "Who played my part?"

"Nobody," she says with her eyes wide.

"Padgie didn't recast it?" I ask.

"Padgie," Ari says, "has taken a mental hiatus."

Briar and I both blink at him.

Mercedes cracks up. She looks great with her curls pulled back in a loose ponytail and a new Brooklyn Industries coat she got for Christmas. "After you guys left and Timber and Kenji took their ill-advised road trip, Padgie lost his cotton-picking mind. The man just wandered around the stage, pulling at his hair, muttering like he was Lady Macbeth"

She does a perfect Mr. Padgett impersonation, muttering, "How could they do this to me?" which makes us all snicker.

"Never mind that the fool had never finished writing the dang musical," Ari adds.

"By the time Timber came to his senses and got back to Brooklyn, Padgie was long gone," Mercedes says.

"Where'd he go?" Briar asks.

"La-la land," Ari says.

"The cuckoo nest," Mercedes adds.

"Huh?" Briar and I both say.

"The man just checked out," Mercedes says. "He was like an empty house. Ain't nobody home."

"Now he's on an extended personal hiatus," Ari tells us. "In Aruba."

"And the performance?" I ask.

Mercy shakes her head. "Never happened."

I reach out for her arm. "Oh Mercy, I'm so sorry."

"I know, right?" she says, shaking her head. "I finally get a decent part and the director flies the coop. But . . ." She smiles big. "I did get cast in that mayo commercial!"

"I'm so happy for you!" I hug her tight.

"But you know what the best part was?" Ari asks.

We all look at him. "Bella got doubly screwed. Mr. Padgett canceled the show, and that weird Clay dude who was her manager split. I don't think I've ever seen her so pissed."

"You were right about Clay and Dawn," Mercedes tells me. "They were creepy."

"Creepier than you can even imagine," I say, and Briar nods.

"They're long gone now," Ari says.

I wish Ari was right. I wish that dark elves were just the bogeymen lurking around the edges of my dreams like I thought when I was a kid. But it's not a joke anymore. The dark elves are real, and Willow still has what they want. They may be gone, but they'll be back. I can only hope that next time we'll be ready for them.

"And Timber?" I ask, refraining from adding a hundred more questions like, oh I don't know, *Is he still my boyfriend, or will the fact that I'm an elf and he's a werewolf put a damper on the whole thing?*

Ari shakes his head. "You haven't talked to him?"

"Not lately," I say.

"And why aren't you guys going to the party with those guys?" Mercedes asks us.

Thinking quick, Briar says, "We want to surprise them."

"Nice," Ari says. "I wish somebody would surprise me once in a while."

The train slides into the Carroll Gardens station. I slip my arm into Ari's. "Somebody will someday," I tell him as we head up the steps.

The streets are packed when we emerge from the station. "Feel good to be back to civilization?" Mercedes asks.

"I'm sorry," Ari says, pulling out his CrackBerry and sending a text that we're on our way. "Alverland sounds nice and all, but aren't you guys bored out of your gourds after twenty-four hours there?"

"It's not as boring as you might think," I say, then Briar and I look at each other and try not to laugh.

"Kenji and Timber said that little town Ironweed was beat," Ari says.

"What are you even talking about?" Mercedes asks Ari. "This place was dead while they were gone. The club was shut down, Kenji and Timber were off acting like nut jobs driving around the U.P. of Michigan looking for these two, the performance was canceled, and we just sat around watching *Dexter* from Netflix for two weeks. I'd rather have been in the woods with you."

"Maybe next time," I say, knowing full well that will never happen.

Ari points down a street. "There it is," he says. We see Levi and Nora walking up the stoop to a lovely old brownstone covered in twinkling Christmas lights.

"Cool," Merci says, speeding up the sidewalk. "I hope this is fun."

Mercedes and Ari immediately head for the kitchen when we get in the door.

"I hope they have shrimp," Mercedes says. "I love me some shrimp."

"Come on, hungry hippo," Ari says, following her. "Let's get you some food before you die of malnourishment."

Instead of going with Ari and Mercy, Briar and I wander around looking for Kenji and Timber, but we can't find them.

"Maybe they're not coming," Briar says as we go back into the empty foyer and drop down on the bottom step of the staircase.

"We could ask Chelsea," I offer.

"I haven't seen her either," Briar says.

We hear voices behind us on the stairs and both turn around at the same time. My heart climbs into my throat when I see Timber walking down behind Chelsea, who laughs over her shoulder. Briar grabs my hand. I stand up quickly and pull her around the corner.

"I can't believe it," I whisper while I peek by the door frame. "Has he been up there with her the whole time?"

Briar squeezes my hand and tugs. "Come on."

I hold back, fearing what happened while I was gone. "No, I can't."

"Yes, you can," she insists, and tugs harder.

We pop around the corner just as Timber and Chelsea get to the bottom landing of the steps where we'd been sitting.

I wish I had a replay of Timber's face so I could decipher every emotion that registers when he sees me. Surprise. Bewilderment. Frustration. Is he still in love with me or is he mad at me, or does he even remember that he was? Then his face settles—eyes bright, mouth swinging upward in seeming delight, his hands reaching toward me.

"You're here," he says.

"And you're there." I point to Chelsea, who leans against the banister with what I could swear is a smirk on her face.

Briar lets go of my hand and gives me a little shove. I trip forward into Timber's open arms. "Oops!" I say, and begin to step back, but he pulls me close. "I didn't know when you were coming back tonight."

When I feel his arms around me, I want to let go of all my doubts about his feelings for me, but not yet. Timber would hug a cactus, so this might only be a friendly hello. I should let go, step back, gauge the situation, but I can't let go quite yet. I hang on, drinking in his fresh piney smell, remembering how elated I was when I found him at the bait shop in Ironweed and my surprise when he leaped out of the woods to tackle Clay, and how my family welcomed him to Alverland, but he doesn't share any of those memories. Then I notice that he hasn't let go of me yet either, so I stay in his arms for another second, tightening my grip against his back.

I catch sight of Chelsea, rolling her eyes from the landing. She plods down the rest of the steps and slinks by. Then Timber lets go of me. "Why didn't you e-mail me or call me to let me know you were home?" he asks, searching my face.

"We just got back last night," I say, but I can't admit that I was too afraid to call him. I don't know which is harder, battling dark elves or explaining myself to an erdler who can't really know the truth about me. "We wanted to surprise you and Kenji," I say, pointing to Briar.

"Well, I'm surprised," he says, but I can't tell if he means in a good way or bad.

"Did Kenji leave?" Briar asks.

"He wouldn't have if he knew you were coming," Timber tells her.

"But I couldn't find him," she says.

"I'll text him." Timber pulls out his iPhone and zips off a text. It buzzes within a few seconds. "Basement," Timber says. "You should go find him."

Briar looks at me. "Should I?"

"Duh," I say. "Yes." But she still hesitates. "You want me to come with you?"

Briar looks from me to Timber and back to me. I know she's as afraid as I was. But then she straightens up and stands tall. "I can handle it."

She goes, leaving Timber and me alone for the first time in what seems like eons.

"I missed you," he says.

"You did?" I can't hide my surprise. Was the affection he had for me before I left purely from the elf circle spell I cast or was some of it real?

"Didn't you miss me?" he asks.

"I thought about you so much, sometimes it felt like you were right there with me."

A grin spreads over his face until his teeth show beneath his lips. My secret wolf boy. My protector. "Really?"

"Yes, really," I tell him.

"That's funny," he says, and takes a step closer to me. "Because I tried to find you."

"I got your e-mails."

He looks at his shoes and blushes. "Yeah, that was pretty messed up what Kenji and I did."

"Did you get in trouble?"

Timber shakes his head and smiles. "Not too bad. My mom loves you. She understood." Then he grabs my hand. "You want to get out of here? Go somewhere to talk?"

My heart pounds. "The last time I left without Briar, all hell broke loose."

"She's with friends," he says, and tugs on my arm. I know that he's right, that I can't worry about her all the time and that I have to trust her to make good decisions. "All right," I say slowly. "But can we go to my house? I have a present for you."

"I have one for you, too!" he tells me.

He talks nonstop on the train ride back to my house. He tells me all about the road trip, how the performance was canceled, and how he was grounded and not allowed to go skiing with his dad for Christmas, then he stops and looks out the train window. We're aboveground now, looking into the harbor where the lights on the bridges, boats, and the Statue of Liberty twinkle like urban stars. "I know I pissed off a lot of people by taking off, but I think driving up to Michigan was good for me." He continues staring out the window. "Something changed in me while I was gone."

I catch my breath and hold it, half afraid of what he might say, but then he shakes his head. "I don't how to describe it, but I sort of feel older in a way. Smarter. Like I understand myself better." Then he shrugs and smiles at me. "Maybe it was just doing something on my own. Getting out of the groove and away from my normal thing."

"I know what you mean," I say. "Sometimes changing up your life can make everything seem fresh again."

"That's exactly it," he says. "No wonder I missed you. You understand me in a way nobody else does." He studies me for a moment, and I feel like a tree unfurling new leaves in the spring under the warmth of his gray-blue eyes. "I swear, sometimes it's like you know me better than I do."

When we get to my house it's already past eleven.

"Nobody's staying up for New Year's Eve?" Timber asks, as we tiptoe through the dark and quiet rooms.

"We celebrated the new year earlier," I whisper to him with a quiet laugh. "Let's go out to the garden so we don't wake anyone." I lead him into the kitchen, then I say, "Wait here, I have to get something."

When I come back, Timber's sitting on a stool, strumming my dad's guitar, which was propped up in the corner. He plucks a few strings, sending the mellow bass notes into the air. I stop in my tracks. "That's funny," he says.

"What?" The hair on the back of my neck prickles with recognition.

"I just got this weird sort of déjà vu, like I've played this guitar before." He plucks the strings again and I hear the notes of "Green Glen Ladies," the old elfin song he and Grove played that night by the fire in Alverland.

I laugh uncomfortably. "Not possible, right?"

"No," he says. "I guess not. Mind if I bring this outside?"

"Sure," I tell him, and walk toward the back door.

"Hey, what's that?" He points to the long skinny gift, nearly as tall as I am that I've wrapped in red linen.

"You'll see," I say as I lead him outside. We sit on the railing of the wooden deck. I look up into the sky, searching for stars, but like most nights in Brooklyn, it's nearly impossible to make out any heavenly bodies because of all the city lights. "You ready for your present?" I hold out the long skinny gift.

Timber takes it from my hands. "What is it, a tennis racket?"

I laugh. "Are you joking?"

"Yes, I have no idea what it could be."

"Open it and find out."

I watch Timber's face as he unwinds the fabric to reveal the intricate carvings of leaves, flowers, and totem animals on my birch walking stick. He looks perplexed at first, then pleased, then confused again, kind of like he's trying to remember something but can't quite pull it out of his cloudy mind. "This is amazing," he says. "But . . ." Then he laughs. "I still have no idea what it is."

"It's a walking stick," I tell him. "My grandfather makes them. I thought you might like it."

"I love it."

"It can come in handy when you're hiking," I say, wishing I could retrace the memories lost in his mind.

He hugs me. "Thank you."

"You're welcome."

"Now, I have something for you, but it's a different kind of present," he tells me. "You know how you're always saying I could make a comeback if I wanted?"

I curl my knees into my chest and hug myself. "I think you'd knock everybody out if you did."

"Well . . ." He straps my father's guitar over his shoulder. "I'm not sure I'm ready for a band, but I decided to write a song." He turns tuning pegs on the guitar, getting each string just right. "Remember all those e-mails I sent you while Kenji and I were driving around trying to find you?"

I nod because how could I forget.

"When I looked back at them later, I realized that they could be lyrics, so I made up a melody and I came up with this song." The notes are light and pretty, like birds singing on a clear, crisp morning in the woods. "It's for you."

I'm quiet, but my heart pounds as he strums the guitar, filling the quiet night with lovely music, then he begins to sing,

Came by your house this morning
no matter how I knocked
no lights came on, no answer
baby, your doors were locked

I think you flew the coop
I think you left the nest
I don't know where you're heading,
but I think you're heading west
I'll fly after you
I'm a crane
I'll come for you
I'm insane
I'll dance and sing
and flap my wings
'cause baby, it's you I've got to find
Crossing the GW
leaving NYC far behind
over rolling hills and fields of green
it's you I've got to find
I pass the lakes as big as seas
I haven't seen anything but trees
and miles and miles of corn and beans
but still you haunt my dreams
From New York City to Mackinaw
Across the country
I've seen it all
but nothing takes the place of you
It's you I've got to find
I ended up in Ironweed
Eating ham and eggs without a lead
you disappeared among the pines
it's you I've got to find
I'm flying after you
I'm a crane

I'm coming for you
I'm insane
I'll dance and sing
and flap my wings
'cause baby, it's you I've got to find
I went on a wild goose chase
just to see your face
and for the chance to see you dance
but I can't find a trace
I don't know where you've gone
or when you will return
but I'll be here, waiting still
my heart will always yearn
I'll fly after you
I'm a crane
I'll come for you
I'm insane
I'll dance and sing
and flap my wings
'cause baby, it's you I've got to find

When he's done, I can't even move. I'm stuck beneath the dark night sky, my eyes welled up and my mouth half open. I shake my head. "I don't know what to say," I whisper.

Timber pulls the guitar over his head and sets it aside. "Because it sucked?" he asks, his eyes squinched up like he's about to be punched.

"No!" I fly to him. I spread my arms and catch him in my embrace. "I loved it."

He holds me close. "Sometimes I feel like I can't explain what's going on inside of me."

I nod, my heart racing, because the truth is, there's more inside of Timber than he could ever imagine. He has no idea what courses through his blood. The mark my grandmother can see. What happened in the woods in Alverland. And I can never tell.

"But when I sat down to write that song," he says, "I could say everything I wanted about you."

I pull back to look into his eyes, those crazy gray-blue wolf eyes. "That's what music should be about," I say. "People think it should be about fame or money or being the best or getting the lead in a musical, but it's not, you know?"

Timber nods. "It's about expressing what's deep inside."

I let go of him but keep my eyes on his. "I see what's inside of you." I press my hand against his heart. "It's fierce and beautiful and when you need it most, what's in your heart will save you."

He covers my hand with his and smiles at me. "Thank you," he says.

I realize then that what's in my heart is more simple than I used to think. I don't have to be the best singer or have Timber so madly in love with me that he can't think straight. I don't have to win every audition or continually worry about Bella or keep tabs on my cousin Briar. As long as my family is safe, we don't have to be together all the time. My grandmother and Willow are still with me, even if they're in Alverland. Dad and Grove can come and go. Thinking I have to have everything all to myself all the time is selfish, and in the end, it doesn't get me what I truly want.

We sit together, underneath the starless sky, his hands on my waist, my arms around his neck. As I'm next to him, the feelings I had when I danced for him come rushing back to me. The world swirls and everything is reduced to just Timber and me. I feel my heart swell with feelings for him. No matter how much I miss Alverland or how worried

I am about the dark elves going after Willow, I am glad to be back in Brooklyn. Selfish or not, this is where my life is right now.

Timber pulls me closer. I shut my eyes and lean my head to the left. Even though we kissed a hundred times when he was under my spell, this feels like the first time ever. My lips meet his and fireworks explode. Above us, the sky erupts into shooting stars, red fountains, and blue rockets.

"Happy New Year!" Timber says.

Just as I'm about to pull Timber in for another kiss, the back door opens. My brothers and sisters come clattering out into the garden with my mom and dad right behind them.

"Look at them!" Poppy shouts, pointing to the sky.

"Fireworks!" Bramble yells.

"Happy New Year," Mom calls to all of us.

They surround us, jumping and screaming for joy. We're caught in the tangle of arms and legs and voices all talking at once, but I don't mind because what I want most in life is right here, right now. I'm happy.

Don't miss the first book
featuring Zephyr

ISBN: 978-0-14-241255-8

$7.99 ($9.99 CAN)